P9-DWJ-584

Zaleski's
Percentage

Zaleski's Percentage

Donald MacKenzie

1974
HOUGHTON MIFFLIN
COMPANY BOSTON

**MIDNIGHT
NOVEL OF
SUSPENSE**

The author is grateful for permission to quote from
"Peregrine" which appears in *Collected Poems of Elinor Wylie*.
Copyright 1923 by Alfred A. Knopf, Inc.

First Printing c

Library of Congress Cataloging in Publication Data

Mackenzie, Donald, 1908–
Zaleski's percentage.

(Midnight novel of suspense)
I. Title.
PZ4.M1562Zal [PR6063.A243]   813'.5'4   73–18233
ISBN 0-395-18465-7

Printed in the United States of America

*For George Corvin-Mlodnicki
(and comrades)*

Zaleski's
Percentage

Chapter One

THE RESTAURANT was on the first floor of what had once been a four-storied residence at the unfashionable end of Fulham Road. Faded velvet curtains emblazoned with the faint pattern of a white eagle blocked the view from the street through plate-glass windows. The name of the restaurant was painted in gold on a black wooden shield that hung above the sidewalk.

WIELKAPOLSKA

A smaller velvet curtain screened the glass entrance door while a narrow, dirty passageway, untidy with litter and milk bottles, led to the upstairs premises. The dingy nameplates on the wall no longer held significance. The building was due for demolition and there were no other tenants. It was six o'clock on a cold January evening. Candlesticks were burning on the tables in the long narrow room behind the velvet curtains. The tables were set against dull red walls decorated with prints of feudal Poland. Noblemen with ermine caps hawking on the outskirts of vast forests, peasants bent under bundles of firewood, children tumbling in the snow.

Food was trundled up from the cellar kitchen on a hand-operated elevator. A small bar was embellished by icons, behind it was a tarnished gilt mirror diagonally set. The red walls and the reflection of the faded curtains gave an impression of cosiness. The Wielkapolska opened for dinner at eight. No lunch was served. The two Spanish waiters came in and set the tables during the afternoon, the Polish chef a couple of hours earlier to prepare his menus. The only person in the building at the moment was the owner of the restaurant, Casimir Zaleski. Zaleski had put his checkbook to use that morning and was wearing his purchases with a great deal of style, a tan cashmere shirt and a pair of elaborately checked trousers. He was sitting with one ankle locked over the other, his shoes old but burnished. Zaleski was a believer in spit, wax and the inside of a banana skin for the best possible polish. But the mixture was an unsavory one for the use of a gentleman, and he relied on a commercial product that could be applied without soiling the fingers. He wore his thick black hair brushed straight back. A prominent nose and high cheekbones protected small deepset eyes the color of wet slate. A monocle hung from a silk cord around his neck while a fold of flesh under his right eye suggested a convenient lodging place for it. The bottle of vodka on the bar in front of him was pinning down a newspaper. Three glasses stood beside the bottle.

He sat completely still, listening to the building creak and groan under the weight of the traffic outside. Suddenly his ears detected a tapping on the street door. He slipped off the stool, sucking in his gut, a stockily built man of fifty-four smelling of *eau-de-Portugal*. He went to the door, opened it a crack then threw it wide, letting in two men of his own age. His gold bridgework flashed behind the smile of welcome. He spoke warmly and in Polish.

"Bogdan — Stanislas! Welcome, old friends!"

Bogdan Czarniecki spread his arms like a polar bear in a zoo pleading for fish. He was six-and-a-half-feet tall and dressed in a long, shabby topcoat worn over oil-stained denim workpants. Zaleski hugged him demonstratively and turned toward the other man, solicitous of the mutilated arm as they embraced. Sobinski's left sleeve was pinned back above the elbow. Smooth white hair and an unlined face gave him the demeanor of an aristocratic cleric. Czarniecki aimed a moth-eaten beaver hat at a chair and shed his shabby topcoat. A North African virus contracted a generation before had left him completely bald. His stretched scalp was the color of old ivory and his neck revealed the scars of skin grafts. His teeth were ostentatiously false, his smile surprisingly gentle.

Zaleski double-locked the street door and led the others toward the bar. Memory tricked the reflection in the advancing mirror so that he saw the three of them once again, boulevardiers in the Cairo redlight neighborhood, the heat of the battle behind them. He filled the three glasses from the chilled vodka bottle and toasted them.

"Zdrowie!"

Sobinski belched unaffectedly. "You will excuse me but it is the food. After twenty-five years in this benighted country, my stomach is still unable to digest mutton fat."

Zaleski nodded sympathy and refilled his friend's glass. Sobinski worked as a ward cleaner in a nearby hospital. In his whole life, Zaleski had never put foot in a hospital, but he had a profound mistrust of all British institutions. He rapped on the bar with his signet ring, assuming the solemnity necessary to the occasion.

"You are wondering why I have asked you to come here this evening?"

The white-haired man said nothing. Czarniecki winked.

"You are going to make our fortunes, again. Either that or offer us jobs as waiters."

Zaleski ignored him. The question had been rhetorical. "I would like to remind you, my friends, of a night in June, twenty-seven years ago." The opening, he thought, had a ring to it, a promise.

Czarniecki extended an arm across the bar. He unscrewed a bottle of olives and filled his mouth with them, firing the stones into the hollow of his hand like missiles.

"Why should we need reminding? Our memories are as good as yours. You talk like an old woman sitting by the fire."

"And you like the child at her knee," Zaleski said calmly. "I am merely putting things in their proper perspective. I will continue. A commando unit attached to the Carpathian Division was parachuted in behind the Gothic Line. Its mission was to attack the field headquarters of the Seventy-first German Infantry Division."

Czarniecki spat out his last olive stone. "Captain Zaleski commanding, Lieutenant Sobinski and Sergeant Czarniecki in loyal support."

Zaleski controlled his irritation. "We were supposed to capture two enemy agents, Italians. British Intelligence supplied us with their names, covers and photographs, but the men were not there. In fact, no one was there. The post had been evacuated an hour before we arrived."

"We fought like tigers," said Czarniecki. He yawned.

Zaleski fitted a cigarette in his holder, seeing ten men with blackened faces crouching outside a monastery stark in the moonlight. They had swarmed in to find abandoned equipment, a safe lying on its side. An abortive attempt had been made to open it as though the keys had been mislaid. He'd given the order to blow the safe, hoping to find documents of military importance. Sobinski had been the explosives expert. Czarniecki had helped him pack the strips of plastic putty into the interstices. The charge had fired prematurely, the explosion driving a piece of steel deep into the sinews and muscles of Sobinski's arm. A smaller piece had scythed the back of Czarniecki's neck. Eight men had pulled themselves up from the dust, staring through acrid smoke at the blackened safe. The door hung by a single hinge. On the shelf inside was a jeweled monstrance, undamaged.

"The monstrance," prompted Zaleski. "You remember the monstrance, surely?"

Sobinski's clear, calm eyes were expressionless. "No, Casimir, I do not remember the monstrance."

Czarniecki grunted. "It is hardly surprising. You were eating morphine tablets in the plane like pieces of candy. But I remember well, Casimir. You disembarked holding the thing high above your head like a missionary bringing the news of Christ to heathens. It was very impressive, all those diamonds sparking in the sunshine. The British major made a touching speech when you surrendered it in the name of the Father, the Son and the Second Polish Corps. He called us 'men of honor.'"

"We were," said Zaleski. "And we still are."

The giant put his tongue between his lips and blew hard. "I will tell you what I remember best about that night. A girl was hiding in a ditch as we went up the side of the hill. She was holding her skirt over her head and I could see her ass, bare in the moonlight. The British had promised us low cloud and no moon."

Sobinski was making wet circles on the bar with the bottom

of his glass. "Ten parachutes, perfect targets for machine-gun fire — drifting down on the hill like balloons at a village fair. We thought it romantic."

A nerve jumped in Zaleski's cheek. The word jarred his sensibilities, reminding him of a recent remark by his bank manager. *The nature of an overdraft, Mr. Zaleski, is that it needs to be reduced. I sometimes have the impression that your approach to business borders on the romantic.*

"What we thought doesn't matter," he said. "What we need now is a pragmatic attitude to the present."

Sobinski fished a package of loose tobacco from his pocket and rolled a cigarette deftly with one hand.

"Thus spake Zaleski. Test the truth any way you like, my friend. We are middle-aged failures, embarrassments to our hosts."

Zaleski leaned back against the bar, extracting full dramatic value from each word.

"Betrayal. Rejection. Hardship. None of these alters the fact that we are still Poles."

Sobinski dropped an eyelid, avoiding the spiral of smoke. "If I had more than one hand I would applaud."

Zaleski's glance was affectionate. His friend's irony was understandable. Sobinski had suffered more than any of them. Zaleski lifted the newspaper revealing the photograph that lay beneath. He held it up so that both men could see it. The glossy ten-by-eight had been carefully preserved. A Ministry of Information stamp on the back bore the date June 1945. The photograph portrayed a group of men sprawling in hot Italian sunshine. Tethered in their midst was a pugnacious looking ram. A young Zaleski had one arm around the animal's neck. He was holding his nose with the fingers of his free hand. A typewritten caption pasted onto the print read

A POLISH COMMANDO UNIT MAKING FRIENDS WITH A
LOCAL RESIDENT SOMEWHERE ON THE ITALIAN FRONT.

He used his thumb to blot out one face after another. "Dead. Dead. Missing. Missing. Dead. Missing. Dead. Out of ten men we are the only survivors."

Czarniecki filled his mouth with more olives, speaking through them. "And of less importance to the British than the blacks or the Asians. They at least have their defenders."

Sobinski peered down at his own image, clicking his tongue. "So young, so brave and so handsome. Well, Casimir, it has been a long day, attacking bedpans in the geriatric ward."

"Wait," said Zaleski. He unfolded the week-old periodical, slotted his monocle in place and started to read in accented English.

THE VIRGIN'S DOWRY GOES HOME

In June 1944, a British commando unit attached to the Eighth Army attacked a Panzer headquarters deep behind the Gothic Line. The primary mission was to capture two enemy intelligence agents. The raid was successful in spite of fierce resistance, and among the booty was a jeweled monstrance known as the Virgin's Dowry and looted by the Germans from the convent of San Marco, near the town of Montefelcino. The origin of the monstrance dates back to 1698 when the widow of a local aristocrat took the veil and gave her fortune to Holy Mother Church. A Venetian jeweler fashioned the monstrance from pure gold and crystal, encrusting it with gems from the widow's collection. Additions were made over the centuries, diamonds, rubies and emeralds being donated by the faithful in recognition of favors received. The jeweled monstrance was valued at over £100,000 in 1940. A conservative estimate of its present-day worth would be in the region of £500,000. Due to the peculiar circumstances surrounding its capture, the constant movements of military units at that time, the monstrance was forgotten by all except the faithful of San Marco. Inquiries were made after the surrender of the Italians, but the years passed without further news of the booty. In August this year, the Virgin's Dowry was found in a store once used by the office of the Custodian of Enemy Property. After a careful inspection by a representative of the Italian government, the monstrance was said to be intact. From the 19th to 22nd inst, it will be on exhibition at the Dante Gallery, Conduit Street. Mr. Paolo Tedeschi who owns the gallery is a native of San Marco and is lending the premises for the occasion. The monstrance will be returned to His Excellency the Italian Ambassador at a ceremony at the embassy attended by officers and men of the Parachute Regiment.

Zaleski widened his eye, letting the monocle fall into his cupped hand. He reverted to his own language.

"A *British* commando unit!"

Sobinski wriggled a shoulder. "So? The British are not famed for the length of their memories or for that matter the depth of their gratitude."

The building shook as a truck lumbered by. Zaleski pushed the vodka bottle to safety. Czarniecki continued to pick the black grease from his fingernails with the end of a matchstick.

"I can remember," he said conversationally, "riding my bicycle as a boy twelve kilometers just to leave a flower on a windowsill. The girl was your cousin Basha, Casimir. Since then I have learned to borrow money from my landlady and at the same time stay out of her bed. She is over fifty and uglier even than I am. *That* is what I call pragmatism."

"You lie," Zaleski said calmly. "You would borrow from

the Jews if you could and go to bed with my grandmother. I ask you both a question. To whom does the monstrance belong — to the church? All the gold in Africa is less than the wealth of Holy Mother Church. To the Italian people? They are communists."

Czarniecki suspended his manicure. "Blood brothers to the commissars sitting in Warsaw. To the gallows with them!"

Zaleski slid the photograph between the pages of the newspaper. "The monstrance is neither the Englishman's to give nor the Italian's to receive. Morally it is ours."

Sobinski spoke with the care of a man asking directions from a stranger. "What do you intend to do about it — summon the press and tell them that three penniless Poles are the rightful owners? You dream, my friend. Night and day, you dream."

"This is no dream," said Zaleski, shaking his head. "What we have done once we can do again. We are going to retrieve this monstrance, dispose of it and share the proceeds."

Sobinski's bright blue eyes were the color of the Baltic. "You are joking, of course?"

Zaleski crossed himself elaborately, touching his thumbnail to his lips.

"Before God I am not joking. This will be a military operation governed by the rules of war."

Sobinski stared at him. "A military operation! Is your brain addled or what? It is what the law of the land says it is, robbery!"

Zaleski waved away the suggestion contemptuously. Where he led, Czarniecki would follow. Sobinski had always been the difficult one.

"The law of whose land?" he demanded. "Not yours, certainly. You *have* no country, Stanislas. An Irish gunman has more claim on England than you have."

Czarniecki's yawn shifted his store-teeth. "For my own part I would rob a bank tonight if I thought I could get away with it."

Zaleski concentrated on Sobinski. "Think positively, Stanislas. We have brains, courage and loyalty. There is nothing we cannot do together. I need your help."

Czarniecki extended his yawn. Sobinski smiled wryly. "For once your logic is irrefutable, Casimir. I have no country, no home, no possessions. But I do have my liberty."

Zaleski pounced like a terrier. "Liberty for what? To collect soiled bandages? To prowl the museums on your free afternoons, looking for some spotty girl to share your bed?"

Sobinski's pallid face colored. "You are being offensive."

Zaleski reached out, patting his friend on the knee. "We are brothers, Stanislas. The years have kept us so. Have I ever failed you? Trust me," he added quickly before Sobinski could answer the last question.

"You sound like a confidence trickster," Sobinski said calmly.

Zaleski forgave him. "I am offering you an end to indignity and suffering."

"Save your breath," Sobinski shrugged. "You win. Of course you must win. My nights would be sleepless otherwise. In any case what do I have to lose?"

Czarniecki put his head back and let go with a bellow of laughter. Zaleski found himself infected. Sobinski joined in. The three men fell about, supporting one another weakly as the tears rolled down their cheeks. Zaleski wiped his eyes and refilled the glasses. They all stood. He toasted them solemnly.

"Never above you, never beneath you but always at your side!"

They drank quickly, upending the glasses as they had done in a hundred bars from Tripoli to Trieste. Sobinski's boyish face was flushed.

"This military operation, when does it take place?"

"Tomorrow night," Zaleski said casually.

The news sobered the looks on the other men's faces. Czarniecki sounded a shade dubious.

"We wouldn't have to leave our jobs?"

"The opposite," Zaleski assured him. "It is essential that we all go about our business in the normal way. Bogdan at the garage, Stanislas at the hospital, me here. We will need a car for tomorrow night. Can you manage that, Bogdan, without it being missed?"

The big man's face was painfully thoughtful. "I think so. I am certain, yes. Fleetline has two hundred vehicles on the road. There are always some in the repair shop. When a car goes out on a test run it leaves by the back way. There is no check on the car or driver."

"What time is the back way closed?"

"Eight o'clock. Men work overtime."

"Good," said Zaleski. "That gives us three hours. We will need a car that is inconspicuous yet big enough for a man to be held down without being seen from the outside."

"Ahah," said Sobinski, looking up from rolling another of his handmade cigarettes. "A man is held down?"

"With a hood over his head," added Zaleski. "I spent the whole of last week reconnoitering the area. The owner of the gallery is a bachelor who lives alone. If he is not home on time there is no one to worry. He closes the premises every night shortly after five and walks back to Berkeley Square where he leaves his car. I have watched him six nights in a row. His routine never varies."

Czarniecki scratched his bald head with a calloused fore-finger. "Starting tomorrow it will. A jeweled monstrance is more than just paint and canvas."

Zaleski looked at him charitably. "It is all in the mind, Bogdan. What we think of as a jeweled monstrance others see as an historical relic. This Tedeschi is no fool. His gallery is well protected — burglarproof locks, an alarm system with the bell hanging outside on the wall."

Sobinski aimed a stream of smoke at his glass. "It gets better and better. Continue."

Zaleski leaned forward, tapping the side of his nose. "I have seen Tedeschi set the alarm. I know where the switch is."

Sobinski's eyes were as clear as pebbles in a mountain brook. "And I know Conduit Street. West Central Police Station is no more than a couple of hundred yards away. There is bound to be some watch on the gallery."

"Agreed," said Zaleski. "But not at five in the evening. Listen. When Tedeschi leaves the gallery, we grab him and take his keys. I go back and open the door. You will be driving Tedeschi around in the car. At six o'clock sharp you dump him somewhere safe and go home. It will be dark, and you will both be wearing disguises. No one will see me entering the gallery. No one will see me leave."

Czarniecki yawned again. Zaleski knew him too well to think that the yawn was prompted by nerves.

"Any questions?" asked Zaleski.

Sobinski looked up. "What happens when we have the monstrance. What do we do with it?"

"Everything has been taken care of," Zaleski answered calmly. "By this time next week we shall be rich men." The scene was vivid in his mind. Cashiers whispering together as he made his way to the bank manager's office. The respect as he flipped open the dispatch case, revealing the wealth inside.

Czarniecki rattled his teeth excitedly. "What does a rich man do with his money? I have never had any to worry about."

The question disappointed Zaleski. "Have you no dreams?" he demanded. "Money turns dreams into reality."

Sobinski's eyes lingered on the giant fondly. "Bogdan has dreams. We can live like princes. Changing our clothes four times a day, drinking champagne, eating only steak."

"There'll be women," prompted Zaleski, still irritated by the big man's simplicity. "Beautiful women of high birth." He kissed the tips of his fingers, winking.

Czarniecki pounded the bar happily. "The first thing I will do is kick the foreman's ass. Then I will go to bed for a week in the Ritz Hotel."

Zaleski cleared his throat. "Then we are agreed. We meet at my flat at sixteen hours tomorrow. Bogdan brings the car and you dress in your best clothing."

He helped both men into their overcoats and saw them to the door. He watched from behind the curtain as they walked away in opposite directions. He put the vodka bottle back on the shelf under the mirror and rinsed the glasses. It was twenty minutes of seven, a time of day he disliked since his separation from Hanya. He imagined her now, sitting alone in her damp apartment by the river, painting china with patient strokes of her brush. A woman of quality, daughter of a general, daubing crockery at twenty pence apiece. He nodded unconsciously, hearing his wife's caustic tongue. Her condition was ascribed to his improvidence, his drinking and philandering. Yet in spite of it all, their relationship was better

than it had ever been. Above all, Hanya was loyal. It would
have been unthinkable to plan the restoration of their fortunes
without telling her the truth. After much argument, her
approval had been given resignedly. Even after that, she'd
continued as devil's advocate, going over every step in his
scheme, challenging him on the very point Sobinski had raised.
What was he going to *do* with the monstrance? The truth was
that as yet he had no answer. But the essence of command was
the use of initiative. Tonight would see it employed. Sam
Gerber had booked his usual table for eight o'clock. Jerzy
Dubrowski had first brought Gerber to the restaurant, a
well-dressed gangster known as Lucky Sam. Dubrowski
worked as a croupier in a casino patronized by big-time
gamblers and thieves. Gerber had become a frequent visitor.
The women he brought with him were always good-looking,
and he spent his money freely without reference to its source.
Zaleski was impressed on all counts. The matter would have
to be handled circumspectly, but the more he thought about it,
the more confident he was that Gerber was his man.

He put on his astrakhan hat and black leather overcoat. The
chef had his own key and let in the waiters. It was a point of
honor with Zaleski that he never appeared in the restaurant
before nine o'clock. He crossed Fulham Road and walked two
blocks south to Waverley Court, a small red brick building
with ten units. The separation from Hanya had left his life
oddly disoriented. There was no longer anything to get away
from. For years he had thought of a bachelor's life with envy.
The first-floor studio flat seemed just what he needed. The
other tenants were young. Girl secretaries, a ménage of male
models, a married couple in television who looked and dressed
alike and talked about "the medium." Zaleski had envisaged a

succession of romantic adventures in which he would star. There was no resident janitor, and Zaleski's front door opened onto the lobby. There'd been this one occasion, months before, when his doorbell had rung at seven o'clock at night. He hadn't been out all day and was still in his pajamas and robe. He'd peeked through the curtains into the forecourt. A tall blonde wearing a white stocking cap on the back of her head was standing beneath the light over the entrance. He'd let her in. A wine and cheese party was going on upstairs, and she had pressed the wrong buzzer. She looked back over the banister at him, her voice husky and exciting. Why didn't he join them — Joe and Joyce would love to have him, et cetera. The hosts were the couple in television. Zaleski had taken pains with his appearance, choosing dark blue trousers and shirt and knotting a silk handkerchief at the side of his neck. He clipped the hairs in his nostrils and rinsed his mouth with a liquid compounded of cinnamon and cloves. He walked up the stairs slowly so that his breathing would not be affected. Sudden bursts of energy left him winded of late. The apartment door was open, the atmosphere in the living room acrid with the smell of hash. People were lying around on cushions, others were in the kitchen drinking. The beat of Brazilian music persisted through the mind-bending chatter. Zaleski sucked in his stomach and slotted his monocle, searching for his hosts. The girl in the white cap was in a corner, dangerously close to a bearded fellow in a shaggy sweater. Zaleski knew the type well. Pretentious and penniless poseurs with a glib line about the arts. He bowed in the girl's direction, trying to catch her eye. She looked at him over the man's shoulder and said something, smiling. Zaleski rolled on the balls of his feet as if struck. His nose thinned.

"Peasants!" he called out in Polish, but nobody seemed to hear him. Back in his apartment, he poured himself a stiff whiskey and water. By the time he had drunk it, anger had changed to outrage. Who did they think they were, these mummers and strollers! He was still young and vigorous, a man of experience and sophistication. He poured another drink from the Scotch bottle and called a cab. He finished the night in the arms of a Swedish masseuse, biting her neck in an exercise of passion and virility. It was the last time he accepted any invitation from within the building. His doorbell had been out of commission ever since.

He turned into the forecourt, observing the new graffiti scrawled on the low wall. He had his eye on the offender, a surly milkman who was without doubt a communist. A party was under way up on the third floor. A bottle of wine had been dropped on the stairs. The floor was still wet. Someone had used the mop in the broom closet to wipe up the mess and the closet door was still open. He shut it and unlocked his apartment. The furniture, paintings and television set were rented. There was nothing of his own in the flat except a few things in the bedroom — his clothes and shoes, two framed pictures of Hanya taken in Cairo years ago. She'd been a handsome woman then, with fire in her veins. The basic trouble was that women aged faster than men. His own appearance had altered little since the old days. There were no gray hairs on his head, he could still quote Plato and the roll of fat around his middle was due to a lack of exercise. In a country besotted by horses, getting up on the back of one was an expensive business.

As winter approached and the days grew shorter Zaleski spent the most of Sunday in bed, surrounded by the newspapers and empty coffee cups. The building started to stir around noon. The English had a preoccupation with breakfast, wolfing great plates of bacon and eggs no matter how arduous the night before had been. They were insensitive, clattering milk bottles and playing their protest songs at high volume. They shouted up and down the stairs before leaving for the pubs around one, annoyingly fresh and clear-eyed. Zaleski maintained a haughty silence, broken only by an occasional skirmish. His phone rang rarely. When the building was empty a deep sense of melancholy settled on him, a nostalgia for something only barely remembered.

He bathed and dressed in the dark suit he usually wore in the evening. It was a long time since he had given his tailor any money, and there was the matter of a county court summons that had gone to Hanya by mistake. She had paid the tailor's bill in full, stupidly using her savings. To protect his honor, she'd said, as if nonpayment of a tradesman's bill could smirch it. Yet when he needed cash she pleaded poverty. A sheaf of unpaid accounts fluttered through his mind. He saw them settled with one grand gesture. Graciously, of course, as befitted a gentleman, a little pained perhaps at his creditors' lack of faith.

It was precisely nine o'clock as he turned the corner onto Fulham Road. Three cars were parked in front of the restaurant. He recognized the red convertible that Gerber drove. A cosy glow came from behind the curtains. The shabbiness of the floors above were hidden in the darkness. He made his entrance, smiling as he assessed his customers. Six of the ten tables were occupied. The Canadian who ran the bookstore further up the road was there with his girl friend. The middle-aged couple holding hands were Sunday regulars.

They chose the same dish each week, drinking a bottle of Hungarian wine with their meal. Gerber's party was at the window table. The rest of the diners were strangers. He hung his hat and coat behind the bar, glancing automatically at the food elevator. The Polish chef was temperamental and given to shouting abuse up the shaft at the Spanish waiters. Zaleski poured himself a quick shot of vodka, drinking it under the bar. He wiped his mouth and straightened up, winking at the Canadian. The girl at the table waved back.

Gerber was a tall man of forty with sandy hair receding from a high glistening forehead. A razor slash had removed the tip of his left ear, leaving a thin line in the scalp behind where the hair had ceased to grow. Zaleski always avoided looking at it. Scars that were not the results of gunshot wounds revolted him. Gerber's clothes were chosen with restraint. He dressed like a merchant banker in dark, natural-shouldered suits, white silk shirts and sober ties. In spite of the disfigured ear, heavy-framed spectacles gave him a donnish look. Zaleski walked across to his table. The redhead with Gerber was wearing a mink hat. A matching coat was draped over the back of her chair. The last member of the party was a thin-faced man in his thirties wearing a double-knit suit and snakeskin shoes. He wore a large ugly ring on the index finger of his right hand and his head was flattened like a weasel's. Zaleski knew him as Benny, or the Bookeeper. If he had other names, they were never mentioned.

Gerber pulled a chair. Zaleski remained standing till the gambler made the introductions.

"This is the owner of the place, Share. Watch him, he's the fastest worker in the business! Sharon O'Donnell."

Zaleski touched the outstretched hand with his lips. The girl's flesh was expensively scented. He knew that his English was fractured. After three weeks at a language school, he'd given up the struggle with syntax and canceled the rest of the course. He still thought in Polish, translating as he went.

"Welcome, mademoiselle. Wielkapolska is honored by such beautiful guest."

Gerber snapped his fingers for another glass. There was a bottle of champagne on the table, an empty one upturned in the ice bucket.

"Sit down, you old goat," he said jocularly. "I told you, Share, watch him! He's a lecher."

Zaleski dissembled his disgust. "Is possible we can talk together?" he asked quietly. "Alone."

Gerber took his hand off the girl's thigh promptly. He thumbed her in the direction of an empty table.

"You too, Benny," he ordered. "Tell each other how you lost your virginities."

The redhead squirmed to her feet, trailing clouds of scent. "Isn't he awful?" she whined coquettishly.

The Cockney accent shocked Zaleski profoundly, but he smiled gallantly as she left, followed by the man in the snakeskin shoes.

Gerber snipped off the end of a cigar with a pair of gold cutters. "What's your problem, Zally — you're not nicked are you?" His references to the law always implied a certain disrespect. He talked openly about his ability to defeat it.

Zaleski scraped his chair closer. "You are gambler, right?"

"I like a bet," admitted Gerber. His lighter was gold like the cutter.

"Money interests you?"

"Pos-i-tively," said Gerber. "I'm fascinated by it." He tilted the wine bottle and filled Zaleski's glass.

Zaleski's sip was no more than a token.

"You are man of discretion as well, I know this."

"Silent as the grave," said Gerber, lowering an eyelid.

Zaleski was picking his way delicately. "Gamblers are taking chances."

"Keep going," said Gerber. "You're doing all right up to now."

Zaleski smiled acknowledgment. "Polish army was good school. I am judge of men, you understand."

"Not a word," said Gerber, flicking ash at the carpet. "If you've got a proposition, make it."

The middle-aged couple had paid their check and were leaving. Zaleski waited till the door had closed behind them. The redhead was giggling with Benny. The other guests were intent on their food. He leaned forward confidentially.

"You are man of world, Mr. Gerber. Friends of mine are having fortune in jewelry. Difficulty lies in selling."

"You mean the gear's bent?" said Gerber easily.

Zaleski blinked. "Bent?"

"Crooked," amplified Gerber, waving his cigar. "Your friends nicked it, right?"

Zaleski glanced up in the mirror hurriedly. Nobody seemed to have heard. Gerber was feeling the effects of the champagne.

"Is complicated story," Zaleski said in a lower voice. "Is difficult to explain but no chance selling jewelry in ordinary way."

Gerber cocked his head. "Like I said, they nicked it."

Zaleski put his finger on his lips, pleading for discretion. He had gone too far to turn back. The fellow had the cunning of his kind and would bear careful watching.

"Are hundreds of diamonds," he whispered. "Rubies and emeralds."

Gerber's eyes were round behind his spectacles. "No kidding! Diamonds, rubies *and* emeralds?"

Zaleski nodded. "Half-a-million pounds' worth. Ten percent for man who arranges disposal."

Gerber drew on his cigar, contemplating Zaleski through a cloud of smoke.

"What exactly do you take me for, Zally — a fool or a buyer of stolen property?"

"My friends are serious people," urged Zaleski. "Is no risk for a man with contacts."

The smoke cleared in front of Gerber's face. "Look, mate, I like you. Know something? A few weeks ago I even thought of throwing a few quid into this place. Benny made a few inquiries. Your lease runs out next year, and you don't have a pot to piss in. That's right, isn't it? So don't give me this cobblers about your friends and the crown jewels."

Zaleski's body was rigid. He looked across the table at the grinning face, trying to find words to answer.

"Drink up," Gerber said kindly. "Don't take it to heart. They all have a go at me, a little con of some kind. I never mind the first time. You're sort of different. I didn't expect it. But if you want a twenty you can have it, you don't have to knock yourself out."

"No," said Zaleski, denying the insult. "Ah this, no!" He picked up his glass and threw the contents in Gerber's face.

Benny was on his feet in a flash, a blade halfway out of his jacket pocket. The redhead's mouth opened in a silent scream. Zaleski backed off against the wall, fronting the man with the knife.

"Hold it!" called Gerber. The blade disappeared again. He took off his spectacles and wiped them deliberately. He laid some money on the table and picked up the mink coat. Benny and the redhead moved to the door. Gerber looked at Zaleski, smiling.

"You should never have done that, mate. You shouldn't have done it." He left the door open. Seconds later, the convertible outside pulled away at full speed.

Zaleski shut the door. The room was completely quiet. The guests had assumed the detachment of the English faced with public unpleasantness. He made his way to the Canadian's table.

"You let me join you, Kirk?"

Fraser pushed a chair forward quickly. He was a tall man on the wrong side of thirty with graying hair worn long over his ears and quizzical blue eyes. His tweed jacket was shabby and spaghetti sauce had dropped on the front of his sweater. He poured a glass of red wine and shoved it in Zaleski's direction.

"Wow! What the hell was all that about?"

The wine was rich after the bubbles of the champagne. Zaleski liked this couple. They were friendly and intelligent, and the girl never forgot that he was a male. In a neighborhood poisoned by scandal and bitchery, they kept to themselves, untouched by malice or gossip. Their bookstore was an oasis where Zaleski went gladly. He lowered his empty glass, apologizing to the girl.

"I am sorry, Ingrid."

She shook back shoulder-length black hair, a graceful movement that employed the use of capable hands. The shape of Ingrid's askew face, her long flowered skirt and shawl gave her a demure, old-fashioned look. Hoops in her ears swung as she shook her head. Her cobalt blue eyes continued to smile long after her mouth was at rest.

"It's you we were worried about. I think you ought to call the police or something. That man was positively evil."

Zaleski shrugged the suggestion out of existence. "Is not necessary. I know this kind of man. Are making noise and nothing else. He will not come back to Wielkapolska."

Fraser's expression was curious. "That sounds like a cop-out, Casimir. Who is the guy, anyway? We've seen him in here half-a-dozen times."

"A gambler," Zaleski said shortly. He took the girl's hand in his and changed the subject. "Why bothering with this Canadian, Ingrid — this backwoodsman?"

Fraser smiled at her fondly. "I'm giving her the best years of my life, and she loves me for it."

The girl's glance caressed him absently. She pantomimed a shiver. "I can't get the look on that man's face out of my mind. It was sinister, horrible. How any girl could allow him to touch her . . ."

Fraser winked at Zaleski. "I don't know," he drawled. "There'd always be the mink to remember."

She pulled her shawl tighter around her shoulders. "No thank *you!* When you're tired of me, Casimir's going to take care of me, aren't you, Casimir?"

"Why waiting?" said Zaleski. "Why wasting time with this immature Colonial?" He refilled his glass, restored by their company. When the time came, they would be high on the list of those to be helped. The urge to drop a hint was irresistible. They had joined hands. He leaned over and clasped their fingers.

"Are too many gray days in London, my friends. You need sun on your bodies."

"Remind me to win the pools," Fraser said wryly.

Zaleski pushed his chair away from the table. "Some day soon," he promised. "You are coming to stay in my house in Italy."

Their joint disbelief left him undisturbed. He took their dinner check and tore it up.

"With Zaleski all things are possible. Tuscany in summertime. So many beautiful colors, herbs growing from cracks in rocks. You'll see." He touched the girl's cheek. "Good night, my dear. Be kind to her, Kirk."

It was after ten and few customers dined late on Sundays. He opened the cash register and removed the takings. He put on his hat and coat and left the restaurant. The chef could lock up. The street was cold, the air raw. He started walking west, past the pubs and the cluster of eating places. A queue was waiting in front of a hamburger joint. The sight gave him peculiar satisfaction. The English were aping the Americans, lining up for ground meat drenched in ketchup. The plight of the Poles was bad, but the English were not much better than aliens in their own land, their traditions dying or forgotten. They were scared of the blacks and the Irish, envious of the French and the Germans. He was walking a little splayfooted, his belly bulging out comfortably over his belt. Hanya would give him something to eat. Living with her again would mean that he would feed well. The chef at Wielkapolska had been a cook in the cavalry corps. A red convertible flashed by. Zaleski skipped aside instinctively, but it wasn't Gerber. If the gangster did cause trouble, he would find that Poles had ways of dealing with ruffians. He opened the phone booth and dialed his wife's number.

"I have to speak to you," he said in Polish. "A change of plan. I will be there in half-an-hour."

He left the booth hastily, flagging down a cab that was passing. He paid the driver off at the southern approach to Putney Bridge and headed for an apartment building a couple of hundred yards away. Mist was rolling off the river, veiling the streetlamps, glistening on the bare trees. He walked around in back of the buildings, over the expanse of hardtop and down the long covered passageway that led to the service access. The third-floor corridor was quiet. He tapped on a door at the end. The woman who opened it was wearing a painter's smock over a woollen dress and comfortable slippers. Her white-streaked hair was parted in the center and scraped back in a coil on her neck. She was inches taller than Zaleski, still handsome in spite of bones blunted by too much flesh.

"Wipe your feet," she instructed.

He shuffled his soles on the mat and stepped inside. The furniture was familiar. A leather sofa and matching chair he had bought when the White Eagle Club closed down. The closure had shocked them all then, but looking back on it, why would the English subsidize a club for Polish veterans when they refused to pay them pensions? The faded Indian carpet had come from the same place. The living room walls were bare except for a framed display of his dead father-in-law's military decorations. The general himself, attired in the dress uniform of the Hussars, glared from a silver stand on the mantel. The plates his daughter had been painting were drying on a rack in front of the convector heater. Mrs. Zaleska's lips tasted of the cachou she chewed endlessly.

She took his hat and coat, speaking with her back to him. "You have been drinking."

He waited till she turned then tapped the face of his watch. "It is twenty minutes to eleven, Hanya. *Naturally* I have been drinking. I would like to continue drinking," he added, sinking down in the chair that had always been his. His wife never used it herself.

She opened a small closet. The bottle of vodka he had brought on his last visit was untouched. The door to her bedroom was ajar, the lights there thriftily extinguished. He needed no light to see the narrow bed with the crucifix at its head, the yellowing pictures of cousins and aunts on the bridge of an old-fashioned steam yacht. The children dressed in white sailor suits leaning over the rails looking down at the Baltic. His wife carried in a tray from the kitchen. He spread the napkin over his knees and forked a mouthful of soused herring.

"It is settled, Hanya. Bogdan and Stanislas are agreed. We do it tomorrow night." He looked up, gauging her reaction.

She was sitting on the sofa, smoking. The Egyptian cigarettes were her one luxury.

"I expected as much," she said calmly. "Three old fools together. But they at least have no wives to worry about them."

He removed a bone from his bridgework and placed it on the side of the plate.

"Enough about fools, Hanya. There is nothing more to discuss. You gave me your word about this."

It irritated him that she smoked without inhaling. The exercise was a waste of time and money.

"I shall do what I promised," she said. "I shall also continue to think what I think."

He pushed his plate away, his appetite suddenly gone. "I told you, there has been a change of plan. The English are not to be trusted. We have decided that the operation must stay in the hands of Poles. So you will take the monstrance to Paris."

She crossed herself hurriedly, holding the cigarette at arms length. "A consecrated relic, *stolen!* This I cannot do, Casimir."

He eyed her belligerently. "Nonsense! People have been polishing the thing with their backsides for a generation. The holiness has gone. You will leave tomorrow."

She looked at him, shaking her head. "It is well that we have no children. Your behavior is hard to defend."

"Listen to me, Hanya," he implored. "It is a small thing to ask of the woman I love."

She made a move of disbelief, but her eyes softened. "And what do I do in Paris?"

"Go to Paul Poniatoski. He will receive you, furnish you with the necessary papers to come back to England under another name on Tuesday. You will arrive here after dark. No one in the building must see you return. They must think that you are still in France. I will bring the monstrance here, and you will take it to Paul. You will never come back to this country again, Hanya."

His wife's tone struck a note of obstinacy. "I will not abandon my possessions, Casimir. Everything I own is here."

He started up, staring about him wildly, the veins bulging in his neck.

"Possessions!" he shouted. "What possessions? Have you taken leave of your senses?"

She extinguished her cigarette carefully. "Behave as you like in your restaurant, Casimir, but this is my home. Do me the honor of remembering this."

The general's daughter was speaking in the fastness of a Silesian manor. He hit his forehead with the heel of his hand and lowered his voice.

"Hanya, Hanya! — Listen to me, please. I am taking you

away from this *merde*. A few more days and you will be living like a queen."

"My father's decorations go with me," she said firmly, "The family pictures. And what is this with Paul Poniatoski, a watchmaker in a Paris slum?"

The slur was on a comrade and brother officer. He warned her of it behind outstretched arm.

"A little respect, woman — careful!"

A look of indifference spread across his wife's face. "Respect for a man who has owed you money for twenty years? A man who offered insult to his own sister-in-law?"

"You know nothing about it," he said stubbornly.

"I know enough," she answered. "It is six years since you saw him anyway. That, too, I remember. Ten days of drunkenness. Ask what you will but respect, no."

His smile was forbearing. Women understood nothing of such matters. Their friendships with one another needed the reassurance of constant contact.

"As you like, but he will be your host. I shall call him tonight and arrange things. He has the right contacts. It is the start of a new life for us, Hanya. We shall assume our rightful place in civilized society. A house with a garden, my darling — remember?"

It was Galicia now he was recalling, his parents' home. Beyond the forests, the Tatra mountains. They had met, courted and married there.

She adjusted her paint-stained smock, looking down at it. "And if the police arrest me?" she asked quietly.

He held up a hand, his face pained and disbelieving. "Do you think I would let you run that risk, Hanya? How many times do I have to tell you — the plan is foolproof. I beg of you to trust me in this."

Her mood seemed to change and she shrugged. "All my life I have done as I was told. My father first and then you. I suppose I must be grateful, if there is peace at the end of it all. However, I would prefer cows and geese to your civilized society."

He crossed to the sofa and sat down beside her, his eyes dimmed by a moment of sudden tenderness. Her smile had sustained him for thirty years.

"There will be concerts, Hanya," he urged, remembering how much he loathed them. "Ballet, the opera. We will read again together as we used to. The house will have poplars around it, and you will be able to see the mountains."

She shook her head, smiling gently still. "You will fill the house with your drunken friends and disgrace me with the maidservants. I have no illusions left, Casimir. Just give me the geese and the cows."

He inflated his lungs and rapped himself on the chest. "There is much to do, I have to go. Remember all I have said. It is essential that the people here do not know of your return on Tuesday. Do not put the lights on. Just sit here and wait for me. Your travel document is in order?"

She moved her head in assent. "Have no fears about me. I shall obey your wishes no matter what."

He looked at her closely, seeing his childhood sweetheart. He would try to reform, manage his *affaires* more discreetly.

"Here is money," he said, giving her the takings from the restaurant. "Eighty-five pounds. Spend wisely till the monstrance is in our hands." He put on his coat and buttoned it up slowly.

She came close, smoothing his lapels. "We could start a new life here. There is room for us both. We need no more than we already have."

He planted the astrakhan cap firmly on his head. "The train leaves Victoria Station tomorrow evening. Travel first-class. You will be in Paris before midnight. I will telephone you at Poniatoski's."

She put her face next to his. "Good night, Casimir. No matter what, I shall always be there."

He kissed her tenderly. The passion of their love might be spent, but something still stronger remained. He hesitated for a moment then shut the door behind him. There was no way of telling her that. She was a proud woman and might not have understood. He managed to leave the building without being seen, unabashed by a feeling of relief. Things would be greatly different once they were out of this godforsaken country. With money they could create a real home for the first time in their lives, a refuge from a world bent on debasing the values they stood for. Hanya would have her animals, the garden, to occupy her mind whenever he made the occasional foray in search of adventure. A hot-blooded man needed romantic adventures, romance without involvement. That much Hanya did understand. All she asked was that his forays were conducted with discretion. He squared his shoulders and walked briskly into the mist that was still rolling off the river.

It was midnight by the time he reached home. The lights were out in the apartment across the lobby. The two girls who lived there were already in bed. He slammed the lobby door loudly, defying them and their new establishment, their criticism of his generation. Sluts in bedsocks who mistook ordinary courtesy for lecherous behavior. He no longer passed the time of day with them. He switched on his radio and dialed Paris. It was one o'clock there, but Poniatoski was still on his feet. They spoke in Polish with the usual expressions of mutual regard. Zaleski was cagey about details. A blow was being struck for the Old Guard. He was relying on a comrade's prudence. A fortune was at stake, and he needed a contact with a dealer in jewels. Someone reliable. If he was Jewish, so much the better. The Jews had imagination. Poniatoski's response was emotional. For an old comrade-in-arms anything was possible though the sum mentioned as a finder's fee was small for the risk involved. It so happened that he knew someone living in Amsterdam. Everything would be arranged with the utmost circumspection. No time was wasted with ethical doubts. Poniatoski would arrange for a false identity card for Hanya, and she would be an honored guest in his house.

Zaleski put the receiver down. Friendship like faith moved mountains. The incident with Gerber was fading from his mind, an error of judgment best forgotten. There was no need for Bogdan or Stanislas to know about it. He ran a bath and soaked in the pine-scented water for half-an-hour, pleased with the way things were going. In bed, he reread the article in the *Catholic Weekly*. The British had no shame. He put out the light remembering the old Polish army story. A Polish parachutist is waiting to drop from a British plane. He opens a sealed envelope containing his orders. "You will proceed to the spot marked X on the map. You will find a bicycle standing under an oak tree." The British flight sergeant signals him to jump. He is halfway down when the Pole discovers that he has no parachute. "Bastards," he thinks. "And I bet they've forgotten the bicycle!" He was still smiling as he slid into sleep, snoring heavily.

Chapter Two

THE DAY DAWNED cold and damp. His first sight was a pigeon huddled on the windowsill. He loathed the birds, their filth and ubiquity, the way they clustered underfoot in the squares. He had once seen one flying out of the tunnel at Camden Town Station a quarter mile underground. He threw a pillow in the direction of the window. The pigeon flapped away lopsidedly. There was no reason for Zaleski to look at his watch to know the time. The banging of doors and smell of breakfast cooking told him that it was past eight. The radio from the apartment overhead reaffirmed his judgment. He yawned, looking for his slippers as the announcer spoke of floods, strikes and traffic delays. Zaleski placed his hands on his hips and tottered into a few shaky genuflections. The effort depressed him as usual. He took his coffee and toast back to bed and stayed there, working out his schedule. He was done making concessions, compromising. He wanted something now unconditionally and was determined to succeed. At half-after ten he called his bank and made an appointment to see the manager at noon.

He dressed in the new cashmere sweater and checked trousers and inspected every inch of his face in the mirror. An unsightly appearance gave rise to doubt and the impression he had to make was important. Not a bristle had escaped the razor. There were no unsightly blackheads, and his scalp gleamed under smoothly brushed hair. He stepped back satisfied. His bank was in South Kensington. He pushed through the revolving doors, picking up a stock survey on his way to the manager's office. Mr. Howard came out of his chair, smiling, a stout man with his cheeks scraped to a high gloss.

"Good morning, Mr. Zaleski, and what can we do for you today?"

The walls of the office were hung with pictures of prize Herefords. The manager had transferred from a country branch, bringing with him the bluff friendliness of a small market town. Zaleski's financial antics invoked a sense of bewilderment in Mr. Howard's mind. Zaleski put the stock survey inside his fur hat and crossed his legs comfortably.

"I am closing business, retiring."

Howard's nose lifted as though detecting some strange rare scent. "You're not telling me you've sold the restaurant?" His tone implied that only a lunatic would have bought.

"Is nothing to do with restaurant," Zaleski said loftily. "My wife is inheriting large fortune."

"I see," said the manager. His fingers strayed toward the file at his elbow, but he thought better of it.

Zaleski knew exactly what was in the file. His life insurance policy, the guarantees for bank loans coaxed from reluctant friends.

"Is highly confidential," he emphasized. English was an appropriate language for this kind of conversation. The words had a ring of importance. "We shall be needing advice about investments."

Howard's expression was a blend of gratification and wariness. "I see," he repeated. "The inheritance is your wife's, you say?"

Zaleski waved a hand airily. "Is same thing. With Polish people, husband is controlling money."

"Yes," said the manager. "Yes, of course." He put his hand on the file as if exorcising some form of black magic that was new to him. "You do realize that the bank would be unable to extend further credit until the — ah — the appropriate documentation is in hand?"

"Is unnecessary." Zaleski fitted a cigarette into his holder. He placed the spent match in the ashtray and smiled. "Lawyers will provide whatever we need. They know nothing about overdraft, of course. Is no need and embarrassing for my wife. I am quite sure you understand."

The manager's voice slipped into professional heartiness. "Of course. Let me offer you my very real congratulations, Mr. Zaleski."

Zaleski took the outstretched hand, shook it firmly then came to his feet.

"Thank you. Is only reason I came here this morning. My wife said first to know should be bank manager. In few days' time, overdraft will be paid off. Now. You are busy, and I must leave you."

Howard accompanied his newly affluent client to the door. The bank manager's expression was slightly dazed.

"About the investments. I am always at your disposal, Mr. Zaleski. It must be a wonderful moment for you."

"Is wonderful," Zaleski agreed, clapping on his hat. "But I am not forgetting that wealth is bringing responsibility. Good day, Mr. Howard."

He bought a copy of *France-Soir* in the subway station across the road and turned into the espresso bar where he normally drank his mid-day coffee. He sipped it slowly, pleased at the way the interview with the bank manager had gone. Poniatoski would provide the name of a French lawyer who could be used if necessary. Gerber he remembered now as a hoodlum he had barred from his premises. Zaleski's bachelor existence was as predictable as that of any suburban straphanger. He simply did different things at different times. It was getting on for one o'clock, the hour when he usually strolled as far as the wine bar on Fulham Road and took his lunch. Today he was neither hungry nor thirsty. He paid his bill and went down the steps to the underground station. Phase one of his plan was in operation. He surfaced at Hammersmith Broadway, losing himself in the crowds along Uxbridge Road. The tinseled saris and bare ankles of the Indian women, the bright colors worn by the blacks, accentuated the gray desolation of the streets. Zaleski could think of no reason why he should be followed, but the idea excited him. It revived memories of Cairo alleys stinking with urine, of doorways in deep shadow, the grunt that accompanied the knife thrust. His contacts with the police were limited to his appearances at the Aliens Office and a couple of visits to Chelsea Police Station. His mental picture of detectives was colored by television series. He thought of them as dour-faced men with North Country accents, beset by domestic difficulties. There was nothing glamorous about the occupation that he could see.

He turned into the warmth of a chain store, a brightly lit covered market with counters loaded with food, hardware, paint, crockery and costume jewelry. He'd picked the place for its anonymity. Once the customer's money was in the cash register, he was forgotten. Zaleski bought three pairs of gloves and some sunglasses with outsize frames. His last stop was at the cosmetic counter. The girl packed his purchases into a cardboard box. He left the store buoyed by a feeling of euphoria that had been with him since he woke. He dropped off the bus at the corner of Fulham Road and Drayton Gardens. The detour he made to avoid the liquor store was with reason. He knew exactly how Czarniecki felt about the foreman at the rent-a-car firm. He intended to settle the liquor store account in the same spirit. The sons of bitches had to be taught their proper places.

Wielkapolska was less inviting by day than by night. The upstairs windows were blank and grimy, the entrance blocked by garbage cans. He opened the door and picked up the Monday mail that had been slipped through the slot. He sorted the wheat from the chaff with practiced eye, pushing the bills into the cash register. The kitchen downstairs was spotlessly clean. The chef's knives glistened on a board, his meat cleaver sunk deep into the chopping block. It was the last thing the man did before leaving at night, a gesture of possession and defiance. The chisel that was used to pry open packing cases was in a drawer. Zaleski pocketed it. Hanya would be in Paris at seven o'clock tomorrow night. She would be back by the same time the next day if she traveled on one of the two morning trains. This meant that he would have the monstrance on his hands for over twenty-four hours. He had to find a safe place to hide it. His first thought had been to use one of the lockers at Victoria Station. The difficulty was the short maximum rental period. After twenty-four hours the lockers were cleared, the contents redeemable only at the baggage office. His final choice of a hiding place had exercised his conscience. He had no intention of telling anyone else where or what it was, least of all his wife.

He closed the restaurant and walked along Fulham Road. It was important that people should remember seeing him in his usual haunts at the appropriate times. He stopped outside the bookstore and rapped sharply on the window. Fraser's back was to the street, but Ingrid waved, smiling. Zaleski blew her a kiss and walked on, working his way south to Chelsea and a quiet cul-de-sac between King's Road and the river. An imaginative use of glass, timber and paint had converted two rows of ugly artisans' dwellings into what the real-estate agents described as "town houses of character." A Rolls and an Aston-Martin symbolized the status of the people who lived in them. At the end of the cul-de-sac was a small chapel behind a gated wall. The stonework was blackened, the bricks mellowed to a shade of mulberry. There was no trace now of the manor or the gardens that had once reached as far as the river. Zaleski had reason to know the history of the chapel. A turbulent Polish priest was buried there, an *émigré* who had followed Charles II from exile. Lodged in a sanctuary near his tomb was the sword of Prior Kordecki, the defender of Czestochowa monastery. Though the chapel was still consecrated, few people worshiped there. It was unpopular with the clergy, cold and difficult of access. A handful of Polish-Americans made the pilgrimage in summertime. Mass was said once a month and Hanya never missed attending. Her mother had been born in Czestochowa.

He crossed the flagged yard and turned the big iron ring that unfastened the front door. Stained-glass windows filtered the daylight, and it was dim inside the chapel. He removed his fur hat and knelt in the back row of pews. A small red lamp was burning in front of the altar. He narrowed his nose against its smell. A part-time verger unlocked the chapel on his way to work, closing it as he went home. The gate to the entrance yard was never shut permanently. An Irishwoman from the council flats on Flood Street swept and scrubbed twice a week. Zaleski had taken care with his facts.

After a couple of minutes on his knees, he eased his buttocks onto the hard wood and peered around cautiously. There was nobody else in the church. The Polish priest's tomb was fashioned out of Carrara marble and protected by a frieze of gilt-topped spears. Behind the tomb was a small side altar and the sanctuary, a structure the size and shape of a meat safe. Pennants bearing the arms of Czestochowa Monastery hung on the walls above a line of thin, unlighted candles. Zaleski pulled himself up and tried the door that led to the sacristy. It was locked on the other side. He stepped over the gilt-topped spears, wearing his gloves. In spite of the cold he was sweating. His mind rejected the word sacrilege, but there was something about the stillness of the place, the Grand Guignol figure of Christ with its exposed heart dripping blood, that unnerved him.

The wooden sanctuary was secured by a small flimsy lock. He inserted the blade of the chisel and pressed. The lock gave with a sharp crack, wrenched from its screws. It dropped into his hand as he pulled the door open. The sanctuary was completely empty. He closed it again, wedging the door with paper. As close as he was standing, it was impossible to see that the lock had been removed. He clambered back to the aisle, outraged at the thought of the Polish prior's sword hanging in the palace of some fat-assed English bishop. It had probably been there for years while the faithful went on mumbling in front of an empty box. The reflection eased his conscience. A small opaque window secured by a flat bar overlooked the yard in front of the chapel. He lifted the bar free of its notches so that the window could be opened from the outside. He collected the packages from the pew and took off his gloves. There was no one to notice as he made his way out of the cul-de-sac.

It was almost four when he let himself into his apartment building. There was no noise from upstairs. It would be a couple of hours before his neighbors returned from work. He poured himself the first drink of the day, put the bottle away and changed into his dark suit. He unzipped the small leather case on his dresser. Inside were some cuff links and a fob-watch that had belonged to his father. Underneath the remaining odds and ends was a regimental badge bearing a bison's head as emblem. He had taken the badge with him on every commando raid he had made in the old days, defying the order about carrying objects that identified his unit. He slipped the badge in his pocket deliberately. Then he sat down facing the window and waited for the others.

Sobinski arrived first. Zaleski let him in. The doorbell rang again almost immediately. Both men had done their best with their limited wardrobes. Czarniecki's suite must have been a dozen years old. He wore it with stub-toed shoes and a raincoat. Sobinski's quilted topcoat covered dark gray flannel. Zaleski offered his hand to each in turn. Czarniecki's fingers were scrubbed, his nails cut short.

"As long as the car is back before eight o'clock there are no problems."

"Stanislas?" Zaleski looked at the one-armed man.

Sobinski plucked a cigarette from the pack on the table, his pale blue eyes impassive.

"I took a walk at five o'clock last night."

Zaleski nodded. "I had it in my head that you would. What did you see?"

Sobinski frowned into tobacco smoke. "The streets were crowded. People were going home from work. Everywhere I looked there was action."

"I know all this," said Zaleski. "I have covered the route not once but six times. What is your point?"

Czarniecki was poking into the cardboard box on the sofa. "It is no place to drag a man forcibly into a car."

Zaleski pushed the giant's arm away and distributed the wigs, gloves and sunglasses. Sobinski's wig was shoulder-length and ginger, Czarniecki's a mass of tight black curls. He placed it on his bald head and struck an attitude.

"Bogdan Czarniecki, queen of all the acrobats!"

Zaleski's mouth tightened angrily. "My liberty at stake and I choose a critic and a clown as accomplices! Call it what you like but this is no charade we're engaged in."

The other two glanced at one another quickly. The big man's homely face sobered.

"Why are you so angry, Casimir? It is my nature to be a clown. I have no criminal training. I joke because I am nervous."

Zaleski's expression softened. "Tedeschi will see you for seconds only and that in a bad light. All he will remember are the glasses and wigs. It takes him between five and six minutes to get from the gallery to where his car is parked. As soon as we see him coming we start to move — pull up in front of his car with our motor running. Bogdan jumps him from behind. Remember, he mustn't be allowed to shout. Then I go back to the gallery with his keys while you two drive him to Hampstead Heath. At exactly six o'clock you turn him loose.

Each of you destroys his own wig, gloves and glasses — completely and without any trace."

He gave Czarniecki the adhesive numerals for the front and rear of the car, the pillowcase that would be pulled over Tedeschi's head. He turned out the lights.

"Don't forget. From the moment we grab Tedeschi, there is to be no talking — not even a whisper. Now let yourselves out, one at a time."

He gave them a few minutes then pulled on his gloves and followed, carrying a blue canvas bag with Olympic Games' markings. The lobby was still quiet, the streetlamps lighted outside. The black Cortina was parked fifty yards away, Czarniecki at the wheel, Sobinski next to him. The false numbers had already been stuck on the plates. Zaleski walked around the car. It was a new model, fast enough for their need and roomy. He plucked a square of paper from under one of the windshield wipers.

THAT WHICH IS BORN OF THE FLESH IS FLESH

John 3:6

He tore the reminder into small shreds and took his place in back of the man at the wheel.

"Let us do what we have to do," he said. It was almost five o'clock as they cruised down the east side of Berkeley Square and stopped between the lampposts. An unbroken line of cars was parked end-on to the railings on the inner side of the square. The sidewalk between was dark and empty. Zaleski kept his eyes on the bottom of Hay Hill. The other two had their wigs and glasses out ready. The clock on the dash measured the minutes — 5:04, 5:05, 5:06. Czarniecki was whistling through his teeth tonelessly. A tall figure in a light-colored coat, wearing a scarf around his neck, stopped under the corner lamp, waiting for a lull in the traffic.

"Now!" said Zaleski.

The Cortina sliced forward, hugging the inside lane, and stopped near the northwest corner of the square, blocking the exit of the stationary Bentley. Czarniecki and Sobinski pulled on their gloves and wigs. The big man unfastened the catch on his door. Zaleski's gesture froze him. A traffic warden limped out of the darkness. For a moment it looked as if he was going to stay by the Bentley till its owner arrived. A horn bleep beyond the trees sent him shambling away. Tedeschi turned the corner and the two men met, the traffic warden touching his cap in salute. Czarniecki slipped out of the car, bending double as he approached the Bentley. The gallery owner stepped off the curb, presenting his back to the Pole as he fumbled with his car keys. The big man took him from behind, cutting off the Italian's breathing with a crooked elbow. A grotesque figure in the curly wig and glasses, he lifted his burden off the ground and ran it toward the Cortina. There was one frantic bawl, like that of a lost heifer, and Tedeschi was in the car. Sobinski was kneeling up on the front seat facing the rear. He leaned over, looking narrow-eyed, and swung his good arm. The judo chop poleaxed the Italian. He slumped on his back, snoring loudly, his eyes shut. Zaleski went through his pockets. The three keys he needed were in a small leather wallet. Traffic was sweeping around the square, past groups of people bustling homeward. The brief flurry of violence had gone completely unnoticed. Zaleski covered the gallery owner's head with the pillowcase and climbed out of the car. Sobinski took his place in back. The last thing Zaleski saw as the Cortina pulled away was the outline of the long ginger wig.

It was 5:24. He was four minutes behind schedule but calm.

He crossed Bond Street avoiding the lighted facade of the Westbury Hotel. The Dante Gallery was on the first floor of a building on the north side of Conduit. Overhead were suites of walkup offices. Drapes across the gallery windows allowed a certain effulgence of light from inside. Zaleski turned into the lobby. The hairdressing salon opposite stayed open until seven o'clock. He approached the gallery door. Two of the high-security locks were sunk into the mahogany at stomach level, the third a couple of feet lower down. People were still coming out of the offices above. He stood square onto the door with his back to the stairs. His eye told him that the smallest key fitted the lock at the bottom. It rotated smoothly. He straightened up, starting to sweat as he made the wrong choice with the other keys. The salon door opened, releasing a waft of warm scented air. A woman called good night. He turned the last set of tumblers and pushed the door open. A split second afterward, the alarm bell on the street started to ring. The whole building seemed to vibrate with the sound. A switch in the paneling near the floor operated the alarm. The noise stopped as his fingers found the button. He shut the door and leaned against it for a second, his mouth dry, imagining a troop of women charging across the lobby, their hair skewered up in bobby pins, arms pointing accusingly at the door behind which he sheltered. Footsteps clattered down the stairs and out into the street. He turned slowly, facing the low-slung lamp hanging from the ceiling at the end of the pine-paneled room. All the paintings had been cleared from the gallery except one. The exception was obvious, a Caravaggio representing the Virgin and Christ Child. A table covered with black velvet stood beneath the lamp. On it was a jewel-encrusted monstrance reflecting the light in brilliant colors, diamond white, ruby red, emerald green. By the monstrance was a card.

THE TREASURE OF SAN MARCO

A visitors' book lay open on a side table. The first signature was that of the Italian ambassador. Representatives of three ministries had signed their names immediately beneath. The lavender silk drapes were drawn across the street window. There was no way in which he could be seen. He tiptoed to the table, holding his breath as he lifted the heavy cross. He wrapped it in the velvet cloth and stuffed the bundle in the blue canvas bag. He could hear people coming and going on the stairs outside, across the lobby. He took a deep breath and opened the door, presenting his back to the hairdressing salon. He bent down and switched on the burglar alarm.

The first key he used turned halfway and then stuck. The need for haste was making his hand unsteady. A woman's voice was loud behind him, talking about an appointment for next week. He pulled the key out and tried again, making sure that the tongue of the lock was leaving the box. The key jammed for the second time. With the tongue of the lock sticking out, the door was impossible to close. The burglar alarm came to life, the high-pitched ringing reverberating through the lobby. He wrenched at the key desperately. It broke in the lock, leaving the shank in his fingers. He ran for the street and zigzagged through the halted traffic. The alarm was a high-pitched jangle overhead, but nobody bothered to look up. The drivers of the cars were watching the signals at the junction of Bond Street. Zaleski was fifty yards away when a couple of uniformed policemen pounded by on the opposite side of the street. One of them was talking into his microphone as he ran. Zaleski skidded into a walk. He had started to blow and his calf muscles were flagging. He drove himself on toward the lights of Regent Street. A cab pulled to the curb at the corner, discharging a fare. Zaleski climbed in and shut his eyes. The pain in his chest was surely his heart. He opened his eyes again as the driver's voice came from a distance.

"I can't sit here all night, mate. Where'd you want to go?"

Zaleski told him. The hack made a left turn back onto Conduit Street. A police car was drawn up in front of the gallery, its light flashing. The burglar alarm was still ringing. He could see that the lobby was full of cops. A cluster of women stood in the doorway of the hairdressing salon pointing. It was doubtful that anyone had seen his face, but he would have to destroy all his clothing. Forensic scientists hanged men with as little evidence as a tooth filling. It was 6:11 when the cab stopped outside Chelsea Town Hall. Zaleski walked away, one hand supporting the bag and the weight of the monstrance. He walked south on Flood Street. Five minutes and he was in the cul-de-sac. The curtains of the houses there had not yet been drawn. Firelight reddened a regency-striped wall. Figures moved with an insouciance born of confidence. A 999 call would ring the neighborhood with police in a matter of seconds, and the people at the windows seemed to know it, right down to the small girl rocking on her spotted wooden horse. Zaleski was into the chapel yard; the creaking gate closed behind him. He waited for a second, making sure that no one had checked on him further. He reached up, still wearing his gloves, and tried the window. It lifted easily. He hefted the heavy bag, holding the swinging window open with his body as he pulled his legs through and dropped inside. The altar lamp was still burning steadily, its glow touching the faces of the plaster statues. He forked the iron frieze that surrounded the tomb and pulled out the wedge holding the door of the sanctuary. He pushed the bag and its contents inside and wedged up the door again. He paused as he passed in front of the altar, a captive to memories reason had long since rejected. If Hanya was right, her Christ gave no one reason to grieve for his fault. By the time he dropped back into the front yard his mind was busy with matters that were more expedient.

He walked north toward Fulham Road. Chelsea had closed the first show of the day and was preparing for the second. The boutiques were still ablaze, but the blare of pop music in them was over till tomorrow. For an hour or so the area was square territory. Residents walked their dogs, bought flowers from the pedlar outside the post office, carried books to the library. It was the brief respite before the nightly invasion. From eight o'clock onward, the pubs and disco bars would be jammed with the brash enchanted young. Zaleski's adrenalin output was peaking. The broken key was unfortunate, but at worst it meant no more than the police starting their investigations sooner — *useless* investigations.

Lights shone at all levels of Waverley Court. He let himself into his apartment. The expanding suitcase on top of his clothes closet was large enough to hold the clothes he was wearing. He took it into the bathroom and started to undress. Everything went into the suitcase. Leather coat, suit, shirt, underwear, socks and shoes. He put the astrakhan hat in last and forced the top of the bag down.

He washed himself from head to feet, scrubbing his fingernails carefully. He'd burn the bag of clothing in the kitchen furnace after the chef had gone. He dressed in his new checked trousers and cashmere shirt, sprayed his mouth and opened his front door. A smell of frying sausages wafted across from the other side of the lobby. He rang the doorbell opposite. A brunette with a fringe answered. She was wearing a flowered robe over flannel pajamas and her nose and forehead were shiny.

"What do you want?" she demanded suspiciously.

It was the first time in months that they had spoken. He spread his hands.

"A man is banging on door this afternoon, asking for you. Why not telling your friends not to disturb me? At a quarter-to-five I am sleeping."

She sniffed. "With your television on full blast? You must be joking. What was his name anyway, didn't he leave a message?"

A second voice called from inside. "Who is it, Myra?"

The girl at the door kept her eyes on Zaleski. "It's the Pole, love, complaining that someone was here this afternoon for us and rang his doorbell."

The second girl appeared, holding a skillet like a weapon. "You know what I'd like to do with this?" she asked.

Zaleski slotted his monocle and inspected her carefully. "Is unnecessary. Are certain things in life I am doing without, trollops are included."

The two girls stood close together. "Are you calling us trollops?" the taller one asked.

Zaleski shrugged. The scene would remind them that he had been at home all afternoon.

"Look in mirror," he counseled as the door slammed in his face.

He poured himself a Scotch and water, heavy on the Scotch, and made himself comfortable on the living room settee. Tedeschi would be with the detectives by now. Not that his memory would be of much use to them. There was no chance of fingerprints being found in the gallery, and the car was safely back in the garage. The police would keep Tedeschi there half the night, showing him pictures of known criminals, probing his mind for some sort of clue. The beauty of the scheme was that there *were* no clues. His brain was floating comfortably on a pool of whiskey. Professional thieves were caught because they refused to accept the possible as being probable. It was just as well that they were caught. A stable society needed law and order.

He picked up the phone and dialed Paris. He was purposely curt with Poniatoski. The shipment would be in Paris on Wednesday. He asked for his wife, and Hanya came on the line.

"It is done," Zaleski said in Polish. "Everything happened as I planned. Paul has given you the necessary papers?"

"Yes." Her voice was strangely lacking in enthusiasm.

His forehead dragged into a frown.

"You have your ticket for tomorrow?"

"I have the ticket. I leave Saint Lazare at ten-fifteen in the morning, arriving in Victoria at five thirty-three and take the nine o'clock train back."

He put his feet up, bringing the mouthpiece closer. "I have had to change our plans again. There is no need for you to go home. When you come off the train, walk through to the hotel. I will be in the bar. We can have some food together, and I shall stay with you till your train goes."

"But I have to go home," she insisted. "I won't be coming

back to England. There are things that I cannot leave behind, things in the flat."

"Why didn't you take them with you yesterday?" he snapped. It was the pictures of her family, her father's medals, she was worrying about. "Hanya?"

"I'm here," she answered.

"You don't really *want* to leave, do you?" he challenged. "Listen to me! It will be a month before I come to Paris. But whatever it is that you want from your flat I can send."

"No," she said. "I must go home. What is the difference? We have plenty of time, nearly five hours. I will meet you later in the hotel."

Her voice had the determination that had frustrated him throughout their married life. He accepted defeat unwillingly.

"Your neighbors know that you are away?"

"Everyone knows," she answered. "I canceled the milk and the newspapers. The janitor said he would keep an eye on the flat."

"An eye," he repeated. "If he sees you going back to that flat, our whole plan is endangered. You realize that?"

"It will be dark," she said composedly. "And I am not a person to be noticed. It was your original idea, remember. As far as I am concerned, nothing has changed since yesterday."

But things *had* changed. The monstrance was in his possession now. Half-a-million pounds were at stake. He could hear her breathing at the other end of the line, unhurried and patient.

"All right," he replied. "We'll do it your way. So take a taxi straight from the station and pay it off at the bridge. Walk the rest of the way and be sure no one sees you going in or coming out. I'll wait for you in the hotel. There's nothing else you wanted to say?"

"Nothing," she answered quietly. "And you?"

"I love you, Hanya," he said impulsively. It was a long time since he had used the phrase, but he meant it. "This is the beginning of a new life for us."

Her voice was like a young girl's whisper, fearful and tender. "Whatever happens you will always be my husband. Good night, my dear."

He put the receiver down and looked over at the clock — 7:20. Almost two hours before he made his appearance at the restaurant. He carried the suitcase out from the bathroom and put it down. A vague memory was niggling in his mind, an impression of something forgotten. He turned out his pockets, staring at each article until the truth finally hit him. The regimental badge was missing, the bison emblem of the Fifth Polish Army. He opened the bag hurriedly and searched the pockets of the clothes he had been wearing. Nothing. Panic set in. He went down on his knees and started crawling across the floor, feeling blindly as he went into the bedroom and bathroom. There was no sign of the badge anywhere.

He remembered his gloved hands deep in his pockets as he walked up Hay Hill. He could still feel the hard outline of the metal badge. He must have dropped it after he left the gallery, perhaps while he was running. The memory grew more vivid as he thought about it. Someone would pick the badge up, a piece of bronze without value. Or it would lie in the gutter unnoticed to finish in the street sweeper's cart. The remaining possibility was too destructive to consider, and he placed it firmly outside his mind.

The keys he had used were on the table in front of him, the jagged shank of the broken one like some primitive arrow. He'd have to think of some safe place to plant them, somewhere beyond discovery. There'd be time in the morning. He shifted the television set to one side, ripped the carpet away from the wall and pried up a floorboard with a screwdriver. He stuffed the small satchel of keys deep between the joists, among the papers that were already there. There was no dust, no wrinkles, no loose tacks when he replaced the television set — nothing to suggest that the floor beneath was a hiding place. At nine o'clock sharp, he carried the bag of clothing across to the restaurant.

Chapter Three

THE DIN SLICED into Raven's sleep like a ripsaw tearing into spruce. He reached out, eyes shut tight, taking the instrument off its stand and holding it at arms length. The only sound now was the creak of the hull as the houseboat strained against the mooring chains. The tide had turned as he slept. The luminous hands of the small bedside clock showed a few minutes after midnight. He brought the earpiece nearer, wincing as he heard the brisk impersonal voice of the police switchboard operator.

"Inspector Raven? One moment, please, I have Chief Superintendent Drake on the line for you."

Raven jammed his thin shoulders against the bunkhead, groping in the darkness for his cigarettes. A disorderly array of objects appeared in the flare of the match. The floor was littered with an assortment of reading material, an empty beer glass and a piece of cheese. A pair of mulberry-colored velvet pants hung from the back of the chair while black buckled shoes pinned down a ski sweater. He cleared his throat, hearing the new voice on the line.

"Raven," he said.

"Woke you up, did I?" The voice was obnoxiously hearty. "Well, that's what it's all about, Inspector — a policeman's lot.

Poor pay, chronic indigestion and a kick up the ass at the end of it all. I'm in my office. How soon can you get here?"

Raven found the light switch, glancing across at the starboard portholes. The glass was filmed with dirt and spray, but he could see the cars parked along the stretch of embankment. The roofs were dry. He yawned, making no attempt to hide his lack of enthusiasm.

"It's five past twelve. There shouldn't be much traffic. Five minutes to dress, call it half-an-hour if that'll be all right. Sir." The hesitation was deliberate and Drake could take it how he pleased. Their mutual dislike was of long standing and no longer concealed.

"As snappy as you can," said Drake. He had a way of ignoring all sarcasm other than his own. "And if there's anything else on your mind, Inspector, forget it." He dropped the phone, ending the conversation.

Raven swung his spindly legs off the bunk and pushed them into the modish trousers. He scratched himself vigorously and pulled the black sweater over his long yellow hair. His gray eyes were deep-set, his nose a mere bridge of skin and bone. A bacon slicer wouldn't have taken enough flesh off his face to feed a kitten. The beer can on the dresser still held a few drops. He trickled them into his mouth, washing away the taste of sleep. Money, car keys and warrant card. The blue Italian raincoat and a new and full cold beer from the galley fridge. He climbed up to the deck, breathing in the smell of mud happily. Arc lamps flooded the chimneystacks of the power station on the opposite bank. Left and right, the lighted bridges spanned the black wash of water. It was the cleanest capital river in Europe. New varieties of fish were returning every year, and there was no other place in the world where he would sooner have lived. The *Albatross* lay in permanent moorings, her top-heavy hull weighed down by a couple of tons of chains. There were three cabins, galley and a so-called saloon. Gulls used the deck as a launching pad and the sparrows clustered on the power and phone lines that linked the houseboat to the shore. He locked the door at the head of the gangplank. Loops of barbed wire discouraged gymnastics. A couple of years before he'd been burgled, an agile marauder scaling the door and making off with Raven's collection of classical records and stereophonic set. He hadn't reported the break-in, preferring to nose around the neighborhood, chatting up the local busybodies. A retired schoolteacher who spent her waking hours checking on the antics of the couple who lived in the next boat remembered having seen a young man with a bicycle. Raven tracked the culprit down to a basement room a hundred yards away. He was a polytechnic student with a taste for Brahms and living on a bread, tea and offal diet. Raven had retrieved his belongings, leaving a badly scared and shaking youth with some cogent advice for the future. Thief-taking was a devious business, and there were times when expediency made more sense than justice.

His black MG was parked behind the chain that marked the limit of the moorings. He screwed himself in behind the wheel, locked the safety belt and tripped the wipers, clearing the windshield of mist. His straight-armed stance for driving had nothing to do with expert tuition. It was the only stance that gave his arms and legs room in the low-slung sports car. The police-tuned motor caught first time. He made the run to Scotland Yard five minutes inside schedule, parked in his own slot and looked across at the high-rise building. The lights there never went out. Someone was always on duty, collecting problems for people like him. He walked through a quarter mile of corridors to C division and took the elevator up to the sixteenth floor. He rapped on a door, turning the handle as a voice called "Come!"

Chief Superintendent Drake was a large, belligerent man with steel-colored hair and the darting, mistrustful eyes of the old school cop. Twelve years on the beat had given him a reputation for fairness. Another fourteen on the Flying Squad destroyed this reputation completely. He was a merciless cutter of corners, a hater of villains, a man who believed that an offender's rights were of less importance than his conviction. A command post had given him a false bonhomie that Raven had good cause to mistrust. Drake was about as benevolent as a boa constrictor. He wore dark blue suits with shiny seats and elbows, a Scotland Yard tie and a blank-shielded signet ring that had sunk deep into his thick finger. There was a dirty metal pot on his desk and a tea cup stained with tannic acid.

He opened his mouth like a wall-eyed pike taking bait. "Sit down!"

Raven unbuttoned his raincoat, aware that the red lining was somehow an offense. He held up the pack of Gitanes, asking permission to smoke.

Drake made as if he hadn't seen, scraping back his chair and touching the buff folder on his desk.

"You're supposed to be a student of current affairs. Did you ever hear of the Treasure of San Marco?"

Raven took the cigarette from his mouth, his expression dead straight. "The book or the film, sir?"

Drake arranged his lips in the squarish shape that was his smile. "I didn't get you out of bed to listen to a comedy routine. Answer the question."

"No, sir," said Raven.

Drake nodded briefly. "I'll *tell* you why I got you out of bed, Inspector — to give you the chance of a lifetime. What do you say to that?"

Raven flicked his cigarette at the saucer that served as an ashtray. There was nothing in the office that wasn't standard issue. The lack of personal possessions was designed to highlight the no-nonsense approach of its occupant. The only decoration on the wall was a calendar supplied by the North Thames Gas Board.

"Am I allowed to answer that frankly, Superintendent?"

Drake waved invitation. "As long as you keep it polite!"

Raven chose his words with care. "Let's put it this way, sir. You hate my guts, and I'll confess that you're not my favorite superior officer. Why would you want to give me the chance of a lifetime?"

Drake's smile was even squarer. He seemed to be enjoying himself. "Fair enough. There's no love lost between us, that's true. But you're still a good cop. It's your style I don't like, Inspector. You seem to think you're a cut above everyone else."

"Too long," suggested Raven, fingering the yellow hair that hung over his ears. "Or is it the clothes, sir — too trendy for a forty-year-old detective-inspector?"

Drake cleaned a pair of executive-type spectacles, settled them on his nose and looked at Raven.

"All of that plus the fact that you live on this bloody houseboat like a Chelsea playboy. Some call it arrogance, Inspector. I've been your coordinator for over three years. I've dealt with some good men in my time. Better cops than you'll ever make. Men who think the same way as I do. They've never been too bigheaded to ask advice when they needed it. But not you."

"No, sir," said Raven.

"No, sir," mimicked the superintendent. "So here it is, the chance of a lifetime."

Raven looked at him steadily. "What you really mean is that you're giving me a chance to cut my own throat?"

Drake cocked his head as though the idea had just struck him. "Just between ourselves, I'd like to think so. I'd sooner you cut your throat than have to write you up for another commendation. The fact is that C Department is in deep trouble. I'm electing you to get us out of it. They tell me that your sister's married to a Pole, is that right?"

Raven's glance was guarded. "She's married to a man who was born in this country. He's a lecturer at London University. His name happens to be Urbanovic."

"A Pole," said Drake. "You know one Pole you know 'em all. You're going into this assignment with ten lengths start, Inspector."

Raven shook his head. "If I called my brother-in-law a Pole, he'd have me up in front of the race relations board. He's as English as we are. Do you mind telling me how my sister's family comes into this?"

Drake opened the folder in front of him. "The Treasure of San Marco. It's a jeweled cross with seven hundred and eighty-two stones in it. Diamonds, emeralds and rubies. The Italian government values it at half-a-million pounds. Just after five o'clock tonight it was stolen from an art gallery in Mayfair. You're going to find it for us, Inspector."

Raven's shoulderblades sank down defensively. "What's a jeweled cross doing in an art gallery in the first place?"

"It was taken there by someone from the War Office."

"Brigadiers and bugles," said Raven. "Well, I suppose that makes sense."

Drake's jowls quivered as he shook his head censoriously. "Let's not be facetious. It's a sly and pointless exercise." The observation was a favorite one. It was the third or fourth time that Raven had heard the superintendent use it, word for word as it came out now.

"I'm just trying to get the picture, sir," he ventured.

"It's coming," Drake said, holding up a hand. "This cross is called a monstrance. R.C.'s use it in their sacrament. It's not only valuable, Inspector, it's holy. This one's been in England since the end of the war. It originally belonged to this church near a place called Montefelcino. Commandos captured it in a raid on German field headquarters. Nobody seems to have heard of it again till June last year when a storeman found it in an Epsom warehouse. They spent four months trying to find out who owned the bloody thing, and the Italians got the prize. Some publicity-minded idiot at the War Office came up with a bright idea. Let's have a full-dress ceremony where the army returns the monstrance to the Italian ambassador. The first C Department knew anything about all this was at eighteen minutes to six last night. Are you with me so far, Inspector?"

The big uncurtained windows offered a view of the river, the Houses of Parliament one way, the lighted face of Big Ben. The four rosy shafts of the power station stabbed the darkness to the west. Each bridge was a step in the direction of home. Raven lifted a bony shoulder.

"I think so, yes. Everything except the bit about the Poles. How do the Poles get into the act?"

"I was coming to that," said Drake. "The commando unit was Polish. The British are taking credit for the raid."

"That sounds reasonable," said Raven. "Since there *isn't* a Polish army any more. Not that one, anyway."

Drake was on his feet, thudding over the floor between the door and his desk.

"The Foreign Office is officially responsible for the monstrance. The Custodian of Enemy Property's outfit has been out of operation for years. The F.O. sanctioned the exhibition. Some Italian who owns an art gallery offered it for free, and a staff colonel was put in charge of security. He inspected the gallery yesterday morning. There are three good locks on the door, the kind of burglar alarm you'd find on Baggott's Bakery. The colonel seems to have been impressed. He called West Central, told them to keep an eye on the place and went back to his crosswords. You can talk now." He perched himself on the window ledge, his back to the enormous pane of glass.

Raven was tempted to knock him through it. "Thanks," he said. "How about insurance?"

Drake grunted. "Not one penny piece. It gets better as you go on, Inspector. I told you, this is a beauty, just for you. The thieves snapped a key in the gallery door and set the alarm off. Somebody called West Central. A couple of patrolmen got there minutes afterward. No monstrance, no thieves. All hell broke loose. The Foreign Office is leaning on the army and they're both leaning on the Metropolitan Police."

"And you're leaning on me?"

Drake looked away. "The commissioner feels that C Department should have known what was going on. A lack of liaison, he says. The robbery's an affront to a friendly nation, and he's expecting prompt action and results. I suggested your name. He agreed."

Raven pulled himself up in his chair. "How can you know what's going on if nobody tells you about it? It's the fault of the army and West Central."

Drake turned again. His smile showed one discolored tooth at the side.

"Don't you start disappointing me, Inspector. The Old Man's expecting big things of you."

Somebody walked along the corridor. A door opened and shut. Raven lit another cigarette.

"You've been waiting a long time for this, haven't you?"

"A long time," the superintendent agreed. "You see, it's something personal, something between you and me. Nobody else knows what's going on in this room. I've been in the game too long to make any stupid moves. You can't screw me, but I've got a good chance at you. If you get a conviction it'll be down to me. If you bugger it up, the blame'll be yours."

Raven dragged deep on his smoke. Old-timers like Drake belonged to a solid freemasonry. They had their own ways of settling scores, of burying hatchets so deep that they came out the other side. A move like this had been on the cards for the last few months. He just hadn't expected it to be made so openly. He glanced down at his buckled shoes.

"The chance of a lifetime. Suppose I went straight home and reported sick?"

"You won't," Drake said, confidently.

Raven's mind was wide awake. "Then I'd better know the rest of it."

Drake lumbered over to the desk and dropped the folder in Raven's lap. "It's all there. I've even done your homework for you. Whatever happens, *that'll* look good. You want three middle-aged Poles who live in the Fulham area. You've got the files there from the Aliens Office, army records, copies of the witnesses' statements. I expect you'll want to have a look at the Scene of the Crime. The gallery owner's telephone number is on the front page."

Raven snapped the elastic band that fastened the folder. "I suppose I could go right to the top, to the commissioner himself."

"You won't do that either," Drake said, shaking his head. "Accusations against a superior officer, a man who's defended you in the past? You're too smart to do anything like that. You'll come at me in a different way. Here, you better take this."

He flicked a piece of metal across the desk. Raven picked it up, a regimental badge fashioned in the shape of a bison's head.

"You're pretty sure this case is going to land me in the shit, right?"

"Right," said Drake. "That badge was dropped in the gallery. But don't get your bowels in an uproar. They were issued to every man in the Fifth Division of the Polish army. And don't worry about prints because there aren't any. The witnesses are useless. There isn't one statement that would stand up to good cross-examination. Your only hope's to get the monstrance back. And you're not going to do it, Raven."

Raven nodded. Drake's game was to cover himself at each step. This information would be one hundred per cent accurate. He held up the folder.

"Who put all this together?"

It was the moment that Drake had obviously been waiting for. "I did. I may not have your advantages, but when it comes to real police work I can run rings around you."

Raven slipped the badge into his pocket. "Do I pick my own team?"

"Not on your nelly," smiled Drake. "It's already been done for you. Ten men under Sergeant Gifford. You know him?"

"I know *of* him," corrected Raven.

Drake closed an eye. "Goes by the book. You have pool

transport and drivers. Any request for additional help must be cleared through me. The commissioner's expecting results. I'll want a progress report every twelve hours."

He turned toward the hat and coat on the stand behind him. Raven came to his feet, his voice too quiet to be heard outside.

"There is just one thing before I go, Superintendent."

Drake's eyes probed, his arms halfway into the sleeves of his overcoat.

"Yes?"

"Fuck you," Raven said deliberately.

Drake plucked his hat from the stand. "Good night, Inspector. And the best of British luck to you."

It seemed a long way from the coordinator's office to the row of elevators. Only one of them was working. He hit the button quickly in case Drake decided to join him. He stopped on the sixth floor. His own room was smaller than the one he had just left and as little like an office as he could make it. He'd brightened the drab green filing cabinets with bursts of paint-spray, hung a Portuguese bedspread on the wall and brought in a couple of black rugs that matched the coarsely woven linen curtains. He bolted the door and threw the folder on the desk. Behind the telephone was a picture of his sister and her two children. It was as near as he'd ever get to a family. Thought of a permanent attachment to any one person gave him instant claustrophobia. As far as he knew he was alone on the floor. He pulled the bottom drawer in the desk and loaded the cassette player with a recording of Berlioz' *Les Franc-Macons*.

Cigarette butts piled in the ashtray as he went through the folder, scribbling on the backgammon scoringpad he used for his notes. The habit irritated his superiors and therefore he gave no explanation. The truth was that he had bought a gross of the pads cheap and liked the quality of the paper. The gallery owner's name was Paolo Tedeschi, an Italian subject with a work permit, forty-two years old and a bachelor. According to Criminal Records, Tedeschi was clean. His statement was short and unhelpful. He'd closed the Dante Gallery and walked from Conduit Street to Berkeley Square. He'd been about to get into his car when a man had attacked him from behind. He remembered being dragged into a nearby vehicle and hit with some kind of weapon. The next thing he recalled was finding himself lying on Hampstead Heath. The keys to the gallery were missing from his pocket. He called the police from a neighboring house, and a mobile unit had collected him. He was unable to give descriptions of his assailants, but he was positive that there were two of them.

Raven turned the page. Natalie Berenson, fifty-four, English, married. Mrs. Berenson managed a hairdressing salon across the lobby from the Dante Gallery. She'd been on the phone, talking to a customer, when she heard the burglar alarm ringing outside. The noise intrigued her since she had seen Tedeschi leave the premises twenty minutes earlier. She cut the call short, but by the time she reached the lobby the stranger was out on the street. She offered a description of a man's back that would have fitted a couple of hundred thousand Londoners. She hadn't seen the man's face. Both she and Tedeschi had been shown pictures supplied by the Aliens Office. Neither had been able to make a positive identification.

Frederick Nudds, fifty-eight, English, married, traffic warden. Nudds stated having seen a black sedan with two women in it near Tedeschi's car at the time of the assault. He wasn't sure of the make of the vehicle. There was no reason for him to have taken its number. By the time he had walked around the square, the black sedan had disappeared.

Raven turned the cassette over. The next batch of papers were old Polish army records and stamped FOR RESTRICTED USE BY AUTHORIZED PERSONNEL ONLY. A terse report described a commando raid on 24/25 August 1944. The attack on the field headquarters of the 71st German Infantry Division was classed as an "incomplete mission." The capture of the monstrance was dealt with in one sentence. An appended history of the ten men in the commando unit gave the dates of their enlistments and details of their military service. Seven of the ten were listed as dead or missing in 1945. The remaining three had been demobilized in the United Kingdom. Each had been wounded in active service. All had been cited for bravery in the field. Chief Superintendent Drake had pinned three Aliens Office photographs to the military records.

ZALESKI, Casimir. 54, married, restaurant proprietor.
SOBINSKI, Stanislas. 54, bachelor, hospital cleaner.
CZARNIECKI, Bogdan. 53, bachelor, garage mechanic.

The pictures were passport-size, the poses of the subjects stiff and defensive. Czarniecki's bald head bulged over a mashed face like a wrestler's. A note from Earl's Court Road Police Station established the fact that Sobinski and Czarniecki had lived at the same addresses for seven and thirteen years respectively. Neither man had a local police record. The report from Chelsea Police Station offered little more. Zaleski had lived at Waverley Court for a little more than two years. His restaurant had been open for five. Neighbors had complained about excessive noise late at night in the restaurant, of garbage cans that blocked the pavement. There'd been some trouble about serving a summons on Zaleski for nonpayment of rates.

The last pages in the folder contained a full description of the missing monstrance, additional photographs — only not in color — provided by the now defunct office of the Custodian of Enemy Property. Receipts traced the transfer of the jeweled cross through August 1944 to November 1973. The last handover slip carried a War Office stamp. Raven closed the file and snapped the elastic band back on the cover. It was getting on for one, but he was no longer tired. The evidence against these Poles was circumstantial. It tended to prove by inference, but by itself was no proof. They must have known it would be like this before they started. Whoever had planned this caper was highly intelligent. These jokers would be loyal to one another. They were comrades, Western Slavs in an alien land and disciplined. One of them had produced the money for expenses. Common sense indicated Zaleski. As a captain he had outranked Sobinski and Czarniecki. And the style in which he lived was a cut above that of the other two. Raven reopened the folder on impulse and read through the closely typed report from the Home Office. It seemed that Zaleski had made no less than four applications for British citizenship over the years. All had been refused. The last rejection was based on the grounds of Zaleski's conviction for nonpayment of rates. A note in the margin added "no further application from this petitioner need be considered." The Pole had been living apart from his wife for two years. Her address was given as Rivermead House, Putney.

Raven closed the covers again. He turned off the cassette player, thinking that Drake's eyes bored in like a car salesman's. The superintendent's scheme was based on the hope that any move made by Raven was bound to fail. The probability was that Drake knew more than was in the files. Some whisper, some hint — something that he could conveniently deny when the moment came. Raven accepted the challenge. At long last they were out in the open. And as long as he kept his head, there was a chance of landing Drake in the shit instead of himself.

He scribbled a note for the clerk who kept track of most of his paperwork. *Contact me through mobile switchboard until further instructions.* The robbery had been well planned and executed. He could see how three men trained in the use of brain and muscle could have pulled it off. It wasn't necessary to have served your apprenticeship in jail. But only a fool would carry a regimental badge on a job like this. A fool or a romantic. And losing the badge at the scene of the crime was beyond carelessness.

He switched off the lights and went outside. There was a radio-phone under the dash of the black sports car. The unauthorized button he'd had fitted was capable of completing the circuit, of sounding the engaged signal at the Scotland Yard switchboard. The device protected his privacy and people weren't on to it yet.

His first stop was a red brick building a couple of blocks south of Fulham Road. Zaleski's apartment was one of two on the first floor. The curtains were tightly drawn. All the lights except his were out at the front of the building. Raven watched the building for the space of a slowly smoked cigarette and then started his motor again. He drove slowly up Fulham Road looking across at the Wielkapolska restaurant. From the outside at least, it was no more than just another shabby eating place. The lights inside showed through the faded velvet curtains, brighter where the fabric was thin. The floors above were empty, some of the windows even boarded. A beat-up American stationwagon was parked out front, down behind on the shock absorbers.

Raven parked in front of the post office, chainsmoking till the lamps were extinguished in the restaurant. Three people emerged. A tallish man wearing a quilted anorak, his left arm wrapped around a long-haired girl in a shawl. The third person was a stocky middle-aged man wearing a beret and duffelcoat. Raven recognized him immediately from the photographs. The tall man and the girl drove off in the stationwagon. Raven ducked down low as the Pole passed the parked car. Zaleski crossed the road, back straight, belly out in a sort of gooselike waddle.

Raven fingered the regimental badge in his pocket, wondering whether Zaleski had missed it. If he had, so much the better. The trick was going to be to knock him off balance and keep him that way.

He picked up the phone and asked for Drake's home number. A woman's voice answered sleepily. Raven identified himself, and the coordinator came on the line, growling like a bad actor playing the part of a cop.

Raven's voice was wooden. "I'm sorry to disturb you at this time of night, but I thought you'd like to know — I'm picking up Zaleski as soon as I've had some sleep."

Drake cleared his throat with a woolly growl. "Picking him up on what charge?" His teeth were obviously out and his diction whistled.

"Failing to notify a change of address as a person subject to the provisions of the Immigration Act, 1971."

"Are you out of your mind?" Drake demanded. "There's

nothing against any of them at the Aliens Office. I made that clear. Read the bloody file again!"

"I don't think I will, sir," Raven said smoothly. "Like that I can still be mistaken."

He heard the unmistakable sound of Drake scratching, then the coordinator talking for his wife's sake.

"Well, you're in charge, Inspector. I'm sure you know what you're doing."

"Yes, sir," said Raven. "Good night and sorry again."

He lifted the phone once more, raising the duty officer at the pressroom. He gave his name.

"You can release this on the Dante Gallery robbery. Quote. The police are now satisfied that this is the work of a gang of professional thieves. A watch has been placed on all boat and aircraft departures. Officers were interviewing a man late last night who is believed to be in possession of information that could be of use to the investigating officers. Unquote and end. Is that Cook on the line?"

"Yes, Inspector."

"Well let's have no vivid rewriting, Sergeant. Give 'em what I said and no more."

Ten minutes later he was back on the houseboat, undressing in the darkness. He let his clothes stay where they fell and found the end of the bunk with cold feet. He thought about Drake. A couple of well-placed karate chops would have put the fellow through the window, spread him across Victoria Street, sixteen floors beneath. The trouble was, he didn't know the first thing about karate. He closed his eyes and composed himself for sleep.

The Village Bookstore was a couple of rooms that were put

together like a T, with the entrance fronting the hospital
buildings on Fulham Road. The lateral bar had once been a
garage. There was an exit onto Hollywood Road. Fraser kept
his junk there. The store itself was a narrow room lined with
bookshelves. Some sketchy work with hardboard divided a
quarter of the space into an office and washroom. Three
kerosene stoves placed down the center of the room provided a
stuffy heat. Throughout the whole of Fraser's first winter
there he had left each night with a mind-shattering migraine.
Five years had gone since then, and he'd grown accustomed to
the smell of kerosene fumes and wet clothing. The time spent
in England had conditioned him to a number of things. He
drank tea for breakfast, smoked straight Virginian tobacco and
had become indifferent to the abrasive incivility of most of his
customers. It was a living. And whenever he thought about it,
he realized that all in all it was a good one. Life with Ingrid
was an easy arrangement of mutual likes and dislikes, in and
out of bed. She rarely spoke of her divorce and seemed to have
shaken her husband out of her system. Fraser's private opinion
was that the guy must have been a moron.

He stood at the window, watching her swing down the
sidewalk toward the bookstore, demure and yet seductive in
the long flowered skirt and fringed shawl. The combination of
hustler and schoolgirl never failed to excite him. He opened
the door for her, taking the newspaper she had bought on her
way from the delicatessen. The headlines offered the same
promise of death, doom and disaster. An airplane had crashed
in France, more people had been murdered in Ulster, thieves
had robbed a Mayfair art gallery. He turned the sign in the
window, displaying the side that said CLOSED and slipped up
the catch on the door. He unfolded the small table while

Ingrid prepared the sandwiches she had bought. Liver sausage
on rye for him, turkey for her. They ate at the back of the
store, out of sight of the people who were passing. This kind
of lunch was a habit that had started when she first came to live
with him. It had been during one of his broke periods. Her
arrival had put an end to his solitary, stand-up snacks in the
kitchen. The can opener was barely used. Eating one big
meal a day had been part of her plan to keep them solvent.
She'd mended, schemed and worried, heavy on the beans,
spaghetti and chili sauce, never asking him for a penny more
than he gave her. She'd entered his life with a beat-up suitcase
and a trust in him that had scared him senseless. It wasn't that
she didn't criticize. She fought like a wildcat for an opinion.
But she never doubted his word. Things had gradually started
to get easier. A lucky buy from a Surrey vicarage produced a
signed, first-edition copy of *David Copperfield*. They'd re-
papered the flat, bought some furniture and a big beat-up Ford
that was just right for going to auctions. He knew that she was
saving money, but he never asked her why. Thought of any
kind of insurance always depressed him. It carried a suggestion of insecurity.

She swung a leg, nibbling round the crust of her sandwich
and frowning.

"I've been trying to think all morning what was bothering
me. It's those trousers, Kirk. Do you really have to wear
them?"

"You're speaking with your mouth full," he reproved.
"What's the matter with these trousers anyway. They're
clean."

She used her shawl to wipe away the crumbs. "That much I
know. I do your washing, remember. But what would you
say if I wore the same clothes, day in, day out?"

"Nothing," he said, grinning. He played the horses once a week religiously. Usually he lost and Ingrid would remind him that the money would have bought a couple of shirts, a new pair of shoes or whatever. As he told her, he'd never heard of a pair of pajamas paying off at twenty to one. "I don't care what you wear. It's what's underneath that interests me."

Her gray eyes brooded. "That's a boringly obvious remark and not even true. If you didn't care how I looked you wouldn't give me money for clothes."

A banging from the back room stopped him from answering her. They glanced at one another questioningly. From where they sat it was impossible to see the Hollywood Road entrance. He looked at his watch.

"Half-after one? Who the hell could that be?"

She put her cup down and shrugged. "I've no idea. Do you want me to go?"

He pulled himself up. "No, I'll get it."

The storeroom was a chilly wilderness of unframed and yellowing prints, moldy leather bindings and cartons of old paperbacks on their way to the local hospitals. A single light in the rafters illuminated a concrete floor ugly with oil stains. He unlocked the back door, stepping aside hurriedly as Zaleski burst past and turned the key. They stood for a moment in an attitude of mutual appraisal. Zaleski beckoned Frazer away from the window. The Pole was wearing a blue duffelcoat instead of his usual black leather and an outsize beret on top of his head. He was short of breath as if he'd been running.

"Hi!" said Fraser uncertainly. He knew what Ingrid meant when she said that she loved the man. Zaleski could change from a ball-breaking bore stamping around in the past to a man who'd cash a phony check for you and take the consequences.

Zaleski pulled him deeper into the storeroom. His breathing was still giving him trouble.

"Are you alone?"

"How do you mean alone?" Fraser demanded. "The store's closed, but Ingrid's here. Why?"

A man passed in front of the window and Zaleski slipped in behind a packingcase. He touched his lips with his forefinger. Fraser looked at him in bewilderment.

"What *is* it, Casimir? What in hell is going on?"

Zaleski shook his head violently and cat-footed back to the window. He put himself flat against the wall and glanced up and down the street. He retraced his steps slowly.

"I need your help, Kirk. I am in bad trouble."

There was an urgency about the plea that worried Fraser. Drunk or sober Zaleski rarely lost his nerve. It was like hearing your grandfather admit to a fear of the dark.

"What kind of trouble, for crissakes?" Frazer found himself looking back at the window expectantly.

"Police!" said Zaleski.

"Police?" Frazer repeated with an air of disbelief. None of the images that came to mind made sense.

Zaleski's feet dragged over the concrete floor. "Detectives are searching for me. They have been to flat and to restaurant."

The new image was sharper, one of gray-faced men in raincoats stepping out of a doorway. Fraser cleared his throat nervously.

"Searching for you to *what*, Casimir! I mean there has to be a reason. How do you *know* they've been to the flat and restaurant."

Zaleski pulled out a handkerchief, releasing a strong smell of *eau-de-Portugal*. He mopped his brow theatrically.

"I left home early, nine o'clock, to go to sauna bath in Knightsbridge. Only my chef is knowing where I am. He telephoned sauna bath. Police have just left, quarter of an hour, asking questions."

Fraser lit a cigarette. For some reason or other his hand had started to shake.

"What *sort* of questions?"

"Where I am, what times I come to restaurant, this kind of thing."

"Look," Fraser said carefully. "You haven't killed anyone, have you?"

The Pole's washed-slate eyes bored in. "No killing. Is nothing. Is police wanting to frame me. You know what 'alien' means in this country?"

Fraser was beginning to feel as if he'd stepped onto a runaway roller coaster.

"How do you mean do I know — I'm an alien myself, but the cops don't go charging around searching for me! Look, Casimir, you're making me nervous. Look at my goddam hands. Call the police and ask them what they want. It's probably some routine inquiry. Something to do with one of your customers, perhaps. That hood who was in on Sunday night, for instance."

Zaleski shook his head doggedly. "I *know!* Listen, Kirk. You say you are my friend. Is why I am here."

A milk-cart passed along Hollywood. Fraser could hear Ingrid moving around in the store.

"All that's well and good, but I'm no good at riddles," he objected. "Why *should* the police want to frame you? Politics? Who the hell takes you that seriously!"

Zaleski dropped his cigarette butt on the concrete and set his heel on it very carefully. He was halfway to the street before

Fraser caught up with him. The Pole shook him off, his mouth set hard.

"What kind of friendship is this? If you are in trouble, I help, not asking questions."

Fraser blinked, shamed by the look in the other man's eyes. "What I'm saying is that we've got to be sensible. I've got Ingrid to think of."

"Ingrid or yourself?" Zaleski asked quietly.

"Or both of us," Fraser admitted.

Zaleski raised his right hand. "If I swear on my honor is no danger for either of you?"

Fraser shrugged. There was nothing left to say. "You win. No more questions. What exactly is it that you want me to do?"

Zaleski drew himself up, speaking with a kind of emotional dignity. "You are true friend. I shall remember."

"Sure," said Fraser. "What do I do?"

"You know where is Grosvenor Hotel in Victoria?"

Fraser smoothed his long hair, wondering what was coming. "I know. It's the one on Buckingham Palace Road with an entrance into the station."

Zaleski nodded emphatically. "Exactly. You must be there at half-past five this evening. Wait in bar, perhaps one hour, two — I cannot be sure. But you must wait. A lady is coming into bar dressed in black coat with fur collar, black hat. Is looking for me. Here is her picture."

The photograph showed a middle-aged woman with dark hair parted in the center. Fraser put it in the breast pocket of his flannel shirt.

"A lady in a black hat looking for you. OK. Then what?"

Zaleski took his time to answer as if the choice of words

were important. "Speak to her. Tell her you are friend of mine. Tell her she must go back home and wait until she sees me or hears from me. Is extremely important, Kirk. *She must go home and wait.*"

Fraser repeated the phrase self-consciously.

"I'll see she gets the message. But shouldn't I have her name?"

"Why name?" Zaleski asked sharply. The nerve in his right cheek was jumping.

Fraser moved a shoulder. "All sorts of things could happen. I might have to have her paged, for example."

Zaleski straddled his legs, looking up at the Canadian. "You ask for Mrs. Hanya. H-A-N-Y-A."

A memory wormed into Fraser's consciousness. "That's your wife's name, isn't it? Is this your wife I'm meeting, Casimir?"

Zaleski nodded. "Is my wife. You must never speak to anyone of this, Kirk. My whole life depends on it."

Fraser grinned, the steam beginning to leave his system. "You're a real ham, aren't you. You'll be in that restaurant tonight doing your usual act and you know it. Look, I'm bad about lying to Ingrid. She'll have heard your voice anyway. She's got ears like sound detectors."

"A secret with a woman is no secret," Zaleski said doggedly.

"Come off it," said Fraser. "Ingrid isn't just any woman. And how about you — you're sharing a secret with your wife, aren't you?"

The Pole replaced his beret. "I must go now. I gave you my word. Now you must give me yours. None of what I have said will go beyond you and Ingrid."

"Guaranteed," Fraser said lightly. "And relax. We'll be in

this evening and I'll buy you a drink. Which way do you want to go out?"

Zaleski nodded toward the end of the room. "You are my friend and I trust you."

He slipped through the door leading out to Hollywood Road. When Fraser reached the window, the Pole had completely vanished. All he needed, thought Fraser, was a cloak to wrap his face in. Ingrid was sitting near the stove, filing her nails with an ostentatious lack of interest that was overdone. She looked up, brushing the hair away from her eyes.

"What did he want?"

He kissed the back of her neck, took the file away from her and sat down.

"He's in trouble with the police, or so he says."

She nibbled a knuckle for a moment, the skin around her eyes creased by frown marks.

"Casimir? You must be joking!"

She'd let the stove smoke, and he turned down the wick. "If anyone's joking it's Zaleski."

The tale as he told it sounded daft and melodramatic, but Ingrid gave him her complete attention, sitting with her feet close together, playing with the fringe of her shawl. She even lit a cigarette for him so that he wouldn't have to stop. He produced the photograph Zaleski had given him.

"That's his wife."

"I know it's his wife," she said sharply. "I've been to her flat. She painted those plates for us last year. What's the matter, isn't she glamorous enough for you?"

He blinked, completely bewildered by her fury. The truth was that Zaleski spoke of his wife from time to time, usually late at night when he was stoned. He'd go stumbling back in time, the vodka filling his eyes with tears, carrying on about Baltic beaches, students dances in Warsaw, boar hunts in the Carpathian forests. The childhood sweetheart who had become his wife was always in there somewhere. Fraser had gradually built up a picture of a svelte, vibrant Slav with tartar eyes who could dance through the night while being toasted by cavalry officers and jump her horse against theirs in the morning. The woman in the picture looked like an overworked cashier in some knitwear store.

"What are you riding me for?" he complained. "You've heard the stories he tells, drinking champagne from Hanya's slipper and the rest. It's just that I expected someone different, that's all."

"Men," she retorted scathingly. "That's all you're interested in, appearances. How that woman could have stuck by Casimir for thirty years is beyond me. Looking at all those dreadful girls and knowing that he'd been to bed with them."

"Hold it," he said, irritated at finding himself on the defensive. "Why are we talking about his sex life? It doesn't mean the same to a man, anyway."

"It doesn't?" she asked, making her gray eyes very round. "Don't start giving me your lecture about genes and chromosomes, women sinking their roots while men climb mountains to see what's on the other side. I may be Anglo-Saxon, my Canadian friend, but I'd chop it off if I found you in bed with another woman!"

He tipped his chair back and reached blindly for a book in the nearest shelf. He glanced at the title page and put the book back. It didn't help that his choice was some feminist diatribe.

"Finished?"

"Finished," she said.

He drew a long, deep breath. "Good. Casimir says that the police are after him."

Her expression softened. "Poor Casimir."

"Jesus Christ," he said with feeling and stuffed the photograph back in his shirt pocket. "Let's apply a little logic to the scene. Casimir doesn't pay his bills, right? Last New Year's Eve, he kicked in his own front door, stoned out of his mind. What else did he ever do, tell me! Yet we're supposed to believe that the police are trying to frame him. It doesn't even *begin* to make sense, Ingrid, and you know it."

"How do you know what he does?" she countered. "It could be something to do with politics."

"Good night all," he said rudely. "You're as half-baked as he is. Politics stopped for Casimir when they did away with serfs." He went to the door and reversed the sign.

She looked at him closely as he came back to the stove. "You read an average of two suspense books a week. You must believe in *some* of them. But when the same sort of thing happens on your doorstep to a friend, it's suddenly ridiculous. Why?"

"On Fulham Road?" he scoffed. "To Casimir? You know what I think, Ingrid — he's losing his marbles, that's what."

She plucked a piece of lint from her skirt, her voice very quiet. "Can you remember telling me a story about lying in bed with pleurisy, long before I came on the scene. The only person who came near you was Casimir. He changed your sheets, fed you, stuffed you with antibiotics for five whole days. You could have *died* there, and nobody would have known."

The memory was vivid enough. There was no need for her

to remind him of it. She was leaning forward, a pose that spread a veil of hair over her face.

"You don't understand these things," he told her. "If Casimir really is in trouble, I want to know all about it. At least, a little more than he's told us."

She parted her hair with one hand, pointing the other at him. "You said he was desperate. If he's a friend, that's all we need to know."

He made a sound of exasperation. The kind of friendship · she was talking about just didn't exist. He'd learned that the hard way. What he was offering was something else.

"You'll see," he promised. "He'll be in the restaurant tonight ready with another cliffhanger. It's in his blood. Everything has to be blown up larger than life. You want to bet on it?"

She'd moved to the window, arranging some books on a stand there. "I don't bet with you any more. It's not worth it. You always lose, and it makes you angry. *Kirk!*" The urgency in her voice brought him running to her side. She was pointing at a red convertible, twenty yards away and traveling west.

"That car," she stammered. "It was the men who were in the restaurant on Sunday night, the men who made the scene with Casimir. The one who was driving looked right at me as they passed. And he said something to the other one."

He pulled her away from the window and held her tight. "Easy does it, honey. Time to start worrying when the men *don't* notice you."

She broke free, her small face disturbed. "Those men are gangsters, aren't they, Kirk?"

He shrugged. "Gangsters, gamblers, heavies of some kind,

certainly. What the hell does it matter? This is Fulham Road. Cars do pass. The guy probably recognized you."

She moved her head from side to side, her mouth tight. "I wish you'd stop saying 'this is Fulham Road' as if it was some kind of children's playground. Those men were looking for Casimir."

He covered his eyes with his hand. "Jesus God, we're *all* catching the disease! Why didn't they stop and come in if they were looking for him? And why here anyway?"

"Phone the police," she said quickly.

He put his hands on his hips, looking down at her. "What do I say to them? Go on, tell me — what do I say? — A man in a car just smiled at my girl friend!"

"You've got to do something," she said stubbornly. "Those men are after Casimir. I know it."

"You're damn right I've got to do something," he said, and unlocked the street door. "I've got to sell some books."

He left the store shortly after five, promising to call Ingrid if anything unexpected happened. He walked south to Kings Road and boarded a number 11 bus, dropping off outside the Grosvenor Hotel. It was the first time he had been inside the place. He buttoned the collar of his anorak as he went up the steps. The lobby was crowded with people who were trying to register. On the right was the porter's desk. At the far end of the lobby, a central staircase led to a gallery. He asked for the bar and found his way along a corridor lined with display cases. It was too early to buy a drink. He pushed his head inside a lounge where people were drinking tea. None of the women resembled the picture he had seen. None was wearing a hat.

He wandered out through a large, doorless exit into the

station. The evening rush had started. People were streaming out of the underground, antlike files heading for the waiting trains. A faintly acrid smell hung in the air as if the essence of last year's fogs was still trapped within the station confines. The girdered glass roof echoed the clank of metal, the announcements over the public address system. Behind the windows of the dreary-looking cafeteria, morose Asians were pushing trolleys loaded with dirty crockery. He bought a newspaper at one of the stands, looking across at the clock. Half-after five. The bar would be open. He walked back into the hotel and bought himself a Scotch at the bar. The only other customers were a couple of big-deal executive types. He carried his glass to a corner and sat down facing the corridor. There was no reason for his sudden fit of depression. But then there never was. It was the same old sense of frustration that his mother had called "the sulks." And there'd been no room for the sulks in the Ontario fruit farm where he had grown up. Life was sternly ordered by an Anglican God with mutton-chop whiskers, and the discipline allowed no frivolities, no fancy swings to joy or sadness. He'd never known the warm certainty of sin and forgiveness.

He refilled his glass four times during the next hour and a half and then moved to the lobby. He took a seat from which he could see both the exit to the station and the steps leading down to the street. He was putting out cigarettes that were unsmoked, and his palms were sweating, but he wasn't up tight, he told himself. Just a little apprehensive and naturally so. People came and went. Two women with a chic that was unmistakably French, a party of Sephardic rabbis just off the boat-train, schoolgirls shepherded by swooping nuns. No one remotely like Mrs. Zaleska.

He was sitting here like a fool, with Ingrid crouching over a

stove and worrying herself sick for no reason. The hell with
Zaleski's problems. He walked across to the porter's desk and
showed them the picture in his pocket. Nobody remembered
having seen her. He tried calling the Wielkapolska. The
number rang unanswered. He dialed again. Ingrid's voice
sounded relieved.

"I've blown it," he told her. "She didn't show. It's either
that or I missed her. Anyway, I'm leaving now."

He picked up a cab in front of the station. Ingrid was
waiting in the doorway of the store, her coat already on. He
walked her as far as the corner and stopped.

"You don't think we should look in at Zaleski's place?"

"I called there half-an-hour ago." Her eyes were oddly
warning.

He unlocked the stationwagon. "And?"

She settled herself in beside him. "A man's voice answered.
It wasn't Casimir. It was an Englishman. He wanted to know
my name."

He backed out carefully, his eyes on the driving mirror.
"You didn't give it to him, of course."

"Of course not," she replied.

"It was probably a friend," he said, believing none of it.

Her hand crept onto his knee. "I'm frightened, Kirk. I'm
beginning to be frightened."

He braked at the junction, waiting his chance to filter into
the traffic. For some reason or other, he felt guilty, and his
only defense was bluster.

"Look," he said. "I've wasted nearly three hours on this
crazy caper. I'd like to get it out of my system now. OK?"

She rode as she usually did, her long legs tucked up under
her on the seat, her dress trailing the floor. She kept silent all

the way home, reflecting his own mood. It occurred to him that sooner or later they were going to have to talk about Casimir Zaleski, about men and the problem of living with them. It would go on from there. Tolstoi. The ingratitude of those who were loved. The suspect quality of friendship. They'd covered it all before, each coming out scarred and unrepentant.

The shabby old house they called home stood on a hill facing Streatham Common. It was a gloomy Victorian mansion dotted with stained-glass windows and mahogany lavatory seats. Elm trees hemmed in the surrounding acre of unkempt grass and shrubbery. According to Ingrid it was the closest you could get to living in a churchyard without actually being dead. The house was converted into three flats. A teacher of violin occupied the top floor, a Kenyan Asian doctor the second, the Frasers lived on the ground floor. An entrance at the side gave them complete independence. The two gates on the road were joined by a half-hoop of pockmarked hardtop fringed by dank laurel bushes. Fraser pulled the stationwagon close to his door. The doctor was on call from one of the big hospitals, and the space out front was reserved for him by mutual consent. When Fraser had first moved in, the way into his flat had been a Charles Addams nightmare of ivy and rotting trelliswork. He'd badgered the landlords into laying a brick path and painting the door and the windowframes. But the apartment had never been a home until Ingrid arrived. He'd landed in England with ninety dollars, Canadian, and a disastrous track record. A failed actor, he'd been sacked as assistant purser on a cruise liner, replaced as manager of a Toronto discotheque. He'd been selling cut-price records out of an Earl's Court bedsitter when the news had come of Aunt

Elizabeth's legacy. It landed with the force of a blockbuster. All he remembered about his uncle's wife was that mention of her name in the township of Truro, Ontario, was enough to give his father the shakes. Captain Andy Fraser had accompanied his barge to the bottom of the Erie Canal, leaving his widow to do what she had always wanted to do, drink. She moved into a downtown Toronto rooming house and started to booze away Uncle Andy's insurance money. A broken leg complicated by pneumonia caught her before she completed the job. It came as a shock to everyone that what was left of her cash went to Fraser. The police found a scrap of paper hidden away among beverage store receipts.

I leave all my property real and otherwise to my nephew Kirk Fraser who has the good sense to prefer fire-and-brimstone to harps. There was no question about her soundness of mind and the signature was genuine and witnessed. After that there were no more communications from Rural Route 10, not even the customary Christmas card. He'd used the twenty-two thousand dollars to buy the lease on the Fulham Road premises.

He hung his coat in the small hallway. Ingrid was already in the bedroom. There were only three rooms in the flat, but they were well proportioned. Two people could live there without falling over one another. He had taken the apartment unfurnished, buying bits and pieces whenever he thought about it. Ingrid had thrown out his purchases, lock, stock, and barrel, replacing them gradually by shrewd deals in unlikely places. She'd found an old German carpenter to make shelves and build closets, disguise the ugly fireplaces. The Wilton carpet in the living room was fifty years old. She had cut and laid it herself. None of the furniture matched, but she created an air of shabby elegance that never failed to impress visitors. A flower painting in the living room was the only reminder of what Ingrid called her previous existence. One of the last batch of German flybombs had orphaned her at six weeks of age, and she'd been brought up by a distant aunt. Part of what drew Fraser to her was her loneliness. Without him she had nobody. It was a condition that he well understood.

The living room windows overlooked the Common, a sloping expanse of muddy turf traced by streetlamps. He turned on the television and drew the curtains. He filled his mouth from the peanut jar, watching the colored images flickering silently

"Your boy's coming up," he called. "Hawaii Five-O!"

She didn't answer. He grabbed another handful of nuts and walked through into the bedroom; this was her own preserve, the last of the rooms to be fully furnished. She must have drawn a hundred sketches before she'd finally gotten it right. A shaggy white carpet, low, wide bed, scarlet frames for the old coaching prints she had found in the Fulham Road storeroom. Her clothes were lying at the foot of the bed. She'd changed into her robe and a pair of his pajamas. Her hair was tied back behind her ears, and she was leaning against the wall near the tallboy.

"Do you see what I see?" she asked quietly.

He glanced across at the bed. The spread was a cut-down crimson velvet curtain with gold fringes. There was a clock by the phone where he slept, his copy of *Pepys' Diary*, some magazines on her sidetable.

"What am I supposed to be looking for?" he demanded.

She lifted a hand, pointing at the tallboy. "Those drawers have been opened."

He cleared the fragments of nuts from his teeth. She had a phobia about people touching her things.

"Mrs. Evans?" he suggested.

Her eyes were like a cat's, fixed and unwinking. "Mrs. Evans doesn't come today. She never goes near the drawers, anyway."

The legs of the pajamas were turned up at the bottom. She looked about sixteen, and his voice was suddenly protective.

"Look, baby. A closed drawer is a closed drawer. There's no special way of doing it."

She sniffed hard and clutched at his arm, her fingers digging through the heavy flannel shirt.

"Somebody's been in here," she said in a thin accusing voice.

The clothes closet doors were of the sliding variety. He pulled the first one back. Whatever they had of value was kept on the top shelf. A leather box with her few trinkets, an old Mark 2 Leica, some savings bonds they had bought between them, hoping to win the sweepstake. Everything was there. He pulled the other door back. The hangers had been shoved along the rail. His suitcases were closed but the locks were open. They both heard the noise in the outside passage at the same time, a telltale scrape as someone dragged the garbage can toward the wall. He switched off the lights in the bedroom and living room. She followed him closely, still hanging onto his arm.

"Don't leave me!" she whispered fiercely.

He disengaged her hand. "I'm going out," he whispered. "If I'm not back in five minutes dial nine-nine-nine."

He grabbed a hammer from the box under the hallway table and eased the front door open. The garbage can was up against the wall, but whoever had moved it was somewhere in the garden. A blackbird scurried from under a bush as Fraser looked, running like an animal. It took off, flying toward the lights in the neighboring house. The bird's chattering alarm was loud in the surrounding silence. Fraser inched forward, gripping the hammer firmly. Someone in the distant darkness was reproducing every move he made, step for step, stopping whenever he stopped. He could just make out a grayish shape close to the wall twenty yards away. He charged, floundering through the dead, clumped flower beds while his quarry broke for the shelter of the elms. Fraser reached the foot of the wall as the other man swung over it. Footsteps pounded down the next-door garden, running for the front of the house. Seconds later came the sound of a car being driven down the hill at speed.

Ingrid was standing just inside the door, holding a bread knife. He took it away from her, switched on the lights again and went into the kitchen. Ingrid followed, watching white-faced as he drank two glasses of water in rapid succession. His heart was banging as though he'd just completed a hundred-yard dash.

"*Now* perhaps you'll call the police!" she insisted.

He wiped his lips on the back of his mouth, still dry. "Nothing's been taken," he repeated obstinately.

"If you don't call them I will," she said steadily. "It's those men who were in that car this afternoon. Something terrible's going on."

"Did you *see* the car?" he demanded. The kitchen window was open a couple of inches. Someone had left a footprint on the Formica beside the sink.

"I heard it," she said. "That's enough. I know I'm right."

He put an arm around her shoulders and led her into the bedroom. "Now you listen to me, young lady. A hood looks at you from a passing car, and we're visited by burglars.

Coincidence! We leave windows open, lights off, it's a wonder it hasn't happened before. These people were beginners. They were probably after the television set. We disturbed them. So no police, please, darling. Or they'll be tramping around here for the rest of the night. OK?"

She was sitting on the end of the bed, hands clasped in her lap. She looked up.

"What about Casimir or is that a coincidence, too?"

"If you'll put your clothes on, we'll find out," he countered. "We'll go to his flat."

She managed a shaky smile. "I don't know why I let you talk me out of these things. But anything rather than stay here."

He threw her tights at her. "I'll have the locks changed in the morning, bolts put on all the windows."

They left the lights burning and were in Fulham half-an-hour later. The Wielkapolska was in darkness, the lamp above the entrance door extinguished. He braked to the curb. There was a card in the window. He could just read the felt-tipped pen script.

CLOSED UNTIL FURTHER NOTICE

"Closed until further notice," he repeated.

"I know," she said. "Let's try his flat."

They'd been there once before, walking back from the restaurant, arm-in-arm with the Pole in the dawn of a summer day. The curtains now were dark.

"It's possible that he's in there with some chick," he said uncertainly.

Ingrid reached across and switched off the motor. "Someone's up in the apartment opposite. Go in and find out what's happened."

He turned his collar up, crossed the forecourt and rang both first-floor doorbells. A door opened on the left of the lobby. A girl with a chopped fringe peered out, clutching her wrapper to her throat. Fraser moved into the light, pointing at Zaleski's apartment. She touched a button and let Fraser into the lobby. He could see now that her door was on a burglar chain. He did his best with a smile.

"I'm looking for Casimir Zaleski. His restaurant's closed, and he doesn't seem to be home. You wouldn't know where he is by any chance?"

She nodded vigorously. "Yes, I do know. He's in the Chelsea Police Station and with any sort of luck he'll stay there." She slammed the door, ending the conversation.

He let himself out and walked across to the stationwagon. Ingrid was holding the door open. He wedged himself behind the wheel and shrugged.

"He's done it all right. He's in Chelsea Police Station."

She caught her breath, fingers flying to her throat. "Didn't she say why? What's he *supposed* to have done?"

"There's one way to find out," he said, switching on the motor. "You've been talking about the police all night."

The police station was a block west from Sloane Avenue. A cruiser barreled up the ramp beneath and took the bend with flashing lights. He pulled over to the curb.

"You want to come in or would you rather stay here?"

Her face was almost hidden in the deep collar of her loden-cloth coat.

"I'll stay," she said.

He went up the steps to a small office just inside the entrance. A red-headed sergeant was sitting behind a counter. An institutional clock was hanging on the wall next to a clip of

WANTED and REWARD notices. A metal door banged in the distance, the sound echoing down the corridor. It was the first time Fraser had been in such a place. The cop heaved himself up on enormous freckled hands.

"Yes, sir?"

Fraser shifted his stance self-consciously. "I believe you're holding someone called Zaleski, Casimir Zaleski?"

The sergeant broke open a roll of peppermints and clamped his back teeth on one.

"That's possible," he admitted.

Fraser cocked his head. The reception was doing nothing for his ease of manner.

"*Possible?* Does that mean that you don't know or that you're not telling? If Mr. Zaleski is here, I'd like to talk to him."

The sergeant blew his nose on a clean handkerchief and wiped his mouth with the edges.

"And your name would be . . . ?"

"Kirk Fraser. I'm a friend of his."

The sergeant took a closer look at his caller. "No visitors. C.I.D. instructions."

There was a suggestion in his tone that if Fraser hung around, he was likely to finish in the cells himself.

"Then can you tell me what he's charged with?" asked Fraser. "Or is that a state secret?"

"Look!" The sergeant held up a hand, his face mock-resigned. "Don't start giving me a hard time. I only work here. What nationality are you?"

"What's that got to do with it?" Fraser asked suspiciously. "Canadian, why?"

"Thought so." The sergeant's breath carried a pungent

blast of peppermint. "It's the way you speak. I got a sister living out there, Fenelon Falls, is it, Ontario? She likes it."

"Is that right," said Fraser.

The cop's manner slipped into friendliness. "Look, your chum was picked up by someone from the Yard. If it had been one of our own chaps that nicked him, I'd have chanced letting you in for a couple of minutes. But it's more than I dare do. This inspector eats 'em alive. That's his instructions, one telephone call to a solicitor, no visits. He's had the call."

"How about the charge?" asked Fraser.

The sergeant glanced at the book on the desk. "Immigration Act, 1971. Failing to report a change of address. Christ knows what the fuss is about. It's only a technicality. Look, don't worry about it, Mister er . . . Do you know where West London Police Court is?"

Fraser shook his head. "You're probably not going to believe this, but this is the first time I was ever even in a police station. As I said, I'm just a friend."

The sergeant cracked another mint. "He's a lucky fellow. You see a lot on this job. Once they're in here, people usually don't want to know. Anyway the court. It's off North End Road up by Olympia. Anyone'll tell you. It's best to get there early, say half-past ten. And by the way, the solicitor's another Pole, name of Pulaski. OK?"

"OK," said Fraser. "And thanks." He opened the door. It was good to feel the night air on his face, to have the right to walk away in any direction he chose. If more people were made to visit a police station, fewer of them would end up inside. He climbed back beside Ingrid and shook his head.

"I don't get it. He's been arrested for not notifying his change of address. When did he *change* his address?"

Ingrid's gray eyes were troubled. "He's lived in that flat for more than two years! What does he say about it?"

Fraser switched on the motor. "I didn't even get to see him let alone talk to him. He's *incommunicado.* I'll have to go to court in the morning."

She picked at a cuticle with sharp small teeth. "*Incommunicado?* They don't do that in England, surely?"

He moved his shoulders. "You know it, I know it. It's just the people in there that don't."

The visit to the police station had shaken him more than he was revealing. All the things that Ingrid had said and suggested suddenly seemed possible. Events were becoming linked in a sinister way instead of just being a series of coincidences. The restaurants along King's Road were still doing business. He slowed in front of a *trattoria.*

"Shall we have a quick bite?"

She turned away, shaking her head. "I want to go home. I'll cook you something."

They were in bed by midnight, lying close together in the big bed with open curtains framing a dark lowering sky. She stirred in the shelter of his arms, her breath on his throat.

"Kirk. What happens to a man when he knows that his last chance has gone?"

"I don't know," he said.

"What do you *think* happens, then?"

"What man are we talking about?" he said, wondering what came next.

She was rubbing the inside of her foot along his shinbone, gentling him like a cat. He could feel the pressure of her nipples against his chest. Her voice was small and remote.

"I'm talking about Casimir. That restaurant's his magic

carpet, Kirk. If they take it away from him, he'll never stop falling."

He slipped his arm from under her neck and came up on one elbow. "Who's going to take it away from him?"

There was enough light to see her enormous eyes staring up at him from a fan of dark hair.

"The police. Those gangsters. Somebody."

"I think we've had enough of Casimir for one day," he said. "I'd like to get some sleep."

Her answer was to reach for him, pulling his mouth down on hers. He stirred gradually, imprisoned in her flesh, whispering the secret language of their love until spent desire left them both exhausted. Then he slept as he lay, an arm thrown across her breasts, his nose buried in her armpit.

Chapter Four

THIS APARTMENT WAS on the third floor of an old-fashioned brick block that overlooked Battersea Park. It had been bought by a firm of lawyers who had never seen it and furnished during the dark hours of two winter evenings. The taxes were paid yearly in advance by the nominees of an alleged Colonel Griffin. Neither water nor power or telephone was connected. No mail was delivered. The electoral register had no record of a voter living at the address. As far as it was possible to determine, the premises were permanently unoccupied.

Heavy curtains sealed all the windows. A kitchen door at the back opened onto an iron fire escape attached to the outside of the building. The evil-smelling and rarely used passage below debouched a couple of hundred yards away in a network of shabby, anonymous streets. Gerber entered and left the place under cover of night, using the front or rear entrance as his nose for such things indicated. He had a good sense of impending danger. He never made a phone call from a booth in the neighborhood, never left his car closer than a quarter mile away.

The apartment was a place of refuge where he could sit in the darkness and do a little bit of scheming. He never took women there, made little noise himself but knew every sound in the neighboring flats. At the moment there were only two other men who knew that the hideout existed. And Gerber had recently decided that he didn't care about them knowing. Like the place itself, the two men concerned had a limited period of usefulness. A revelation had come to Gerber during his one and only prison sentence. No villain with class should go out breaking people's doors down or running around banks with shotguns and pickaxe handles. You put yourself on show. It was better to stand well back and let the mugs take the chances. He came out of jail with his new-style thinking honed to a fine edge. During the months that followed he used it assiduously and with growing judgment. The neighborhood bars and billiard halls provided a pool of prospective talent. This Gerber investigated thoroughly, rejecting the ex-cons and reformatory graduates as chumps who thought that they knew it all. He was looking for men who would accept his teachings as gospel truth. He didn't want to be told about the larceny that was in their hearts. He wanted to expose it to them, to offer a lucrative future based upon his wisdom. It was three months before he made his first choice, a twenty-eight-year-old boardman in a local betting office. Benny the Bookkeeper had potential: a natural viciousness, deep respect for anyone able to outsmart him and the moral standards of a Congolese freebooter. The perfect foil for Benny was Junior Murphy, a meat porter at the time, humping frozen carcasses twelve hours a day in a refrigerated warehouse. He was strong, greedy and stupid.

Gerber both planned and bankrolled their first coup, a daytime assault with tear gas on the bullion room of a small platinum refinery. His protégés performed with a mixture of coolness and savagery that was to stamp their coming exploits. The proceeds were cut up five ways, one each for Benny and Murphy, three to the organizer. The same ratio had applied ever since. To offset what Gerber called his "philosophy-planning" it was agreed that he took no active part in a caper. He disposed of the loot and arranged "insurance." The notoriety of the team grew with their success, and the police pulled them in for questioning regularly. There'd been one occasion when the trio was taken as far as the Central Criminal Courts, charged with conspiracy to steal and burglary. A deal with two of the jurors resulted in an acquittal.

Gerber selected the coups himself, walking away firmly from tips and inside information. He trusted nobody completely, including a rum-swilling mother who removed the loose change from his pockets as often as he slept in her house.

It was almost midnight and the three men were sitting in the front room of the Battersea Park apartment. Gerber was lolling in a chair by the oilheater, conservatively clad in dark blue hopsack. The watchful stare from behind the executive-type spectacles belied his apparent somnolence. Junior Murphy was flat on his back on the chintz-covered sofa, his blond curly head buried in a cushion and wearing his usual uniform of black pants, sweater and shoes. His face had the fresh beefy appearance of a rural Irish priest. Benny was squatting on the floor, surrounded by newspapers, elegant in his knitted suit and maroon shoes with two-inch heels. His flat narrow head was shaped like a wedge carried on a long, slender neck. He tapped the newspaper in front of him with a large agate ring worn on his right forefinger.

"See what I mean, Sam. They all say the same thing. The Dante Gallery robbery's down to a gang of international jewel thieves."

"You don't listen, do you," Gerber said, shaking his head at the man on the floor. "How many times do I have to tell you, what we have here is a case of the law boxing clever."

"Right," said Murphy from the sofa. "And we know how clever that can be."

"You're like a bleeding parrot," Benny said resentfully. "If it wasn't for Sam you wouldn't *have* no ideas."

"A couple," said Murphy. "Know something, Benny. You sit just like a bird does, all legs and ass."

Benny flashed sideways, coming up behind the sofa. His curved palm held a three-inch blade close to Murphy's jugular.

"One of these days," he breathed malevolently, "I'm going to open you up and let out all that wind and piss."

Murphy's hand came up slowly, encircling Benny's slender wrist in strong fingers.

"Cut it out, the pair of you," Gerber ordered from the depth of his chair.

The blade snapped shut. Benny kicked through the newspapers and stood near the window, glowering across the room.

"Then tell this bog Irishman to keep his big mouth shut."

Staccato pips and voices sounded from the FM radio on the ground at Gerber's side. The set was specially built to receive police broadcasts. The notebook lying on top of it contained the code signals of all units operating within the Metropolitan Police area. Gerber turned the volume lower. The walls and ceilings were thick but his nature inclined to caution.

"Look at him!" Gerber mocked. "He pays eighty quid for his suits, twenty for his shoes, and he goes about tooled-up like a Soho ponce! How many times I got to tell you, Benny, get rid of that blade. It don't impress no one and if Old Bill ever catches you with it, they'll do you for carrying an offensive weapon. Now pick up those papers and siddown."

Murphy spread his arms wide, looking like an overweight choir boy.

"It was only meant to be a giggle! It's always the same with him. As soon as there's work to be done he's up tighter than a pig's ass. A bleeding prima donna, that's what he is."

"Shuddup," said Gerber, looking at each man in turn. "Let's go over this thing once again. OK. I made a mistake. I don't make many, but Sunday night was one. That Pole offered us half-a-million quids' worth of jewelry, *pleaded* with me to get rid of it for him, and I took him for a false pretenser."

Benny was hanging over the back of a beechwood dining chair. His expression was still sullen.

"Do me a favor, will you? All we know is that the stuff's been stolen. You got no proof that the Pole's got it."

"*Proof?*" Gerber repeated sarcastically. "What do you want, a statement from him? Sunday night he's talking about a fortune in jewels; Monday night this gallery gets ripped off. Use your imagination."

"Then why hasn't he been done for it?" Benny objected. "Instead of being done for some chickenshit charge about not reporting his address to the law?"

Gerber hitched his spectacles up on his nose. Moments like this he enjoyed.

"I'll tell you for why, Benny. It's because Old Bill ain't got nothing on him, no evidence. Or maybe this pinch is just a coincidence. Whichever way it is, we're going to cover ourselves."

Murphy scratched inside the neck of his sweater. "I'm with you, Sam. Zaleski's got that gear, it stands to reason. And I'll tell you something else, this Canadian's in it as well. He's a pal of Zaleski's. It makes you sick, a couple of mugs pulling off a thing like that."

"A couple of mugs," said Gerber. He tilted the chair back and shut his eyes. The lamps, like the heaters, burned kerosene. Their soft hissing was a background to the conversation. There was a quiet about the building at this time of night that reminded him of prison. Now and then he had a glimpse of the other tenants, the ones whose names were on the board down in the entrance hall. Retired admirals and like that, all of them in their seventies, creeping out into the park with their bleeding dogs. At eleven o'clock they were in bed, lights out, doors double-locked against people like him. He squinted under half-closed eyelids. Benny was still riding the chair, his chin lodged on top of the backrest. Murphy was playing with a key ring, whistling soundlessly. They both jumped as Gerber suddenly snarled.

"You think you're so fucking smart — high-class operators! Yet you go and screw this geezer's drum like a pair of teenage tearaways. And even that's not enough. You let him see you at it!"

Murphy muttered something and then louder. "It was you who said to take a look where Fraser lived. And the window was open, wasn't it!"

Benny glanced up from clipping his nails. "The bastard must have *something* to hide. He didn't even phone the law. We doubled back to the house to make sure. Fraser and the bird left. No law." He shook the newspaper full of nail parings into the stove. The room stank like a farrier's smithy.

"Get that bag you live with to trim your nails," said Gerber. "You talk like morons both of you. Of *course* Fraser's in it. But he's not going to keep half-a-million pounds' worth of bent

gear in a tin box on top of the kitchen dresser. What we have
here is a couple of real shrewd articles and you call 'em mugs.
I'll tell you something. It's just in the cards that Zaleski got
himself nicked on purpose — to have the law running round in
circles with him safely inside."

Murphy thudded a fist into the palm of his other hand.
"You know, Sam, I've been thinking about that."

Benny's mouth thinned to a vicious slit. "Good night all!"

"Shuddup," said Gerber. "And I'm getting sick of saying
it! It's possible that Zaleski's a whole lot smarter than what
you are in many ways. There's only one thing we *can* be sure
of — the law's not after us. We got a license to float about as
we like. You're sure Fraser didn't speak to no one at
Victoria?"

Benny's voice was resigned. "I already told you three times
what happened. All he done was sit in the bar and drink. He
didn't speak to no one except the hall porter."

Whenever Gerber thought about it, the memory of the
scene in the restaurant made him want to spit blood. He'd as
good as had a fortune in his hands and given it back.

"Do you know what you're looking for, either of you? This
bleeding monstrance weighs over thirty pounds. It ain't the sort
of thing you stuff down your trousers. OK, Fraser wasn't
carrying it yesterday so why *did* he go to Victoria? I'll tell you
why. He had a meet with someone."

They moved their heads in quick assent, eyes watchful.

"Someone who's in this thing with him," he continued.
"Someone who didn't show. The question is, *who?*"

Murphy frowned, his face wrinkled in concentration.
Benny was quicker off the mark.

"Zaleski's wife?"

"Right," said Gerber swinging around. "Now we know where she lives. What we're going to do is put the frighteners on. Pay them all a little visit. One of you'd better go to the court in the morning. You, Benny. Fraser's almost sure to be there. Zaleski's wife, too, possibly. Have a word with the Canadian first, after you've left the court."

Benny grinned, back in favor and pleased with the prospect. "What do you want me to say to him?"

Gerber closed an eye. "Lean on him a little. Tell him we know the score. That we'll move the loot for them, no sweat, no bother. All we want is a fair piece of the action — like half."

Murphy whistled like a starling. "You must be joking, Sam. They're not going to go for that!"

"I know they're not," Gerber said easily. "But it'll give them something to worry about. What's the first thing you do when someone has a go at your wallet?"

"Move it to another pocket," Benny said promptly.

Gerber grinned. "Exactly. And that's what's going to happen here. If it doesn't, we'll think again. The thing to remember is that we're in the clear. Whoever it is that Old Bill's looking for, it isn't us."

He let them out, one at a time, watching the street from the window. Fifteen minutes later he was going down the fire escape.

Chapter Five

IT WAS TWENTY-FIVE minutes after ten as Fraser drove up North End Road. He could see the blocked streets long before he reached the police court. Cars were bumper-parked on both sides. He left the stationwagon up against a brewery wall and walked back with the smell of hops chasing him on the chilly wind. He was carrying his anorak and wearing a tie with his leather-patched sports jacket. It was Ingrid's idea. The fact that his only tie had been bought to wear at a funeral made no difference, she said. He had to make a good impression. The courthouse was a one-story building with a cheerless exterior like a public abattoir. He made his way into a lobby lined with benches where people sat, smoking nervously, silent and preoccupied. Others showed the desperation of shame. A couple of stunned girls were holding hands, a red-faced father was haranguing his teenage son. A drunk sprawled solitary on a bench, reeking of urine and last night's booze, attended at a safe distance by a spruce, hatless cop.

The walls sprouted a rash of signs.

PROBATION OFFICER   SILENCE IN COURT   FINES

A typewritten list gave the names of people to be tried that day with a description of their offenses and the times when their cases were to be heard. Zaleski's name came fourth. A uniformed attendant answered Fraser's inquiry, nodding across the crowded lobby where two men were talking together. Fraser pushed his way toward them.

"Mr. Polaski?"

The shorter of the two men was wearing the livery of a police-court lawyer, black jacket and striped trousers, a stiff, white wing collar that left an angry weal around his neck. Thinning hair swept back from a high forehead over busy black eyes and a questing nose. His English was faultless.

"I am Pulawski."

"I'm a friend of Zaleski," Fraser said. "Kirk Fraser."

The second man was tall and stood like a crane. His yellow hair was worn in a Friar Tuck arrangement, long over the ears and with a fringe. He had a gaunt hungry-looking face, the eyes of a soapbox missionary and modish clothes. His regency-styled jacket matched his velvet trousers and there were buckles on his square-toed shoes.

"Detective-Inspector Raven," he said, introducing himself.

Pulawski consulted a small flat watch on the end of a gold chain. "Inspector Raven's in charge of the case," he volunteered.

Raven's inspection left Fraser with the feeling that his pocket had been picked.

"I imagine it was you who called at Chelsea Police Station?"

"That's right," said Fraser. "I went there as soon as I heard Zaleski had been arrested."

The inspector's smile was a token display of well-kept teeth. "Of course. Well, I'll leave you to it. We're on next. It shouldn't take long. Incidentally, Mr. Pulawski, I've left my phone number with your client just in case."

The lawyer's grin was equally professional. "You know better than that, Inspector. In case of *what*?"

Raven's outstretched hand floated the question for a second. "Nothing in particular. I thought that he might want to get in touch with me. These things do happen. Well, I'll probably see you later."

Pulawski's gaze followed him across the lobby and into the courtroom. The lawyer's manner went with his smooth, shadowed face. There was an aura of certainty about him, a hint of familiarity with those in high places.

"There's something about all this that I don't quite understand," he admitted confidentially. "Raven's from the Yard. I don't see what he's doing on a case like this."

The stench from the deadbeat sprawled on the bench behind them was atrocious. They moved away and Fraser shrugged.

"Don't look at me. I wouldn't know one cop from another. I came because I thought Zaleski might need someone to stand bail for him."

The lawyer's head moved briskly. "That won't be necessary. This is no more than a technicality. I don't know what the police are up to. Zaleski's been in the country for nearly thirty years. We'd better go in. You go through there." He nodded at the public entrance to the courtroom.

Fraser walked across. There was something tremendously depressing about the scene, the hangdog appearance of the prisoners and their friends, the businesslike indifference of the officials. This wasn't high drama. It was nail-biting, hopeless misery. He opened the door. A brass-railed barrier behind the defendant's stand divided the paneled room into stage and auditorium. A collection of vinegar-nosed citizens in out of the cold occupied the public benches, trying to appear at ease. Fraser took a seat against the wall, facing the magistrate's rostrum. The witness stand was over on the left. Pulawski was in the seats reserved for counsel. A couple of reporters sat behind him. Raven was standing by the door leading to the cells. The magistrate was an irritable-looking man with a nose on the order of the late W. C. Fields and was wearing a pink polka-dotted bow tie. The clerk came to his feet.

"Number four on your list, sir. Casimir Zaleski."

The magistrate adjusted his spectacles as a jailer ushered Zaleski into court. The Pole stalked to the stand, belly pushed out resolutely, his duffelcoat over his arm. He stood at strict attention, eyes fixed on the coat of arms over the magistrate's head. The clerk read from the card he was holding, ignoring the punctuation.

Casimir Zaleski you are charged in that on the 24th day of January as a person subject to the provisions of the Immigration Act 1971 you failed to notify your change of address as required do you plead guilty or not guilty?

Pulawski came to his feet, leaning on the bench in front of him. "I appear for the defense, Your Worship. The defendant pleads not guilty."

Zaleski screwed his head around as he sat down. There was just time for Fraser to smile and hold up a thumb. Raven took the stand. He refused the Bible, made a simple affirmation and brought his mouth closer to the microphone, reading from his notebook.

"John Raven, Your Worship. Detective-Inspector attached to Tactical Force, Scotland Yard. Subsequent to information received, I proceeded to premises at Elm Park Gardens and took the accused into custody at approximately seventeen hours twenty yesterday. After having . . ." He broke off as the magistrate held up his hand. The stipendiary screwed his face into an expression of weariness.

"One moment, Inspector. I take it that you've never appeared in this court before?"

"This court, no, sir."

The magistrate signified understanding. "That accounts for it. We make a practice of using simple language here. We *go* to places instead of proceeding and seventeen hours twenty is twenty past five. Please continue."

Raven closed his notebook, his thin face untroubled by the interruption. "I told the defendant why I was arresting him and took him to Chelsea Police Station. He was subsequently cautioned and charged. He declined to make a statement and asked to see his solicitor."

The magistrate propped himself on his elbows. "What you're saying is that he made no reply to the charge. Is this correct?"

"That's correct, sir," replied Raven. "Later on he said, and I quote, 'Why making fools of yourselves, Officer,' unquote. That's as far I'm able to go at this stage, Your Worship."

His expression remained impassive as laughter exploded in the courtroom. The clerk elongated his neck like a browsing giraffe, whispering to the magistrate who looked from the dock to Raven.

"I understand that you're asking for a remand in this case, Inspector?"

Raven's yellow hair rose and fell as he ducked his head. "That's right, sir. There are a number of inquiries still to be made."

Pulawski was on his feet again, his manner assured. "Then I must ask for bail to be set in a nominal amount, Your Worship. The defendant has a complete answer to the charge. He's a man of unblemished character who has conducted a business at the same address for a number of years."

The magistrate sneaked a look at his watch speaking to no one in particular. "There's no objection to bail, I suppose?"

Raven blew out his hollow cheeks. "There is indeed, Your Worship. The defendant's wife is abroad, and there is strong reason to believe that he might join her there."

"Without bloody passport!" shouted Zaleski. "Is ridiculous!" The jailer quieted him and he sat down, the back of his neck a dull red, still muttering in Polish.

"Really, Your Worship," Pulawski intervened. "I must insist . . ."

"I'm the one who insists in this court," snapped the magistrate. "You'll be remanded in custody for eight days, Zaleski. Your solicitor knows the remedy if you so wish. Next case."

The silence lasted for thirty seconds. Coughs and the rustle of papers broke the tension. The despair in Zaleski's eyes was plain as he turned back at the door leading to the cells. "Bastards!" he shouted.

Fraser hurried out after the lawyer, catching him in the lobby. "That was a great performance. Eight days in jail for nothing!"

The lawyer swung his briefcase with the resilience of his kind. "We were unlucky. The magistrate was in one of his moods. We can always go to judge-in-chambers. I'll have a word with Zaleski. It costs money, of course."

"How much?" demanded Fraser. His eye caught Raven on the way out to the street. The inspector waved back in friendly fashion.

Pulawski's shoulders wriggled. "It depends on who we brief. Junior counsel would do. Forty or fifty guineas, I suppose. It's a routine matter."

Fraser's control snapped. "That's the second time you've given me this bit about it being a routine matter. I'll tell you what it is — a man's sitting in there with the key turned on him. Now you go in and talk to him. If he doesn't have the money I'll pay."

Pulawski's eyes slid away. "There's no guarantee, you understand. The unblemished character's a bit of an exaggeration. He's been fined for not paying his rates. All in all, the circumstances are such that a High Court judge might well take the same view as the magistrate."

"*What* circumstances?" Fraser asked, his voice dangerously quiet.

The lawyer lifted his arms. "He's an *alien*, Mr. Fraser."

"So am I," retorted Fraser. "Now you get in there and talk to him. Tell him we're going to get him out."

Pulawski knocked on the door leading to the cells. The jailer opened it. Only a few people were left in the lobby. One of them was a man sitting on a bench near the Probation Office. The top of his head just showed over a copy of *Sporting Life.* He lowered the newspaper as Fraser glanced across and their eyes met for a second. The stranger came to his feet, stuffed the newspaper in the pocket of his belted jacket and winked deliberately. Then he walked outside to the street. There was something unpleasantly suggestive about the way it was done, as if their mere presence in a police court warranted some sort of camaraderie. Fraser had a vague memory that he'd seen him before. A few minutes passed before the lawyer bustled back across the lobby.

"Well that's that," he said. "No need to worry about the money. It's all taken care of. He wants to have a word with you. I've arranged things with the jailer. I'll be in touch, then." He smiled knowingly and disappeared.

Fraser rang the bell. A thickset officer opened the heavy steel door, looked Fraser up and down, and led the way into a glazed-tile corridor smelling of disinfectant. He flicked a spyhole in a cell door, turned a key in the lock and leaned against the opposite wall.

"You've got five minutes. The van'll be coming to take him to Brixton. No foreign languages."

Zaleski came out of the cell, blinking. His jacket had clearly been used as a pillow and there were stains on his trousers. Fraser pulled his cigarettes out, looking at the cop for permission. The man glanced away, swinging a bunch of keys on the end of a long chain. Zaleski cupped his hands around the flame, squinting up at Fraser.

"You delivered my message?"

"She wasn't there," said Fraser, leaning away from the rising smoke. "Either that or I missed her."

Zaleski's face was pale under the stubble of beard. "Is impossible that she is not there."

Fraser shrugged. "I did my best. I'm sorry."

Someone in a nearby cell started banging on the door. It was the drunk, his voice still blurred.

The jailer turned his head, lengthening his chain so that the bunch of keys crashed against the door. Zaleski used the split second to place a warning finger over his lips. His arms were at his side when the jailer looked again.

"You know where this lady is living?" Zaleski asked carefully.

"Ingrid does," answered Fraser.

"I see. Then you must go there today. Is extremely important."

Fraser shifted his feet. "You can go yourself. Pulawski's getting you out of here."

The jailer joined in. "Not today he isn't. These things take time. He won't be out till tomorrow, earliest. If then."

Zaleski's voice strained. "You must see her today. Tell her she must go back and wait till she hears from me."

Fraser glanced over his shoulder. The cop's expression was bored, as if he'd heard it all before, the floundering hints and hopes that in the end changed nothing. Fraser had started to sweat. He resented it. Most of all he resented being involved in something that he didn't understand.

"Look," he said. "I've heard about police making mistakes, but this is ridiculous. What are they trying to do to you?"

Zaleski reached inside the neck of his sweater and pulled out a small gold medallion. His eyes were steady.

"Was my mother's, Kirk. I swear on it that police are making mistake. I *made* that report. You will go to see this lady?"

"I'll go," said Fraser. "Is there anything you need?"

Zaleski shook his head quickly. "Is nothing. Just doing what I ask."

The jailer heaved himself up from the wall. "That's it then. Things always seem a lot worse than they really are. It all comes out in the wash is what I always say." He shut the door on the Pole, pleased with his homespun philosophy.

Fraser emerged on the street, grateful for the smell of fresh air. He threaded his way through the line of parked cars toward the corner. He was about to turn it when he noticed Raven sitting in a sports car. He wheeled around on impulse, anger blocking his better judgment. The sight of Raven lolling behind the wheel while Zaleski sweated it out in a cell was somehow intolerable. The cop looked up as Fraser approached as if seeing him for the first time. Fraser leaned through the half-open window. Music was coming from a cassette player next to the phone under the dashboard.

"There's something I wanted to say to you, Inspector."

Raven turned the volume down. "Do you know — I thought there might be."

Fraser felt his cheeks coloring. "That was my first time ever in a police court. I didn't like what I saw."

Raven shifted his long legs, twisting in his seat so that he faced the window.

"Few people do," he remarked casually. "Was that all you wanted to say to me?"

There was an expectancy in Raven's eyes that infuriated Fraser. As if he was waiting for some kind of praise.

"I get the impression that you like pushing people around," said Fraser, "people like Zaleski. There just might be an answer to that. I intend to find out."

Raven's bony fingers were drumming in tune with the muffled music. "An interesting statement," he said finally. "I'll remind you of it the next time we meet."

The window went up, and he started the motor. As the car pulled away, there was a glimpse of Raven's smiling face. The memory was still in Fraser's mind twenty minutes later as he jockeyed the stationwagon up behind the bookstore.

Ingrid let him in. She had coffee and sandwiches ready. They sat at the back of the store eating, the stove between them. She listened as he talked, her head bent, her face screened by her hair. Finally she pulled it back, her gray eyes challenging.

"That's not all, Kirk. There's something else, I can tell. Something's bothering you."

The tone of voice, the pose, the steady gaze that pierced

through subterfuge, all were familiar. The trouble about living with Ingrid was that every single experience had to be shared. Anything less was disloyal. There was no hiding place. The shelf above her head held the volumes of *Ornithologia Brittanica,* the 1840 edition with colored plates. He remembered leafing through them at the auction room. A raven was a bird of prey.

"I'm not too sure," he said. "But my feeling is that I've just been threatened by a cop, on the street and in broad daylight."

Her hand flew to her mouth. "But why?"

He stretched his arms till his shoulder blades touched. "It's this inspector — the one in charge of Casimir's case. He was sitting in a car outside the court, you know, playing the hard-nosed cop. One thing led to another and words passed. I don't know what got into me but a friend he is not!"

"In other words you lost your temper," she said, collecting his cup and plate. "Trust you to antagonize the wrong person. And that's supposed to be helping Casimir?"

He listened to her clattering the crockery in the small washroom sink. He held a cigarette against the stove till the tobacco started to smolder. He dragged the salt burn deep into his lungs. At the moment his last worry was cancer.

His voice was bitter as she came back into the room. "It never fails," he announced. "If a guy sticks his fist into my nose, it's my fault for having my face there in the first place."

"You say this man threatened you," she said frowning. "There has to be a reason."

He drew a long breath. With Ingrid there had to be a reason for everything, even a head cold.

"It can't be the hair this time," he argued. "His is as long as mine. Maybe it's the accent."

The phone rang in the office. Ingrid answered it, standing in the doorway and holding out the receiver.

"It's for you."

The Cockney voice was unfamiliar. "Fraser? Look, mate, you and me's got some business to talk over. I'm just up the street. I'll be over in five minutes."

The line went dead. Fraser hung up and shrugged. "Business, he says. A porn salesman from the sound of him."

She made a face, rummaging through her suede satchel for the dog-eared notebook she used for everything.

"You wanted Mrs. Zaleska's address."

The entry was written in Zaleski's bold handwriting. He copied it down. Rivermead House, Putney, Block A, Flat 12.

"It's the third floor," she said. "Are you going to tell her that Casimir's in jail?"

He put the slip of paper in his pocket. "No I am not," he answered deliberately. "What I'm going to do is deliver his message word for word. After that I'm through running errands that I don't understand. He'll probably be out on bail himself in the morning, anyway."

She drew her shawl tighter round her body, her voice unconvincingly casual.

"I know you hate me criticizing your friends, but you've got to admit that it's all a bit strange. Casimir's hiding something."

It was almost two by his watch. "You're right on two counts. It *is* strange and I don't like my friends criticized. Come to that, I thought he was a friend of yours as well."

"He is," she said, reversing their roles composedly. "I'm just not so fanatical about my friends as you are. Look, darling, you're more important to me than Casimir is. If there's anything sinister, I don't want you mixed up in it."

Her possessiveness never failed to provoke him. "Why don't you say what you mean?" he demanded. "What do you *really* think he's done, robbed a bank or something? Do you think it was the police searching our flat last night, looking for the loot?"

"I don't find that even mildly funny," she retorted.

"A pity," he said, shaking his head at her wearily. "I was hoping that you would."

She turned away. "What's the use! It's no good talking to you when you're in this mood. Do whatever you think best." She vanished into the washroom.

"That's exactly what I'm going to do," he said to her back. He reversed the sign on the door and unlocked, noticing the man across the street sheltering in the entrance of the pizza parlor. Now there was no mistaking the weasel face on the long, slender neck, the lissome body in the knit-wool suit. It was the man who had smiled at him in the lobby of the police court, one of the two men who had been in Zaleski's restaurant on Sunday night. Fraser knew instinctively that this was to be his visitor. The stranger zigzagged across the street into the bookstore. He shut the door with an economical movement of his foot and peered into the empty office. The door to the washroom was shut. He rested his right hand gently on Fraser's sleeve. He was wearing a ring set with a chunk of agate on his forefinger. Fraser removed the hand as he might have done an insect. The stranger grinned menacingly.

"I got a message for you, mate. You people don't want no trouble nor do we, right?"

He talked from both sides of his mouth with equal facility. Fraser's rudeness was deliberate.

"I don't know what you're talking about and what's more I

don't even *want* to know. Now if you'll get out of here . . ."
He held the door open.

The stranger continued to grin but his face had reddened.
"Tell your friend that there's enough in it for everyone. All
you got to do is . . ." His flat head swung around warily as
he broke off. Then suddenly he was gone, darting through the
traffic like a fox breaking cover. By the time Fraser reached
the sidewalk, there was no sign of him. But crossing the street
was Detective-Inspector Raven, his long legs lifting like a
heron's. His bare head was even yellower in the grayish
daylight.

He nodded pleasantly, peering through into the store. "I
thought I'd drop by." He made it sound the most natural
thing in the world.

Fraser blocked the doorway determinedly. "You don't
come in here. Not unless you have a search warrant."

Raven stepped nearer the storefront. "That's kind of heavy,
isn't it? I came about your friend's bail. I got the impression
that you were offering yourself as surety or am I wrong?"

"That's right," said Fraser guardedly, still blocking the
doorway.

Raven moved out of the way of a woman passing with a
baby carriage. He smiled as Ingrid emerged from the
washroom.

"That's what I thought. Well, you'll appreciate that the
police have to make inquiries in cases like this. We have to
find out if you're a person in good standing, able to pay up
should the bail be forfeited."

Fraser's eyes sought the length of the street. There was no
sign of the stranger.

"Does that mean that Zaleski's going to make bail?"

Raven moved a bony shoulder. "That's up to judge-in-chambers. I hear that Pulawski's making an appearance in front of him tomorrow morning. Do you rent these premises or do you own them?"

Fraser took a long hard look at him. Every writer in the genre exploited the classic police approach, the quietly spoken, sympathetic character opposed to his roughneck partner, ready to slam the victim around the cell. Raven seemed to use both approaches more or less at the same time.

"I own this place lock, stock, and barrel," said Fraser, careless of the people who were passing. "Any cop on the end of a phone could have found that out for you. So what *did* you come here for?"

"To see you," said Raven innocently. "You know, it's becoming increasingly interesting. I'm sure we'll meet again."

Fraser watched him go with a feeling of relief. There was an undertone to the inspector's easy manner that was distinctly disturbing. Fraser shut the door hurriedly as Ingrid came out of the washroom.

"And *that* was your policeman?" she smiled. "I thought he was rather dishy in a funny sort of way. The velvet suit was way out. What did he want?"

"To see me," said Fraser. "He claims he finds it interesting."

"Perhaps he does, darling." She started to laugh. "Perhaps he fancies you. If he telephones again, you'd better let me talk to him."

He realized then that she thought it was Raven who had called the store earlier. She hadn't even seen the weasel-faced stranger, which was just as well. She was nervous already, and there was no sense in giving her more to worry about. He ran the facts back in his mind, remembering the things that Zaleski had said after the scene in the restaurant on Sunday night. The fact that the two guys were high-power hoods accounted for his visitor taking off the moment that he saw Raven. There was no longer any question of coincidence. Whatever was happening was linked somehow to that hassle in the restaurant. Weasel-face had been present then. He'd been at the courthouse that morning and now here.

Fraser picked up his anorak. Ingrid held the quilted sleeves for him. "Why do you have to go yourself? You could phone — send a telegram, even.

"No way," he said, turning and kissing her cheek. "But if I'm not back by five o'clock, call the law!"

He'd said it as a joke. The sudden tears in her eyes alarmed him. "A joke," he explained, throwing his arms wide. "For chrissakes, Ingrid! I'm driving three miles to deliver a message, not going up the Amazon!"

She followed him through the storeroom to the back way out onto Hollywood Road. She was at the window as he drove away. Her directions were specific, a right turn at Putney Bridge then four hundred yards west along the embankment. The brick towers of the ugly complex were wreathed in mist that billowed off the river. Visibility was down to a few yards. He drove slowly. Three blocks radiated from a central building where watery lights glimmered. He wheeled the stationwagon onto a waste of hardtop behind, cut the motor and started a cigarette. He could just see a children's playground and a tennis court. Mist clung to the surrounding brickwork, veiled the lighted windows. It was a damp hand that left its clammy touch everywhere. A few parked cars were spaced out near a covered passageway that gave access to the rear of Block A. There was no need for him to go around the front, and he was glad of it. There was bound to be someone there who'd ask questions, a building manager or janitor. He wanted to deliver his message and get the hell out of it.

A feeling was growing that Zaleski was mixed up in some kind of gambling operation. The empty floors over the restaurant would be ideal for housing an illegal game. People could come and go unnoticed among the diners and the action would guarantee big money. Maybe Zaleski was already involved and trying to back out. Or maybe the police were on to the racket and using Casimir as bait to trap the hoods.

God knows that a child could punch holes in the idea, but it was a possibility and would account for some of the antics. One thing was sure and certain. Wherever it was that Zaleski was being taken, it wasn't where he wanted to go. Fraser could just see the far end of the passageway looming out from the mist. The cars nearby were empty. There was no one else in sight. He buttoned his anorak to the neck and walked across to the passage door. The heat inside came from a laundry room where a battery of washing and drying machines droned unattended. He followed a series of stenciled arrows to a swing door. Beyond this was a service staircase. He climbed it to the third floor. Chrome numerals identified the apartments on each side of the sisal-carpeted corridor. Number twelve was on his immediate right. He put his thumb on the door buzzer and waited. There was no reply. He tried again without success then bent down, lifting up the mail flap. A piece of felt inside blocked his view. He could hear no sign of life from within the apartment. He straightened his back, looking at the Yale-type lock with a sense of frustration.

Zaleski's wife seemed determined to avoid him. He touched the door handle tentatively, surprised when it turned in his grip. The door was unlocked, the apartment in darkness. The faintest of lights indicated the windows beyond drawn curtains. It was cold as if the heating had been turned off, and the room smelled very faintly of chypre. He groped along the wall, feeling for the light button. Someone else found it for him and the door was closed quickly.

Fraser blinked in the sudden blaze, recognizing the woman sitting on the sofa. She wore her white-streaked black hair with a center parting and had a handsome nose above dark, terrified eyes. Draped across her knees was a black coat with a fur collar of some kind. Standing behind her was a beefy blond man in wide trousers and a ribbed sweater. He was holding a snub-nosed revolver close against her neck. Benny stepped away from the door, his thumbs hooked in the belt of his jacket. He swung his slick, flat-topped head like a weasel approaching a rabbit.

"What did your friend want, Kirky boy?"

Mrs. Zaleska's eyes were following every move that Fraser made. He noted the length of cord dangling uselessly from the phone on the table.

"Which friend is that?" he heard himself say stupidly.

"That fucking copper, Raven."

Pieces were sliding into position, building up a whole. "It was you in my apartment last night, wasn't it?" challenged Fraser.

"Keep your voice down." Benny's sharp-angled face was malevolent. "I'll ask the questions. I asked you what that ponce Raven wanted."

"Information about you," Fraser improvised. His mouth

and tongue were dry. "He wanted to know what you were doing in the store — how long I know you."

"Bollix," said Benny. An airplane droned high overhead, the sound scything into the mist-shrouded apartment building. The two men exchanged glances.

Murphy straddled his burly legs, smiling like a vicious choirboy. "He's a real quick thinker, isn't he?" he asked in a tone of admiration.

Benny came forward stealthily, clicking his tongue. "That bastard don't even *know* me. I'm the one who knows *him*."

"He's got your picture in his pocket," Fraser said, licking his lips at the end.

"Not mine, mate," Benny said, shaking his head. "Why don't you have a little think about being sensible. Like I told you, there's enough in this for everyone."

Fraser's shoulders rose and fell. He stood quite still, facing the mirror as Benny searched his pockets expertly. The hood felt beneath his belt, turned the black knitted tie inside out and made Fraser take off his shoes. Mrs. Zaleska watched like an owl, a fixed vacant look that disturbed Fraser.

"It'll be all right," he said over his shoulder. "Don't let 'em scare you."

Murphy leaned over the back of the sofa, nuzzling the barrel of the pistol into Mrs. Zaleska's hair.

"She's scared, all right. But that's because she's sensible. Right, Auntie?"

Her dark eyes stared up dumbly. "A couple of cheap hoods," put in Fraser. "They're not going to do a damn thing."

Benny's arm flashed. The karate chop sent the Canadian staggering. He found the wall and clutched at his neck, his eyes blinded by tears of pain. Benny floated away like a ballet dancer.

"And I wasn't even trying. Now belt up and listen to some sense. Nobody's going to get hurt, not as long as you people behave yourselves. We don't have to make no deals, Kirky boy. We got you where we want you. But my friend's a fair man. In spite of what that stupid Pole done on Sunday, he's still fair. Give 'em fifty per cent, he says — so that's what it is — half. Comes to a lot of money. More than you mugs deserve."

Murphy knitted his eyebrows. "It's more than fair if you ask me, considering we're the ones with the contacts." There was a sort of deadly reason about the way he spoke.

Fraser was no longer so sure of his courage. Tortured nerve ends racked his head. He worked his jaw painfully.

"How many times do I have to tell you that I don't know what you're talking about. You might as well be talking Abyssinian. If all this has something to do with the restaurant, Mrs. Zaleska will tell you — I don't have a nickel's interest in the place."

Benny was chewing gum. He flicked it from his tongue to his teeth, bringing his face close to Fraser's.

"Where's your girl friend, Kirky boy?"

The question seemed to drop from a great height leaving a deep hole from which Fraser's answer crawled.

"What do you mean, where is she? She's in the store, why?"

Benny wagged his ringed index finger. "She was, mate. But she ain't there no longer. A friend of mine's taking care of her."

The words acted like a shot of adrenalin, filling the

Canadian's head with blinding anger. He lurched forward, arms outstretched. Benny skipped away, his face contemptuous.

"Don't be a fucking hero, mate, or I'll slice your hooter off. Your girl friend's all right. She and Auntie here's going to have a nice little rest while you fix things up with Zaleski." He put the naked blade away in his pocket.

Fraser saw himself in the mirror, wild-eyed, tangle-haired and ineffectual. He made one final plea.

"I swear to God I don't understand what this is all about. That's no cop-out. It's the truth. Tell them, Mrs. Zaleska," he pleaded.

She was crying silently, the tears running from her cheeks onto her woollen dress.

"Ask *her?*" said Benny. "Don't make me laugh. She only went to Paris to see an old friend. She don't know nothing either. But she's got a return ticket in her bag and a forged bleeding identity card!"

Mrs. Zaleska looked away, the tears still running. Benny turned the corners of his mouth down.

"You must think we're a couple of right charleys. What's *your* story, anyway? What are you supposed to be doing here, reading the gas meter?"

"I came to deliver a message," said Fraser. His eyes sought forgiveness from the woman on the sofa. "He wanted you to go back to Paris — to stay there till he got in touch with you. He's in prison."

Her eyes flickered, then she covered her face with her hands. Benny's hand shot out accusingly.

"Are you trying to tell me the Pole gave you nothing to hold for him? No parcel — a key of some kind?"

"He gave me nothing," said Fraser. "Nothing at all. All I did was run a message."

Benny glowered. "You know what I think, mate. I think you're a bunch of fucking liars, the lot of you. Now I'm going to tell you something, and get it absolutely straight. You got exactly forty-eight hours to work things out with your pal. We'll get rid of the gear and there'll still be some left for you. Are you with me?"

There was nothing to do but nod. Benny nodded back approvingly. "That's more like it. Because if you people *don't* come across, we're going to feed your girl friend and Auntie here to the pigs. Into the old slicing machine and into the troughs. And that is no joke, mate."

Fraser looked around, his mind too stunned to do more than register the plain evil of the man's threat. Murphy scooped the scattered contents into Mrs. Zaleska's bag and motioned her to her feet. Benny's tone was mock-kindly.

"Now you behave yourself, Auntie. Junior's going to put his pistol away, but one sound out of you and he'll shoot. He's a very rich boy and don't mind spoiling his clothes."

Zaleski's wife moved toward the door, offering no sign that she either heard or understood. Benny shifted his gum and held up a warning finger.

"Don't do nothing stupid like going to the law, Kirk, mate. We're partners now. And tell the Pole no messing. It's the loot or the chopper. Understood?"

"Understood," said Fraser for what seemed the tenth time. The image was gruesome, but he recalled that these people mutilated one another with bacon slicers, crushed each other's genitals. Killing for them was no more than an exercise in expediency.

Benny fluffed up the cushions on the sofa and looked around. "Careful how you leave this place. Auntie here's supposed to be in France. We'll be in touch." He opened the door, peered up and down the corridor and motioned the others outside. A couple of minutes later Fraser heard the sound of a car pulling away. It was too misty to see anything. His mouth was sour and he felt like vomiting. He put his head under the kitchen tap and kept it there until his brain started sending recognizable messages. He explored the rest of the apartment. The bedroom was sparsely furnished, a long mirror reflecting the strip of worn red carpet. Some photographs lay on the bed, their yellowed edges showing where they'd been removed from their frames. He lowered himself on the living room sofa, seeing that he was wrong about the phone lead having been cut. The instrument was the type that could be carried from room to room. It had simply been pulled from its socket. He pushed the plug back in place and the phone purred like a tomcat. He dialed 999. An impersonal voice answered right away.

"Scotland Yard. Information Room."

The voice repeated itself. Fraser hesitated. Then he replaced the receiver like a man adjusting a very fine balance. The hoods were right. There was no way he could risk calling the police. He took a fresh hold on himself, opened the door on an empty corridor and ran. He drove back to Fulham, staring through the windshield at the traffic that rushed from the opposite direction. The pubs were emptying into the raw, gray afternoon. He left the car on Hollywood Road and walked around to the front of the store, his numbed brain registering the familiar sights. The Half-Moon sign of the corner pub, the line of restaurants — The Great American

Disaster, Wine and Kebab to Take Away, Colonel Bogey's Southern Fried Chicken — the alleged portrait of the owner looking like a racetrack con man with his white hair, mustache and goatee. A queue had formed in front of the butcher shop. A neighborhood drunk lurched around the corner on his way home for his afternoon snooze. It was the peepshow that he and Ingrid watched every single day of their lives. It seemed somehow false that she wasn't there now, to laugh away his fear and explain that this was all one big put-on.

The sign in the door had been reversed. Someone had put out the lights and extinguished the stoves. The store stank of kerosene fumes. Ingrid's coat and suede shoulderbag were gone. There was a final and definite emptiness that depressed him intensely. He overturned a stand of books in his haste to reach the shrilling phone. The voice was unfamiliar, a new and sinister sound to remember.

"Fraser?"

"Yes?" he answered. He had a peculiar feeling that he was somehow being watched.

"Here's somebody wants a word with you," the voice said. Fraser's fingers tightened as Ingrid's whisper sounded against a background of street noises.

"Kirk?"

Fraser took the instrument as far as the cord allowed. The three phone booths up the street were empty, but the feeling that he was being watched persisted.

"Don't worry, honey," he soothed. "Everything's going to be all right."

"I'm frightened, Kirk."

He could see her in his mind, hands cupped, wrists close together, waiting for the miracle that he would perform.

"Everything's going to be all right," he repeated.

The man was back on the line, hoarse but authoritative. "Fraser? Now listen to me. You get out there to the nick right sharpish and talk to the Pole. The women are safe enough, tell him, as long as he delivers. You get my meaning, do you?"

"I get your meaning." Fraser's neck muscles ached like rotten teeth and his mouth still tasted of bile.

"I hope you do, mate," said the voice. "For the women's sake, I hope you do." The line clicked and then was dead.

Fraser searched through the L–Z telephone book. He found the address he needed.

H.M. PRISON
BRIXTON (office)   Jebb Avenue   S.W.2   01-674-5656

He flexed his fingers like a pool-hall shark and dialed. "Good afternoon. You have a Mr. Zaleski there. I'd like to come and visit him."

"A remand prisoner, is he, or convicted?"

"Waiting for bail," said Fraser. "That's really what I wanted to see him about."

The official was helpful. "Visiting hours are from eleven to twelve-thirty in the morning, two to three-thirty in the afternoon. Fifteen minutes duration except by permission of the governor. They'll tell you all about it at the gate."

Fraser locked up the store and drove south through Battersea and Clapham. There'd been a time when he and Ingrid used the route to go home. An incident one summer evening had convinced them that it was no longer healthy. Traffic signals had held them in Clapham Park. A teenage black had darted from the sidewalk, reached through the open window and snatched Ingrid's purse from her lap. He was gone as fast as he'd come. As Ingrid said, it could have been a whole lot worse — her head could have been razored off. Militant Negroes proliferated in the neighborhood, and cops were handing in their warrant cards. There were more muggings on the new southern spur of the underground railway than in the rest of the underground system put together. Evidence of the Caribbean takeover abounded and the whites were moving out. Grocery stores displayed West Indian food. A billboard in front of the Chapel of Christ The Rock proclaimed that JESUS IS BLACK. Madame La Zonga read palms, took care of fallen arches and conked hair. Brightly dressed women with enormous buttocks plowed along ponderously, watched from the shelter of sad tea rooms by their hip and wary offsprings. Men loitered in front of the poolrooms and labor exchanges, their dark skin tinged the color of an elephant's ear by the cold.

The dreary approach to the jail was flanked by a coal depot on one side, the warders' quarters on the other. The road went nowhere else. Fraser parked outside the governor's house. Everything he'd ever read about British prisons, the pictures he'd seen on television, suggested that they'd all been designed by the same manic Victorian architect. False turrets and meaningless embrasures enclosed massive, studded entrance gates. The boundary wall was twenty feet high. A bygone committee of side-whiskered penologists had drawn up the precise amount of breathing space needed by a felon. It was the dawn of the scientific age and everything was carefully measured. Bread, porridge, tea, meat and vegetables were issued in prescribed amounts of pints and ounces. A line on the side of the bathtubs indicated the level of water permitted. There was a thermometer to test the temperature if necessary.

Once through the gates, there was no question of a prisoner having rights. Any concession was referred to as a privilege. A representative of God reinforced the message at the compulsory church services. The cells were exactly the same in 1973 as they had been ninety years before. The only difference was that the carefully calculated living space was now occupied by three men instead of one. Three was the magic number supposed to weaken escape plots and threats of insubordination and repress homosexual tendencies. Two might but three wouldn't.

Fraser rang a bell. Keys clattered inside. A postern gate opened, offering a glimpse of the cobbled courtyard. The jailer had on a police-type uniform with a peaked cap and H.M.P. shoulder flashes. Barred gates at the back made the courtyard a sort of limbo between the street and the jail proper. Lights were burning in an office where bunches of keys hung on rows of hooks. A slate on the wall displayed the prison roll in a parody of some first-grade mathematical problem.

REMAND PRISONERS	306
CONVICTED PRISONERS	210
(AT COURT)	28
TOTAL	544

A trusty hurried across the yard beyond the bars, identified by the red band he wore on the sleeve of his gray battle-dress top. Fraser wrote his name and address in a book and took a seat in the waiting room. A coal fire was burning in the small grate. A printed list of instructions to visitors hung above the fireplace. The only other person in the room was a stout woman hugging a bulging shopping bag. She took a hard look at the jailer's retreating back and sniffed. Then she whisked a small medicine bottle out of her bag, uncorked it and halved the contents in one determined swallow. She stoppered the bottle again, releasing a strong odor of neat gin. Fraser stared out through the window, depressed by what he saw. A cell-block dominated a low cluster of offices. The flat tilted bars outside each cell protected a metal framework with tiny glass panes. He counted them automatically. Three rows of eight made twenty-four. You'd know how many steps there were from the wall to the door if you lived up there.

"Airs and graces," the woman said, nodding toward the courtyard. "Him on the gate's a right bastard. Searched me bag last week, he did."

She planted her stout, booted legs challengingly, drawing the ratty fur coat about her with the air of an outraged duchess. She leaned forward, her voice a hoarse whisper.

"Ex-soldiers, the bleeding lot of them. Military police. Like my old man says, they been saluting for the breakfusses all their lives."

Fraser lit a cigarette. Her breath stank.

Her manner became confidential. "Come to see a friend, have you? What's he in for?"

He watched the paper curl back from the smoldering ash. He knew the type well. A relic of the tumbrils, familiar with misery, at home with disaster.

"Being a foreigner's part of it," he replied.

"Ah," she said reflectively. "Foreigner yourself, are you?"

The arrival of a second warder saved Fraser the trouble of replying. The jailer looked up from the slips of paper in his hand.

"Visitors for Zaleski and Watts. No smoking in the visiting boxes."

Fraser threw the butt at the fireplace and followed the man through a small gate in the massive bars, down a concrete path to a shedlike building. It was split down the middle by a line of cubicles. Each cubicle had a large pane of glass and wire mesh separating prisoner from visitor. Conversation was conducted through the mesh. If you saw, you heard badly and vice versa. Most of the booths were occupied. Zaleski was waiting in one of them, wearing his duffelcoat as if he was on his way to the street. There was an air of indomitable jauntiness about him that infuriated Fraser. He leaned against the wooden partition, his carefully prepared speech completely forgotten.

"You bastard!" he said deliberately.

Zaleski blinked, his welcoming smile vanishing into the pouches under his eyes.

Fraser put his mouth close to the mesh. A spill of paper lay between the sections, testimony to some forlorn attempt to pass contraband.

"Those hoods who were in the restaurant Sunday night, they've grabbed Ingrid and your wife. Do you understand what I'm saying — *abducted* them!"

The wire sagged under Zaleski's weight. His face appeared at the glass, completely devoid of color.

"Tell me, please, quickly."

Warders were patrolling the narrow walks behind them. The voices from the neighboring cubicles droned on, strained chatter that was full of false assurance on both sides. Fraser pitched his voice low, cramming recent events into a bitter attack on his listener. Zaleski heard him out with bowed head.

"Is long story," he said at last. "Is story from war."

Fraser snarled back at him. "Don't give me any more of that kind of crap, I'm warning you, Casimir. I've had just about all I can take. We've got forty-eight hours. I want whatever it is that these hoods want. And you're going to give it to me or else . . ."

Zaleski picked at the end of his nose. "*Or else?* Why talking to me without respect, Kirk?"

The warder rattled his keys against the wooden door.

"Five more minutes."

Fraser shook his head. The Pole hadn't shaved and his eyes were bloodshot.

"I'm talking about your *wife,* Casimir! These hoods are threatening to feed her to the pigs and you talk about respect! I'm desperate! We can't go to the police. What *can* we do except what these people want."

Zaleski placed both palms against the glass. "Tomorrow I fix everything. Tomorrow I am free man. Don't worry."

"You'd better be on the level," said Fraser. "Because if anything happens to Ingrid, I'm going to have to kill you."

"Many people are trying," Zaleski said, nose lifting like a hawk's beak. "But is difficult. I am man of honor, Kirk. No bail tomorrow, I give you what you want."

The warder was holding the door open. Zaleski and Fraser faced one another, molding the split second into a moment of absolute comprehension. Each man knew that from this time on there would be no room between them for concessions. Then Fraser turned away. The dark sky had pulled in over the road outside. Squally bouts of wind drove the rain at the people hurrying away toward the hill. Umbrellas ballooned. The slate roofs of the jail were washed to a dreary covering.

Fraser had no heart to go back to the bookstore. He turned his stationwagon south in the direction of Streatham. Lights were on in the house though most of the tenants were still at work. He had a glimpse of the doctor's wife at a second-story window. She was a slim figure in a sari with a tattooed forehead, a woman who scuttled away like a scared deer whenever they met. He opened his front door, shaking the wet from his anorak and scrubbing his feet on the mat as he looked around. He walked through the twilit rooms, opening each door very carefully as though Ingrid might be behind it, waiting there in the darkness to surprise him. He stretched out on the bed with his hands behind his head. He was living in a city of eight million people and not one he could go to for help. He was no better off than Zaleski lying in that stinking cell. He turned over, burying his face in Ingrid's nightdress. He slept, waking to a completely dark room with the rain thrashing against the window. The smell of curry coming from the apartment overhead told him it was near dinnertime. His phone was ringing. He stumbled into the living room and grabbed the receiver. The voice was the new one, assured and somehow sinister.

"OK, now listen carefully. When I tell you, put your phone down and dial one-seven-five followed by your own number, got it? Then hang up and wait."

"Got it," said Fraser. If they'd told him to stand on his head he'd do it.

The instructions continued. "Your phone ought to ring again. You'll hear someone saying 'Testing, testing.' Then hang up and wait for me to call you back. Go ahead, *now!*"

Fraser held the dial to the light of the barred heater, spun it and cradled the receiver. He sat there cross-legged on the floor, waiting for the promised ring. A minute went by, two. Three stretched into five before the bell shrilled. The stranger was back on the line.

"What happened?"

"Nothing," said Fraser. The headlamps of the doctor's car arriving swept the ceiling. He heard the street door open, footsteps going up the stairs.

The voice was relaxed and knowing. "You're bugged, mate. Don't use that phone no more and stay off the one in the store. Old Bill's probably attended to that one, too."

Fraser swallowed hard, but the lump stayed in his throat. There was something shocking about the thought of a tape machine turning quietly, recording conversations and silences alike, one as guilty as the other.

"Up theirs," the voice said cheerfully. "And don't worry about it. We'll get to you."

Fraser climbed to his feet and went to the window. The bare trees dripped in the radiance from the upstairs apartment. Beyond that he couldn't see. He imagined faceless men flattened against a wall somewhere, watching the house, water running down the backs of their necks. He poured himself a tumbler of Scotch and water and sat in the darkness, listening to the sound of the jets on their run down to Heathrow. It was going to be a long night.

Chapter Six

IT WAS EIGHT o'clock at night and the onslaught of rain had dispersed the riverside mist. The steady fall battered down into the leaden ebb tide, filling the gutters and runnels, washing the deserted sidewalks. Raven leaned against the wall that divided Mrs. Zaleska's bedroom from the living room. The immigration post at Folkestone reported her as having left the United Kingdom two days previously. There was no record of her return. All the ashtrays in the apartment were clean. There was neither bread nor milk in the kitchen, and none of Mrs. Zaleska's neighbors had seen her since Monday. She lived apart from her husband and the building superintendent claimed that he had never even seen Zaleski. Raven's methodical search had revealed nothing more compromising than a couple of hire-purchase agreements with the payments up-to-date. The rest of the woman's papers were a history of work done and money received, an elliptical record of a struggle to maintain a modest standard of living.

His visit had been made on the spur of the moment and unauthorized. Applications for search warrants were for the most part a waste of time, a declaration of intention. All a cop really needed was a ready wit and the necessary tools. His stubborn refusal to conform left him with few friends at the

Yard. Other cops tended to avoid him, scared that his heresies might attach to them. Raven spent a great deal of his spare time in the Metropolitan Police Laboratories on Holborn. The detective branch in general employed the help of scientific officers with a hint of condescension, occasionally with outright disbelief. But Raven respected the experts. Their empiric approach to police work was the same as his own. For years he'd made a habit of dropping in at the old-fashioned building. He talked with veterans, learning about the detection of forged documents and handwriting up on the sixth floor, about guns and ballistics on the fourth, about the locksmith's skill on the floor below. He could knock on a dozen doors in the building and ask for help without going through official channels. The bunch of skeleton keys in his velvet jacket were proof of it. There wasn't a lock in Scotland Yard itself he couldn't have opened, given the need. The idea gave him a certain amount of satisfaction.

He straightened a rug thoughtfully, making sure that he had left no visible sign of his visit. If he'd had the time, he'd have stayed in the apartment, sitting there in the darkness and just waiting. The phone might have rung, someone might have tapped on the door. His hunch was that something *would* happen here. In spite of Mrs. Zaleska's absence, instinct told him that she was in some way concerned with the robbery. He'd put out a check on her whereabouts, but the way Interpol was functioning it could be days before he had an answer. He shut the door carefully and made his way out through the back entrance. The rain was coming down like stair rods, pinging off the waste of hardtop. He covered his head with his Italian slicker and ran for the shelter of his car. He sat for a while, staring up through the swishing wipers at the windows of the second-floor apartment. He should have left the place under surveillance, but he just didn't have the men. The squad Drake had assigned to him had been pulled off other jobs and resented the fact. The coordinator covered his tracks well. He'd always be able to say that he'd acted with judgment. Any failure attached to the investigation would be Raven's responsibility.

Raven slotted the gearshift into reverse and backed across the tarmac, still looking up at the darkened apartment. Police work was essentially a chase. And the nature of the game was that a cop must always be as lonely as his quarry. It was something that a natural-born sergeant-major like Drake would never understand. The streetlamps on Elm Park Gardens illuminated stretches of glistening deserted pavements. The sound of church bells reminded Raven of the Suffolk village where he'd been born. Summer and winter, the tolling bells sent their message across the flat green fields into the chestnut wood where he played alone.

He left the car parked on a double line, taking his chance of a ticket. There were several ways in which he might have indicated his status to a traffic warden, but he used none of them. He paid his fines without claiming the money back on his expense sheet. A couple of times, the sports car had been towed away to the police pound, but that too was part of the game. The results of his work were there to be fed into the computer. The way in which he arrived at them was his own affair.

The brick front of Waverley Court was completely soaked. Rain cascaded down into the forecourt from a broken piece of guttering. It was exactly twenty-four hours since he'd walked out of the building with Zaleski under arrest. His first impression had been that he'd picked up an innocent man. Zaleski's manner had been just right, disbelief hardening to indignation as he found himself on the way to the police station. He'd emptied his pockets without fuss, answering questions with weary resignation, insisting that he was the victim of some unhappy mistake. But Raven had detected and remembered the underlying confidence. Zaleski was acting like a chess player who knows that he's three moves ahead of his opponent. Once his prisoner was in the cells, Raven had gone back to the apartment building. He'd knocked on doors and made inquiries, but the results were negligible. For his neighbors, the Pole was a middle-aged lecher who kept late hours and that was all.

Raven chose two of the keys on the bunch in his pocket. The first one let him into the small lobby. A strip of burlap on the tiled floor had soaked up most of the filth tracked in from the street. There was an overpowering smell of several suppers cooking. Television and radios had been switched on by people who were determined to stay in for the evening. He slipped in quickly through Zaleski's front door and sat down. Enough light filtered through from the illuminated portico for him to see what he was doing. It had taken him seven hours to get the authority to act. The G.P.O. was getting sensitive to public opinion. Four phones had been monitored. The Canadian's two lines, Zaleski's flat and his restaurant. The other two Poles had no phones. He sat down and called the post office engineers, giving a code identification. Only one of the bugged lines had been activated. It was the Canadian's home number. Two calls had been made there. Raven asked for the tape to be played. By the time it was over, he was sitting up straight, trying to put a face to the voice of Fraser's caller. Finally, the long hours spent at the police laboratory paid off. He'd been up on the second floor, listening to tapes with the scientific officer in charge of electronics. The subject was a man called Sam Gerber. The conversations recorded were full of thieves argot and double-talk, almost incomprehensible and useless as evidence. But the voice had stuck in Raven's mind. The brutal arrogance in it offended him deeply. He'd gone back to the Yard and pulled Gerber's file in the Criminal Records Office. A lot was known about Gerber. His dossier described him as an active thief, an organizer of armed robberies, a fence with foreign connections. A red paper star on the cover of the file marked him as dangerous. His one conviction was years ago. Since then no less than five attempts to prosecute him had failed. There was a history of a whole series of abortive searches of his premises.

Now Gerber was calling Fraser. Raven was sure though only a voice-pattern test could determine it. He thought about the implications for a while. The combination of Gerber, Zaleski and the Canadian was an unlikely one. A bunch of amateurs was being manipulated by a vicious thug who would stop at nothing to achieve his ends and the outcome was inevitable. The Poles and Fraser must have done the fetching and carrying. Gerber's role would be to fence the monstrance. It was like giving a hyena a haunch of beef to hold on trust. The tape he'd just heard suggested that the thieves were still haggling among themselves which meant the moment of truth was delayed. Fraser's girl was missing which might have some significance. But Raven's hunch was that Zaleski still controlled the missing monstrance. Four of Raven's men were working shifts on the two Poles who were still at liberty. The results were discouraging. Sobinski and Czarniecki had met once briefly in a Fulham Road pub, talked in Polish and then separated. Neither appeared to show the slightest interest in the men who were shadowing them.

The one sure thing was that Zaleski's presence in jail would hardly reassure his partners, Gerber least of all. Raven picked up the phone again on impulse and called his office at the Yard. The sergeant who clerked for him had already gone. Raven had the call transferred to the Legal Department.

"Detective-Inspector Raven. There's a man called Zaleski remanded in custody this morning from West London Police Court."

He heard the rustle of papers, the duty officer's voice. "Got it. Casimir Zaleski, charged under the Immigration Act, 1971. There's a note here that his lawyer's applying for bail at eleven o'clock tomorrow in chambers. That the man?"

"That's the man."

"The hearing's set in front of Justice Killigrew. We're opposing bail, right?"

"Cancel it," said Raven remembering that everything he said was being taped for the record. "I'm the officer in charge of the case. We no longer object to bail in any reasonable amount."

"OK," the voice answered. "I'll see that the word's passed on. Is there anything else, Inspector?"

"One thing," answered Raven. "If the defense puts up a man called Fraser as surety, he's acceptable. I've checked him out personally."

"The judge'll probably want to have a word with you about that if you're in charge of the case."

"Not with me, he won't," said Raven. "I won't be there."
He hung up, staring at the rain-washed windows yellowed by

the light from outside. As often as he felt he'd gained ground a hand seemed to pull him back. He'd gone through Zaleski's apartment twice already, taking four hours about it the last time. Short of pulling up the floorboards and stripping the paper off the walls, he could see no possible hiding place. Yet the doubt persisted.

His gaunt face was thoughtful as he composed the fresh set of numbers. The outburst at the other end caused the diaphragm to vibrate. He shifted the receiver away from his ear.

"Just what do you think you're playing at?" Drake shouted. "I've been trying to reach you all day, wasting valuable time. You don't answer your phone and no one's seen hide nor hair of you!"

Raven leaned back against the wall. "I should tell you that this phone's on a G.P.O. 11, sir."

"I don't give a bugger what it's on," shouted Drake. His tone changed dramatically. "A *G.P.O. 11?* You're a senior police officer in charge of an important investigation, and you're making a report on a monitored line?"

"I had to reach you urgently," said Raven. "This was the nearest phone. I'd like to meet you somewhere out of the building, sir, as soon as you can make it."

Drake's chair scraped back. "What's the matter with coming here?" he asked suspiciously.

"It's a question of time again, sir. There's been an entirely new development that I'd rather not discuss over the phone."

Drake grunted. "Where do you want to meet me?"

"The Phoenix." A man hurried across the forecourt, avoiding the cascading water. A shadow crossed the strip of light at the bottom of Zaleski's front door. Someone ran up the

staircase. "It's a pub off Cromwell Place, near South Kensington Underground Station. I'll be waiting in the saloon bar.
You'll see the sign outside."

"I don't need a guide dog to find a saloon bar," snapped
Drake. "What time?"

The illuminated dial of Raven's watch showed ten minutes
of eight. "Could you make it in half-an-hour?" he asked
tentatively.

"Half-an-hour," said Drake, high in his nose and hung up.

Raven made his customary check before he slipped out of
the apartment. He hurried around the corner, protecting his
head against the rain that was still lashing down. He drove
west on Fulham Road spraying the pavements with slush.
Handbills in the doorways of the Wielkapolska gave the
restaurant a deserted look. There were no lights in Fraser's
bookstore either. Raven wheeled right and stopped on
Hollywood Road, looking at the back entrance. If he'd known
about it, he could have had someone covering both exits from
the corner. As it was, the girl had simply vanished. A chance
glimpse of her by a cop on the beat suggested that she had left
with Gerber. The number of Gerber's car would be on the air
at any moment now, but little could be hoped from it. Three
years ago, one of Gerber's teams had burgled Kennington
Lane Police Station and removed thirty-two exhibits together
with the entire case for the prosecution. A man capable of
organizing this sort of caper would hardly be using his own car
at a time like this.

He reached South Kensington at ten minutes after eight,
walked through the arcade over the underground station and
into the pub. Firelight played on a polished mahogany bar.
The tables and chairs were shaped like barrels. A warm,

yeasty smell with a hint of tobacco hung in the air. Raven put his blue coat on a hook, glancing at himself in the mirror. His long hair was wet at the ends. He combed it through fastidiously. Drake came through the door as Raven was ordering a drink from the Irishman behind the bar. The coordinator peeled off his topcoat, scowling as he shook the moisture from his hat. The homburg was an affectation that went with the shiny blue suits and Scotland Yard tie. He forced his big butt into the barrel seat and sank the Scotch that Raven had bought for him.

"All right, let's have it. What's this new development?"

"Sam Gerber," said Raven.

"Gerber?" Drake whipped off his spectacles, peering across the table intently. "How do you mean, Gerber?"

"I'm having a voiceprint done of a recorded conversation. If I'm right and it turns out to be Gerber talking with Fraser, then he's involved in this robbery. And you know what that means."

Drake put on his spectacles again, shoving up the bridge with a square-nailed forefinger.

"This wouldn't be some kind of alibi would it?"

Raven put his glass down. The watered Scotch had no bite. His fight with Drake was down to the cut-and-thrust of cutlass work.

"You're going to do your best to break me," he said quietly. That's all right. I don't think you have the equipment. I don't *need* any cover-up. Gerber's my ace in the hole. I just wanted you to know it."

"Bollix," said Drake. "You're still running around in circles. Look — the pressure's being applied on me from above. They're leaning hard, Inspector. The commissioner, the Foreign Office and the War Department. Do you know what I'm doing? I'm looking at them and smiling, I'm telling them that I've got my very best man on the job. When the time comes, you can talk to them about Gerber, but you'll find that all they want is that monstrance. I don't want you to disappoint them."

Raven rose and carried his own glass to the bar and bought a refill. Drake greeted him, grinning.

"What do you think you've got up your sleeve, Raven? Some kind of conspiracy charge? It won't matter a fuck without that monstrance. You can walk on water to the people in Whitehall, but if you're not carrying the cross you're finished. Through!"

He widened his lips over stained bicuspids.

"The thought's never out of my mind," Raven said steadily. "In fact it keeps me on my toes." The cliché put him in mind of his father, a slow-moving East Anglian who sold paint, oil and candles and who had once tamed a badger. For as long as Raven remembered his father had used clichés in times of emotional disturbance. Drake's chair creaked as he shifted his buttocks.

"Do you know what it is that I *really* dislike about you?" he asked quietly.

Raven shrugged. "Everything. And the thing is that it's mutual. It's getting to be an obsession."

The superintendent's heavy face was morose. "I'll tell you why. It's because you don't *belong* on the force. All this is some kind of a game for you. You don't give a fuck for your fellow officers or discipline, and you're smart enough to con the people who matter. But I know you for what you really are. That's why, one way or another, I'm going to have you, Raven."

Raven pocketed his cigarettes, the gesture marking a

decision that he'd probably remember for the rest of his life. Drake was right. He had no sense of comradeship, no real belief in his job or the laws he was supposed to enforce. The only thing he'd ever been dedicated to was the chase. And this one was going to be concluded successfully, come what may. His expression revealed nothing of what he was thinking.

"Time's running short. If it's all right with you, I'll be on my way."

Drake lifted a hand. "One thing before you go, Professor. Where does a man *buy* a suit like that?"

Raven looked down at the braided velvet jacket. "Topper's in Jermyn Street. You'd probably find it expensive, but then I'm a single man. Good night."

He left the bar, turned into the station arcade and ran down the steps into the long, badly lighted tunnel. He came up at the south end of Exhibition Road. The wide thoroughfare was slick under the rain, the lamplit stretches of pavement empty in front of the closed museums. Traffic coming from the park swished by a big black Jaguar parked close up against the curb. The car door opened as Raven approached. He slipped in beside the driver. A small light shone above the two-way phone on the dashboard. Raven made room for his long legs, looking sideways at Gifford. The detective-sergeant was wearing a snap-brim hat and a scruffy raincoat. Put him on a suburban station at eight-twenty in the morning and you'd lose him in ten seconds. He had that kind of face and appearance. Everything about him was nondescript except his eyes which were brown and melancholy like those of a bloodhound. It was the first time Raven had ever worked with him, and he recognized a plodder who offered no threat to more ambitious comrades. He was the kind of cop who went wherever he was sent, never volunteering, doing all the donkey work without complaint. Sergeant he was and sergeant he'd stay. Yet twenty-four hours with him had given Raven an appreciation of the other man's reliability. There was a reserve and respect that had nothing to do with subservience.

The inside of the car was warm though the motor was switched off. The Jaguar had obviously been driven for some time. Gifford dropped the front of the glove compartment and handed Raven some papers.

"Everything's there, sir. The rest was unimportant. There's a message from Interpol, but it's not what you want, I'm afraid."

Raven held the papers under the light. A cable from R.C.M.P. headquarters in Ottawa advised that Kirk Fraser had no police record in his home country. The background details supplied added little to what Raven already knew. The Interpol communication offered a list of Polish criminals known to be operating in Europe. None of the names meant anything to Raven. The envelope at the bottom of the pile was addressed to him in person and marked CONFIDENTIAL.

"What's new from the post office engineers?" he asked.

Gifford had a slow, uncertain smile, as if he was unsure about its propriety. "I checked only a couple of minutes ago, as a matter of fact. There've been five calls. The two to Zaleski's place you know about, the other three were to Fraser's flat. And incidentally I got the result of the voiceprint. There's no question about it, it's Gerber all right. The patterns match perfectly."

Raven fitted a yellow Gitane between his lips and leaned back. "I knew it, George. Let's hear those tapes again — the ones where he's talking to Fraser."

He shut his eyes, listening to Gerber's voice and then touched the stop button. "The 'testing, testing' bit is recorded. The engineers use the one-seven-five call to test a faulty line. The thing is that you can't have two electronic devices working on the same phone at the same time. So if there's no recorded voice it means that your line's bugged. How would a bastard like Gerber know a thing like that, George? That's what disturbs me." He offered the pack of cigarettes.

Gifford shook his head. "I don't, sir, thank you. How does he know? A contact somewhere, an engineer — ours or the post office's. There's always one rotten apple in the barrel. Some of the things he's got away with are incredible. I'd break fifty laws to pin a man like that. Have you ever actually met him, sir?"

"Never," said Raven. "But I will." He leaned forward and restarted the tape machine. Fraser's third call was timed at 19:37 and was from Zaleski's lawyer. Pulawski talked about his client's bail. Fraser's answers sounded decidedly edgy, but by then he'd have known that his line was bugged. He offered himself as surety and the two men arranged to meet at Lincoln's Inn Fields at ten-thirty in the morning. Raven stopped the machine and tucked one leg up. He jerked his head at the pile of gardening magazines on the back seat.

"Is that your hobby, George?"

Gifford grinned diffidently. "I wouldn't say hobby, sir. It keeps me from growing fat and that's about all. Where I live there's six inches of topsoil on solid clinker. It's the challenge, I suppose."

Raven wound down the window and flicked the butt into the wet night. "How do we stand on our round-the-clocks, George?"

Gifford consulted his notebook. "I've got two men on Fraser working twelve-hour shifts, four more with Sobinski and Czarniecki — these bloody names are breaking my jaw. There's no activity there at all and Gerber's a dead loss. This mews house of his is off Redclyffe Gardens, but we can't get anywhere near the front door. You said there was to be no confrontation, you'll remember, sir. The lights in the house go on and off, but there's no way of knowing who's inside."

"Any other way out?"

"A possibility," admitted Gifford. "All those houses have been converted from stables and garages. They're small, bang on top of one another with flattish roofs. An able-bodied man could go from one end of the mews to the other without being seen."

Raven was staring out at the rain, listening with half an ear. "There's no sign of the girl, I suppose?"

"Not a whisper," said Gifford. "It's just possible that she's at Gerber's place. She's certainly not back with Fraser. Too bad Crane had to lose her this morning."

"Nobody wins them all, Sergeant," Raven consoled. He weighed the buff envelope in the palm of his hand wondering how Gifford would take the news of his decision. Probably with contempt. Resignation from the force was a display of disloyalty to your comrades. The only excuse acceptable was to get yourself crippled by some hoodlum. It was better to put no strain on the sergeant's loyalty. Raven ripped the envelope open without removing the contents.

"We're going to nail these jokers tomorrow, George. I've got a few surprises lined up for Mr. Zaleski. Where do *you* think the monstrance is?"

Gifford cocked his head at the hiss of the passing tires. "There's no evidence one way or another, is there, sir?"

"I'm not talking about evidence," said Raven. "I'm talking about an opinion. Use your crystal ball if you like."

Gifford's tone was unsure. "It would have to be Zaleski, wouldn't it? It seems to me the only explanation for Gerber's still being around. A villain like that doesn't waste his time with mugs."

Raven's hand shot out, touching Gifford on the arm. "Precisely, George. And it'll be Zaleski who leads us to the loot. What's the matter, you don't like the idea?" he challenged. Gifford's expression was less than enthusiastic.

The sergeant worried an oil stain on his raincoat. "It's not that. I just don't understand it, sir."

"Same thing," said Raven. "Tell me, since we're in the mood for frankness — is there anything else about me that you don't understand?"

Gifford raised his head, meeting Raven's glance frankly. "That's a loaded question, Inspector. You're putting me on a spot."

"I'd still like an answer," Raven insisted.

The sergeant offered his diffident smile. "OK. I think you're sort of romantic, sir, and I don't understand romantics."

"What's that supposed to mean — that I'm not practical?"

"You're twisting my words. No. It has to do with imagination. You have it, I don't. It's as simple as that."

Rain drummed on the roof of the car. Raven nodded. "I know my reputation, Sergeant. Uncooperative, stubborn, the whole lot. Tell me something else — how did you feel when you heard that you'd been assigned to work with me?"

Gifford rested his arms on the steering wheel. "After seventeen years on the firm I take each one as it comes. It's all the same to me who I work under. I just do as I'm told."

Raven looked at his nicotine-stained finger with disgust. Thirty pence a pack and he coughed his lungs up each and every morning. He'd have to give it up.

"What would you have done in my place, George?"

Gifford gave the question thought before replying. "I'd have thrown the lot of them inside and turned the key."

"Without a charge?" demanded Raven. "Where's your evidence? You hold them forty-eight hours and then what?"

Gifford moved a shoulder. "I told you, sir. Imagination isn't my strong suit. But I think that forty-eight hours would have been enough. One of them would have coughed by them."

"But not the one who mattered," countered Raven. "Not Zaleski. *There's* your romantic, George. I remember reading somewhere that a man can get anything if he wants it absolutely. It's a kind of innocence, I suppose. Most people only want something *if* . . ."

Gifford's expression was stolid. "That's beyond me. A villain's a villain, the way I see it, and I don't care where he comes from. When the pressure's on they'll talk. It's a question of offering the right kind of bait. Honor among thieves is like saying absence makes the heart grow fonder. It sounds good, but it doesn't work."

"You're a cynic, George," said Raven. He'd gone as far as he could with the sergeant. Gifford's ideas of a police investigation were rock-ribbed. "That's it for the night. It'll take them a while to fix Zaleski's bail. They'll have to drive from the City to Brixton Prison. He won't be out much before noon. In the meantime, keep things going as they are. I want a round-the-clock watch on them all."

Gifford nodded. "Understood."

"OK," said Raven. "I'll call you about eleven on the mobile circuit. Bye, George."

He opened his door. By the time he reached the entrance to the tunnel leading to the underground station the big black car was lost in the traffic. He drove south, careful on the greasy surface, filtering through the rain-washed residential streets till he reached the embankment. The houseboat was rolling on the swollen ebb tide. Wind whipped the waves, showering him with spray as he climbed up the creaking gangway. He hurried below, drew the saloon curtains and switched on the fire. He was home for the night. He set the coffeepot on the stove, exchanged his buckled shoes for slippers and switched on the stereo set, the volume low. His choice of record matched his mood — Chopin's Piano Concerto no. 1. He stretched his lanky frame on the garden chair he favored and read the contents of the buff envelope. The fact that it was written on an electric typewriter gave the announcement added importance.

> Serious Crime Squad
> Office of the Coordinator

Detective-Inspector Raven
Scotland Yard
S.W.1

A meeting has been called in the office of the Commissioner of Metropolitan Police at 10:00 A.M., Friday, 26th January. The purpose of the meeting will be to present to representatives of the ministries concerned a progress report of the investigation into a robbery from premises at 276 Conduit St. W.1

> Edward Drake, Detective-Chief Superintendent.

(Copies to: Ministry of Defence, Ministry of Foreign Affairs, Home Office)

He put the letter back in its envelope and tore the whole thing into precise pieces. The block was ready, the axe sharpened. When the headsman swung, Drake intended to leap nimbly sideways wearing an expression of pious regret. But it wasn't going to *be* like that. He walked into the galley, worked some Stilton into a Welsh rarebit and ate standing at the stove, washing his meal down with good Costa Rican coffee. He belched gently and reached for the bicarb. He gave the tablets a couple of minutes to settle before sitting down at the phone. His sister answered right away.

"It's me," he announced. "Are you alone or is the security risk with you?"

The remark was no more than a weak standing joke. His brother-in-law's politics were negligible.

"I'm alone except for the children," his sister replied. "What is it you want? You only phone when you need something."

"It's a good relationship," he said. "I'm handing in my resignation. Just as soon as this case I'm working on is closed."

She sounded profoundly shocked. "You're doing *what?* I suppose that means you're in some kind of trouble?"

"No more than I always am. I've had enough, that's all."

"But what will you do?" she put in quickly.

He could hear the Highgate matron protecting her home and brood from the visitations of a profligate brother.

"Look around. You were the one who was against my joining the force in the first place, remember. I wanted you to be the first to know. Keep it under your hat. Not a word to anyone, not even Jerzy."

"Does this have something to do with those Poles?" she demanded. "The ones you were asking Jerzy about?"

"Not a thing," he lied. "What it has to do with is imagination. Good night."

He flipped the record and took off his slippers. The warmth from the heater cheered his cold feet. The cloud of tobacco smoke swirled in the hot air and vanished into the ventilator. He wondered again what it was that Zaleski wanted so absolutely. If he only knew that, success in this particular chase would be a certainty.

Chapter Seven

THE ALARM CLATTERED and skeetered on the polished surface of the bedside table. Fraser ungummed an eye and fastened it on the clock face. 7:30 A.M., 25 January. The clock was made in Scotland and a legend next to the date read BURNS NIGHT. He struggled up in bed, stabbing at the button that silenced the bell. The light beyond the window was no more than a pale shade of gray. The rain had stopped during the night, but the trees and shrubbery outside still dripped. He'd slept badly, burrowing into the sheets and blankets, disturbed by flashes of dreams that had no continuity. BURNS NIGHT. His mind hurdled the years back to the Owen Sound farmhouse frozen into the rock-hard ground. He remembered the barn chores done, the cows content under the milking machines, sweet-breathed and patient-eyed. Snow shifted on the roof as the heat engendered by the bodies of the beasts warmed the air. He and his father would make their way along the paths cut through snowdrifts. A big log fire blazed in the living room. The masks of trapped and slaughtered animals grinned from unplastered walls. The radio was playing the music of the massed bands of pipers from the Mapleleaf Stadium. A deep voice read with nostalgic emotion:

> How can ye chant my bonnie birds
> And my heart so full of care . . .

All that had gone with the rest. Old men sitting in the sunshine by the courthouse, the kids' first hockey game, the Bellamy sisters' school of instruction behind George Dougill's back barn. He swung himself off the bed, aware that he was becoming maudlin. The leaden sky outside was low over the soaked shrubbery. The wail of Bengali music and tom-toms drifted down from upstairs, incongruous in the dismal grayness of the morning. It was the first time in more than two years that he'd made his own breakfast. He spooned coffee extract into a bowl and boiled an egg. He ate in the sitting room, averting his eyes from the whiskey bottle. It was half-empty, though thank God he had no hangover. He'd started in drinking right after Pulawski had called. He hadn't dared tell the lawyer that the line was bugged in case it in some way affected Zaleski's bail. Once he'd hung up, his compunctions had been for the opposite reasons. He owed it to the lawyer et cetera.

A letter shot through the mail slot, landing well out on the hallway carpet. He picked it up apprehensively, but it was no more than an insurance reminder. He bathed, shaved and dressed in his one good suit. He gave his hair a couple of swipes with Ingrid's brush and polished his toecaps with the underside of the bedspread. No matter what happened, he was never going to be the same again. All he'd wanted to do was help, no sides taken, no moral issues involved. Two days later he found himself in a world of freaked-out hoods and sadistic cops. As if that wasn't enough, Ingrid was out there somewhere in fear of her life. Bastards, the lot of them.

There was a London guidebook in the bureau where he kept

his papers. Kings Bench Walk lay between the Embankment and Fleet Street, an area given over to the practice of law and, said the book, "a place of residence for several judges of the laws of this realm." *Judges of the laws of this realm.* It made a big fat sound till you remembered people like Benny and Murphy and Gerber. He left his breakfast things in the sink and wrote a note for the cleaning woman.

> Mrs. Fraser is away for a couple of days.
> Please change sheets, pillowcases and towels.

All he was managing to do was put one foot in front of the other, hopefully but without being too sure where they were taking him. He slammed the front door behind him. He still hadn't had the locks changed but so what. Gerber and company could walk in any time they felt like it. Dr. Bulchand was squatting by a wheel of his car, testing the tire pressure. He treated each morning run to the hospital like a vital stage in some rally. Every device and possibility was checked and rechecked before he fastened his seat belt. He smiled shyly as Fraser passed, the whiteness of his teeth making his cheeks a dirty yellow. Ingrid's gloves were on the shelf under the windshield along with a magazine she'd been reading the day before. Fraser switched on the motor. Beyond the fringe of trees a man was exercising his dog on the sodden turf. A despair almost unbearable weighed him down. What the hell was he going to do if Zaleski didn't make bail?

Kings Bench Walk turned out to be a street of eighteenth-century houses that bore the signs of their current use, dull paintwork, curtainless windows, worn steps washed only by the rain. Each door bore a cluster of brass plates — solicitors, barristers, Queen's counsel and benchers. He was ten minutes

early. He jumped the stationwagon up on the curb, close to
the railings that protected the grass. He was on his second
cigarette when Pulawski appeared, bustling down from the
direction of Fleet Street. He was black and shiny like a crow
and carried his dispatch case under his arm. He greeted Fraser
briskly.

"You're on time, good. Killigrew won't stand for un-
punctuality."

They climbed an uncarpeted staircase to the second floor
where two men were waiting in an anteroom. Both were
dressed alike, black jackets and wing collars worn with white
ties. One of them greeted Pulawski. The window overlooked
a patch of dirty grass with a chipped stone basin where
sparrows were bathing. A door opened and a clerk beckoned
them into a warm, book-lined room with an Adams ceiling and
fireplace. A gray-haired man was sitting behind a desk. He
looked up through half-lensed spectacles as the two barristers
approached the desk. The informality of the proceedings
surprised Fraser. There was a brief exchange of questions and
answers . . . section two of the Immigration Act, 1971 . . .
remanded for eight days . . . no previous history.

The judge's well-bred voice lifted testily. He glanced
around the room as if used to a larger audience for his remarks.

"I don't understand the police tactics in this matter. Why
did they object to bail in the first place?"

The crown lawyer leaned forward deferentially. "My
instructions are this was due to a misunderstanding, M'Lord."

Justice Killigrew removed his spectacles deliberately. Without them he looked like an actor made up for the part.

"Very well. Bail is granted in the amount of two hundred
pounds. The defendant in one surety of a hundred and one

other. These proceedings have been a waste of everyone's time, Mr. Rawlinson. I shall make my views known to the Director of Public Prosecutions."

The clerk bustled out with the bail papers. The opposing lawyers were already halfway down the stairs, chatting to one another amicably.

Fraser wrote his name in the spaces indicated. Pulawski dropped the papers in his dispatch case. "I'll take a cab to the prison. I'm due in court in an hour's time."

They were on the steps when the lawyer touched Fraser's arm. "I almost forgot. There's a message for you. A man called my office just before I left. He wants you to meet him at four o'clock this afternoon in the Tate Gallery. He said it's important." He raised his arm as a taxi turned the corner.

"There must be more than just that, surely," said Fraser. "Didn't the guy leave a name?"

"He said you'd know," answered Pulawski. He climbed into the cab and gave the hack his directions.

Fraser went the short route to the prison — Battersea, Clapham Common and up Brixton Hill. The message the lawyer had given him was much on his mind. The way these hoods operated was unbelievable. They set up meetings in public places as if they were calling a Salvation Army assembly. Ah well — it was still hard to believe that Zaleski would be free in half-an-hour in spite of what had happened in the judge's chambers. Fraser wheeled right onto the cheerless piece of road leading to the prison. A trusty was sweeping up piles of damp leaves in front of the gates. A guard watched him from the open wicket. It was some time before the cab arrived. Pulawski hurried across to the stationwagon.

"This won't take long. You can wait here if you like."

Fraser slid out from behind the wheel. "I might as well get my money's worth. I'll come."

The lawyer identified himself. The gate hack let them into the courtyard, indicating the room where Fraser had waited the previous day.

"If you'll take a seat in there. I'll tell them in the front office."

"They should know already," said the lawyer. "The judge's clerk was going to call the police."

It was too early for visitors and they were alone. Fraser kicked the coals into a blaze and went across to the window. Remand prisoners dressed in their own clothes were walking around in twos and threes. A queue had formed outside the row of latrines. The comings and goings there were supervised by jailers standing on concrete blocks. Suddenly he saw Zaleski, talking to a warder with a paper in his hand. The Pole's head moved vigorously and he vanished into the cell-block. Pulawski's voice came from behind.

"He'll be glad to get out of there. Those men represent a couple of hundred years in jail. It's a salutary thought."

Fraser turned away from the window. "What happens when he comes up next week?"

Pulawski shrugged. "He'll be discharged," he said. "I've been to the Aliens Office. There's no doubt that Zaleski did make his reports. I have the photostats right here." He tapped his dispatch case.

Fraser did his best to sound offhand. "They wouldn't cook up something else, would they? I mean another charge?"

Pulawski was clearly startled by the question. "What do you mean, another charge? I don't understand."

"It's Raven," said Fraser. "He was over at my place yesterday, chucking his weight around."

Pulawski pounced. "You mean he was threatening you?"

Fraser shook his head. Whatever Zaleski's secret, the lawyer obviously didn't know it.

"It wasn't exactly a threat. It was the more the way he acted — as if he had something up his sleeve."

"Bluff," said the lawyer, his face clearing. "You're new to all this if you don't mind me saying so. The police hate to admit a mistake. I'll tell you something in confidence, Mr. Fraser. I wouldn't much like to be in Inspector Raven's shoes at this moment. This is a clear-cut case of wrongful imprisonment. The Police Fund will pay any damages allowed, but it wouldn't let Raven off the hook. There's bound to be a Court of Inquiry."

The jailer poked his head through the door. "Your man's on his way over from Reception."

A gate clanged a couple of times. Zaleski came into the courtyard with the air of a king returning from exile. He seized the lawyer's hand and greeted him demonstratively in Polish, gazing deep into the man's eyes. Then he wheeled sharply, grabbed Fraser by the shoulders and kissed him square on the forehead. A bemused jailer let the party out through the gate. Zaleski bounded forward, arms extended, inhaling deeply. Fraser watched the performance critically.

"It's only been two days. Everything's just as you left it."

Pulawski waved good-bye from the cab. Zaleski waved back, smiling. "Is fool," he said to Fraser. "No head for important matters."

They went across to the parked stationwagon. Fraser switched on the motor, glancing over at his passenger. Zaleski was looking at Ingrid's gloves, shaking his head and muttering.

"Is all right, Kirk," he said out loud. "I give my word. You believe me?"

The Pole's voice rang true, but then it usually did. That was the trouble. Even now his charisma was hard to resist.

"You'd better know what you're doing," said Fraser. "That cop's on to you. They've had my phone bugged since yesterday."

"And Gerber?" Zaleski's slate-colored eyes bore in on Fraser.

The name was no more than an uncertain memory, a relic of something once said. And then suddenly he had it. Gerber was Benny's boss. The man who'd had the hassle with Casimir on Sunday night. The Cockney voice that issued the instructions. The man who was holding Ingrid.

"He called last night. He was the one who told me my phone was bugged. I'm supposed to be seeing him in the Tate Gallery at four o'clock this afternoon."

"Four o'clock," repeated Zaleski as if the time had some special significance. "And Inspector Raven, what is Inspector Raven doing?"

"I told you, he's on to you. Everybody's on to you except me."

"Is no place for talking," Zaleski said quickly. "We drive to my flat."

They came to the river by way of the dreary wastes of southwest London. The Victorian buildings served makeshift purposes. Terraces of semi-detached houses awaited the deft hand of the property developer. Sad lights burned behind dingy curtains, although it was no later than noon. Billboards advertised products that no longer existed. The faces of the people on the streets reflected a kind of acceptance of failure. Zaleski surveyed the scene like a man inspecting some newly acquired territory.

Fraser cocked an eye at the driving mirror. "I've had this feeling since yesterday that someone's on my tail. I don't see them, but somehow I know that they're there."

"Is possible," said Zaleski easily. "Always at such times is better you pay no attention. In Cairo . . ."

"No Cairo," Fraser said firmly. "I want to keep my mind in one piece."

Their route brought them north into the noontime bustle of Fulham Road. Zaleski clicked his tongue at the garbage cans standing in the entrance to Wielkapolska.

"Tonight we eat together," he announced. "Ingrid, Hanya, some friends. Is celebration."

They were held at the traffic signals. Fraser watched as his passenger folded his arms, the top half of his body going into some wild Polish dance.

"You are dangerously insane," Fraser said dourly. "What do you want here — a brass band playing 'Hail the Conquering Hero'?"

He wrenched the wheel sharply, drove south and parked. They walked across to Zaleski's apartment building. A dumpy woman with red hair was putting her cleaning things away in the broom closet. Her face split in a grin of delight, and she put both hands on her hips.

"Lawd love yer, I knew it. I told those madams in number one. They won't keep Mr. Zaleski locked up, I said. It's a mistake, I said."

Zaleski helped her on with her coat. She lowered her voice confidentially as he pushed coins into her reluctant palm.

"A man come round here an hour or so ago, asking for you. He *said* he was from the bank, but if you ask me it was a copper."

Zaleski opened the lobby door for her and unlocked his apartment. A batch of mail was lying on the carpet. He picked it up and threw it on the table unread. He peered in the corners of the room, nose questing, head held high. Something about the way he carried himself reminded Fraser of Raven. Both were like hound-dogs, hunting by sight.

"The woman was wrong," Zaleski said. "Why police are coming here? Nah — police are waiting and watching, not showing themselves. This man was from bank. The English are uncivilized."

Fraser sat down on the sofa, loosening his coat. One hour's freedom and the Pole was restored completely, unregenerate and seeing life as he alone could see it. Fraser tapped a smoke on his thumbnail.

"You're going to have to talk to me now, Casimir."

Zaleski nodded absently. There was no other indication that he'd heard. He made his way into the bedroom. Fraser could hear the drawers being opened and closed, then the Pole was in the kitchen. He came out, smiling broadly and holding a chisel. He drew the curtains and bunched powerful shoulders as he lifted the television table to one side. Then he was down on his knees. A swift wrench freed a section of the carpet from its tacks. He chiseled up a couple of floorboards near the wainscoat. Underneath was a small key wallet and a thick manila envelope. He tossed the envelope into Fraser's lap.

"Read!" he instructed.

Fraser unfolded the batch of clippings. Inside was a glossy photograph taken of a group of men sprawling around a goat in brilliant sunshine. The years had thickened Zaleski's body and taken toll of the youthful good looks. There was something debonair about the way in which he grinned at the camera, something that still remained. The first lead headline provided the clue that had been eluding Fraser. His mind registered key phrases as he scanned the paragraphs . . . *British commando units . . . German field headquarters . . . a gold monstrance weighing thirty pounds encrusted with five hundred diamonds, two hundred and fifty emeralds, one hundred and seventy rubies . . . present-day value estimated at over three quarters of a million pounds.*

He pushed the clippings and photographs back into the envelope and stared at Zaleski. The news flashes, the television interview he'd seen on "Police Five," took on a fresh and startling significance. This was no "gang of international jewel thieves." It was a pot-bellied Pole with a ridiculous monocle, grinning like a teenager who's just made out with some chick. There was no shame, no suggestion of guilt.

"Is big surprise, no?" challenged Zaleski.

Fraser gave the envelope back, shaking his head. "You're beyond me, boy. Dragging your wife into a caper like this."

Zaleski's face was puzzled. "But Hanya does as I tell her. You think this was robbery, Kirk?"

"You're damn right it was robbery," Fraser replied.

"Nah," said Zaleski shortly. "Restitution not robbery."

The taste of tobacco was bitter. Fraser stabbed out his butt. "Let's try and get this together, Casimir. I don't give a goddam if you rob the Bank of England. I'm only concerned with Ingrid. You've no right to involve us like this. And with Gerber of all people. Since when is he a Polish hero?"

Zaleski put a match to the buff envelope. He carried the blazing paper into the bathroom. The toilet flushed. He came back wiping his hands on a silk handkerchief.

"I fix something to eat," he said, winking. Fraser heard him in the kitchen, humming away to himself. It was like trying to communicate with a head-hunter from Borneo. Zaleski's thinking just didn't relate. The Pole shoved his way through the kitchen door carrying a tray set with ham and sausage, rye bread wrapped in foil, butter and a couple of fluted glasses. He made the trip back to the kitchen and came out blowing the cork from the champagne bottle at the ceiling. He filled both glasses.

"To friendship!"

Fraser looked down at the worn napkins embroidered with some heraldic device. The champagne probably wasn't even paid for. Suddenly he found himself on his feet, his voice shaking.

"Friendship, you phony bastard!"

Zaleski put his empty glass down very carefully. His green black eyes were perfectly steady.

"Don't hit me, Kirk," he warned. "We fight on same side not against."

Fraser let his arm drop slowly. "You're insane. Don't you understand, I can only take so much of this goddam charade."

Zaleski smiled, coming forward like a cat investigating unknown territory. He pushed Fraser gently down onto the sofa, put the plate of food on his knees, the glass of champagne in his hand.

"Drink, old friend!" he ordered.

The wine was straight from the icebox and the chill set Fraser's teeth on edge. "Are you going to tell me what's behind all this? I have to know even if I beat your head in, Casimir."

"Sure," soothed Zaleski. "So we eat and then I tell you." He dragged a chair in front of the sofa so that he was facing the Canadian. He wolfed the food, refilling his glass as though he were drinking water. Finally he belched and massaged his belly.

"Now I talk." He did so for the best part of twenty minutes, starting his tale about a monastery on an Italian mountain. He jumped the years to a handful of Polish veterans marching down Whitehall to the Tomb of the Unknown Warrior, their last farewell to a dead and gallant commander ignored by the allies whose cause they had made their own.

Zaleski spread his hands. "Is the same for all Poles in this country. Are outcasts without respect. Germans, Italians, Japanese, Russians — even new Poles — all are friends of British. But not old Poles. You saw what newspapers are saying, even that is lie. Monstrance recovered by *British* commandos. What British? Our past has been taken from us and we have no future. And you want to call me thief, Kirk?"

The words of a poem persisted in his mind. *Liar and bragger, he had no friends except a dagger.* Zaleski came back into the room, smelling strongly of his *eau-de-Portugal.*

"So, Kirk. Do you condemn me?"

"Forget it," Fraser said wearily. "I don't condemn. I just want out."

Zaleski poked his thumb through two fingers, making an obscene gesture. "Scum. Why treating these people with importance?"

Frazer's amazement was genuine. "Because they put the fear of God into me, that's why! You should have seen your wife's face as they took her out to the car. She knows the truth even if you don't."

"But I *give* Gerber the monstrance," Zaleski said reasonably. "Of course I give."

Fraser drew the longest breath of his life. He'd sat in so many bars, heard so many things said and suddenly he wanted to hear no more. The champagne was working in his head and belly. He pulled himself together.

"Then what are we waiting for?" he asked simply.

Zaleski laid a cautionary finger alongside his jutting nose. "Tactics. Is necessary, you see, to think carefully what we do. These men are primitives. Troglodytes."

"They're killers," amended Fraser. "Killers that you brought into my house."

"Please," said Zaleski, his face pained and holding up a hand. "You suffer, I suffer. You are not inventing love, Kirk."

"Bullshit," said Fraser. His hands were trembling like an old man's. "I've told you before. I've only got so much self-control. I can see myself now, up here in my head, listening to you as if you were some sort of fucking prophet instead of a dangerous psychopath. I want that monstrance by four o'clock, Casimir. I'm going to hand it over to Gerber and get out of there just as fast as I can. Away from the lot of you. Does that make sense?"

"You are upset," Zaleski said calmly. "Is natural and I am not offended. Listen to me, Kirk. We are not brutes, you see. Are men of breeding exposed to classical educations. No good for dealing with people like Gerber. We must crawl with him, use his kind cunning. You think that is simple? You think we exchange monstrance for Ingrid and Hanya like some piece business in a supermarket."

"Your syntax is going to hell," said Fraser. He added truthfully, "I don't know *what* I think! What I am sure of is that I'm starting to fill up with you. OK. Suppose we do it your way, what am I supposed to say to Gerber?"

Zaleski crossed the room, sat down beside the Canadian and talked earnestly for some minutes.

"No using telephones except in public places. Be on lookout for police. They are bound to be following. Be careful going into Tate Gallery."

Fraser glanced up at the mirror. As far as he could determine there was no visible sign of what he was going through. Maybe his brain was too dull to register real emotion any more."

"You mean police are going to be following me?"

"Of course," Zaleski said swiftly. "Are following everyone and probably Gerber. Make no mistake, Kirk. Are not walking with big feet and clubs. Are pretty girls smiling in subways, polite gentlemen asking for cigarette lights. All kinds disguises. Be careful. I am used to it."

"I know. In Cairo," said Fraser, coming to his feet. "Meet me in the public bar of the Antelope at half-after five."

Zaleski shut the door and walked across to the window. The scene outside was a familiar one for the time of the day. A delivery wagon was in front of the block across the way. People were returning from shopping. A street sweeper was pushing a broom lethargically along the gutter. Zaleski watched Fraser's retreating back as far as the corner. The fact that no one seemed to be following him meant nothing. The police would be trained in the art of shadowing suspects. Nevertheless, it was difficult to stay on the trail of a man of resource who knew what was happening. In spite of the Canadian's jibes, it wasn't too much different from Cairo in the old days, the intelligence agents of five supposedly friendly nations chasing one another all over the city. The mood Fraser was in was just right for the part he had to play, bewildered, aggressive and ready to be led.

Zaleski ran a quick bath. He could still feel the touch of prison on his skin. These barbarians had treated him as a common criminal even though his offense was supposed to be a technicality. He changed into cavalry-twill trousers, cut to reveal his well-developed thighs and calves, and donned one of his crew-neck cashmere sweaters. The keys to the Dante Gallery were on a table in the living room. He wrapped the wallet carefully in a handkerchief so that it didn't chink and pinned it in the lining of his duffelcoat sleeve. The chance of being caught with the keys in his possession was one that he had to take. He let himself out of the apartment building and hurried north to Fulham Road. It was a few minutes after one and nearly all the stores were shut for the lunch hour. He walked toward the restaurant, ignoring the waves of a group standing in the window of the wine bar. They were friendly enough now, but which of them had as much as come to the police court.

He unlocked his restaurant and carried the empty garbage cans inside. He shut the door again and looked around. The waiters had laid the tables before they left. The checked cloths were slightly starched, the glasses gleaming. He looked behind the bar, noting the alignment of the bottles on the shelves, the fact that the cash register drawer was half-open. It was the same downstairs. Whoever had searched the place had done the job thoroughly. The contents of the deepfreeze had been shifted from one end of the chest to the other. Canisters had been emptied, flour spilled. He ran back up the stairs and opened a chink in the faded velvet curtains. A bearded man he knew by sight was across the street talking to a slovenly sculptress. A bus removed them from view briefly. When Zaleski looked again, past them this time, he saw the man standing in the dentist's doorway. The stranger had stationed himself in front of a strip of mirror so that he had a two-way view of the street. Zaleski took his fingers away from the curtain.

He unlocked the wine store and put a couple of bottles of export vodka in the icebox. The bastards were communists, but they used the old methods. He added four bottles of vintage champagne. Defeat or victory, the occasion was one that must be celebrated. A ten-foot wall enclosed the small yard at the back of the kitchen. He placed a couple of boxes against it and clambered up awkwardly, bringing his eyes level with the top of the wall. The neighboring yard was littered with junk, headless statues, tables without legs, a chaise-longue with the upholstery ripped to shreds. The owner of the antique store ate his lunch in the pizzeria up the street. There was no one to see Zaleski drop, arms crossed against his belly, legs relaxed as if falling from a height instead of a few feet. He negotiated two more walls without being spotted, ending up in a big yard behind the corner dairy. A youth in an apron, wearing hipboots, was hosing down a milk-cart, with his back to Zaleski. The Pole hurried out through the open gates onto a side street that was fifty yards away from his restaurant. He waited in the porchway of the convent school, bowing courteously at a nun who came out. He scanned the announcements of novenas, an Easter excursion to Lourdes, one eye on the street he had just left. The only living objects were the nun and an overweight Dalmatian relieving itself against a lamppost.

Zaleski descended the steps, square-shouldered, his belly thrust forward confidently. A cab took him to Fulham Broadway where he spent a quarter-hour in the post office.

The telegrams to Czarniecki and Sobinski were written in Polish. The telephone book supplied the address he wanted.

GERBER Samuel. 36a Redclyffe Mews s.w.5 01-352-0606

His call was to another number. He identified himself in his own language, spoke for thirty seconds and hung up. He left the post office, making his way through the rotting fruit along North End Road onto a street of cut-rate stores, laundromats and shabby dwellings. The place he was looking for was a narrow building wedged between a fried fish shop and a Moravian chapel. A shabby panel truck was parked out front. The store window displayed a haphazard collection of pots and pans, hacksaw blades, axe heads and dusty toolsets. A homemade sign hung from a length of lavatory chain.

LOCKSMITH   KEYS CUT

A bell jingled as Zaleski pushed the door open. He took a quick look behind him and threw home the bolt. A stocky man wearing dirty overalls came from behind the counter. His Polish was spiked with the unmistakable accent of a Silesian.

"Casimir, old friend!" He held Zaleski at arms length in a powerful grip. "Nah, Casimir!" he chided, shaking his head. His hair was powdered with some form of white dust, and he stank mysteriously of tallow.

Zaleski disengaged himself firmly. They met perhaps once a year, at a marriage or funeral. Wladimir Scheel always treated the occasions as if they hadn't seen one another since their school days. Scheel lived alone, mistrustful of events that had turned a budding concert pianist into a locksmith and seller of cheap hardware. But his contacts with the world he cared to remember were always given the ceremony that they deserved. Zaleski came to the point quickly, knowing his man.

"I need your help, Wladimir."

Scheel's eyes slid away so quickly that they appeared to vanish completely, returning after a second as if by sleight of hand. He reached under the counter and produced a couple of glasses and a bottle. The fingers of his right hand were crooked, the joints smashed thirty years before by blows from a rifle butt. He offered a glass to Zaleski who wiped his mouth with his handkerchief before and after drinking.

"Your health, old friend," said Scheel. "And how is Hanya?"

"Well enough, I thank you," said Zaleski. "It is I who needs help."

Scheel cocked a thoughtful eye at a moulting canary in a cage hanging from a shelf.

"Whatever I have is yours, old comrade. The fact is I am penniless. In this godforsaken country I manage to do no more than exist. Like a dog I exist."

Zaleski cleaned the top of a chair and sat down fastidiously. "Eleven months ago you won three thousand pounds in the football pools. And I happen to know that you own the deeds to this rat-infested barrack. But no matter, old comrade. Since it is not money that I need, I accept your offer of help gladly."

Scheel's expression was that of a man relieved of an intolerable weight of loneliness.

"You have only to tell me how I may serve." His face closed tighter and tighter as he listened to Zaleski's earnest argument. "What you ask of me is difficult," he said at length. "I live surrounded by thieves and vandals, teenage bandits who have no respect. The police are always coming here asking questions. Did this one request a key to be made, did that one buy a housebreaking instrument? You see, old friend, I have to obey the laws."

Zaleski stopped his drumming on the dusty counter. "There are other laws, Wladimir. I hope for your sake that you do not make me invoke them."

Scheel scratched the back of his neck. The rasping sound and a tentative twittering from the caged bird disturbed the sudden silence.

"Aiee!" he said at last.

Zaleski turned his hand over. "You look, judge and supply whatever I need. It is a simple and innocent expedition. I shall tell Hanya you were kind enough to ask after her."

"Yes," Scheel said thoughtfully. "I kiss your wife's hand. You say I look and then pass judgment. Yes. And where is this house?"

"In Redclyffe Mews," said Zaleski. "Your telephone?" The instrument turned up hidden under a metal hood designed to cover roasts.

He rang Gerber's number three times. It rang unanswered on each occasion. He put his beret on his head and nodded at the door.

"We shall go in your vehicle. Wear the dungarees. They are eminently suitable."

The truck shuddered to a halt on the south side of Redclyffe Square. Zaleski pointed over at the arched entrance to the mews.

"Make no mistakes. There can be no return."

He watched Scheel shuffle away, a mysterious length of sash cord trailing from the back pocket of his overalls. The locksmith stopped outside Gerber's house, bent down and made some obscure measurements in the region of the drainpipe. Then he turned round very slowly, his eyes on the door in front of him. He came back to the truck and wedged himself behind the wheel, shaking his head. He switched on the ignition and the truck shuddered violently.

"Impossible," said Scheel. "This lock is a Janus. Anyone using a skeleton key or picklocks will only jam the mechanism. I am sorry, Casimir. There is nothing more I can do for you."

"How is it that you know about these locks?" persisted Zaleski. "What makes you so sure?"

Scheel shifted from first to third, second gear apparently missing. He steered the truck out into the traffic like a man pushing a punt from the edge of the river.

"I know because I have installed many of these locks. Each one is guaranteed burglarproof."

"What happens if people lose their keys?" persisted Zaleski. "They surely do not break the doors down! Of course they don't. They call a man like you. And what do you do, Wladimir?"

It took Scheel some time to answer and then only in a reluctant mutter. "There is a master key."

"Of course there is," Zaleski encouraged. "And you have one, do you not?"

Scheel gave him a nervous glance. "There is a book, Casimir. The manufacturers insist that any time a master key is used the circumstances must be recorded."

"Quite rightly," observed Zaleski. "I shall borrow the key and on this occasion you will forget to write in the book."

The truck swerved as Scheel took both hands off the wheel. "Aiee!" he said bitterly.

Zaleski righted the steering. "Calm yourself, man. Everything will be all right. You know my reputation. I shall return this key before nightfall."

They spent the next twenty minutes in the store with the

street door bolted. Scheel unpacked a new Janus lock and produced the master key. Zaleski practiced the quick stab and turn until it was perfected. He touched Scheel's shoulder, smiling.

"Unbolt the door, Wladimir."

Scheel spoke in a high, unnatural voice. "Just an envelope through the letter box. I would sooner not see you again today, old friend and comrade."

"An envelope through the letterbox," Zaleski agreed. "Perfect. And I shall remember your cooperation. Till we meet again then, Wladimir."

A cab took him back to Old Brompton Road. He was dangerously near his flat and the restaurant, but it was unlikely that the police would be combing the neighborhood. He dialed Gerber's number again from a booth on the street. As before, it rang unanswered. A man like Gerber, he reasoned, would plan an abduction in detail. In this case he didn't even have to worry about the police. The suggestion that Hanya and Ingrid were being held somewhere in the country was almost surely false. Gerber would have them near at hand. About that sort of thing he would bluff. About murder, assault and battery never.

Zaleski turned into the mews, the master key concealed in his gloved hand. A confident entrance was necessary to lull the suspicions of any neighbor who chanced to be at the window. Gerber's front door was painted a bright shade of yellow. Crocus shoots showed in the window boxes. Beyond the heavily lined curtains Zaleski could see a well-appointed sitting room. Whoever had done the decor had applied Gerber's money with taste. The impulse to walk on by was strong, to peer into every doorway as far as the end of the mews. What looked like a small furniture removal truck was parked there, the cab empty. He stopped, the movement of his hand swift and direct. The key slid home, the tumblers lifted easily and the door opened. Zaleski stepped in quickly. The white-painted hallway was small. A short flight of stairs in front of him led up to the second story. A gouache painting of a thoroughbred horse hung on the wall, the jockey poised high on the animal's withers. The faint smell of cigar smoke had no apparent source, as if it was sprayed from a pressure can. Zaleski ran up the thick-carpeted staircase. There were two bedrooms, a bathroom with a sunken bath between them. Zaleski moved on the balls of his feet, whistling through his teeth tonelessly. He was carrying the wallet of keys, his eyes searching the bedroom for a place in which he could hide them. After the almost effeminate luxury of the green-tiled bathroom with its spouting dolphin faucets, black marble fittings and silver-topped bottles, Gerber's bedroom was monastic. A clothes closet with sliding doors occupied the entire length of an inner wall. The two windows overlooked the cobblestones outside. Directly beneath them was a narrow bed. Whoever slept in it would only have to raise his head to have an uninterrupted view of the mews in both directions. The only picture was an aerial photograph of Dartmoor Prison.

Zaleski wheeled sharply, his heartbeat accelerating as the adrenalin pumped into his bloodstream. There had been the slightest noise as if something or someone had moved. He tiptoed out onto the landing and peered down over the banister rails. He could neither see nor hear anything. Then the cistern was flushed in the neighboring house. The sound was clear through the dividing wall. The noise that had disturbed him had probably come from the same source. The second bedroom had an enormous bed with a silk spread and a basket-weave head and foot. The make-up on the dressing table, the fashion magazines by the bed, showed that the room was used by a woman at least some of the time. There was the same type of clothes closet as in Gerber's bedroom. Some dresses were hanging inside, a couple of mothproof plastic covers. He unzipped one of them. The silver mink coat had a small pocket in the lining. He dropped the gallery keys into the pocket and zipped up the shroud again, smiling to himself happily. He'd accepted the final loss of the monstrance ever since Fraser had left the jail the day before. The brief dream of a refurbished life was over. Now, all that remained was to erase the memory of defeat. Revenge was no shoddy emotion. Its absence was a sign of an effete society. Czarniecki and Sobinski would understand: Poles, gentlemen and gamblers. The strangest thing was the way he was thinking now of Hanya. He thought of her love as a blanket that covered his imperfections, a flame that both seared and yet warmed with a gentle heat. It was all part of an almost forgotten sonnet he had written to her a generation ago — "To My Love from a Bridge Across the Vistula." She was also a good cook.

He was still staring into the big gilt-framed mirror when he heard the noise again. His eyes narrowed, losing themselves in the pouches of flesh high on his cheeks. A fully grown chow dog was standing in the doorway, softly growling. Zaleski wheeled with infinite caution. The growl deepened in tone and intensity, the dog's top lip trembling over fearsome teeth. Zaleski broke out in a sudden sweat. The animal must have been lying in the kitchen or sitting room. He put out his gloved hand tentatively, trying to recall commando practice.

Grab the dog by the front legs as it springs, wrenching them apart so that the heart bursts from the rib cage. If you missed, of course, you had no throat.

"Is good Rover," he said in a low voice, an uncertain memory prompting the name. Goddam the English and their repulsive domestic habits. In Poland, dogs were kept outside the house with the rest of the animals. The chow went down on its haunches, neck fur bristling, its amber-colored eyes watching every move. The tip of its purplish tongue was caught between two teeth giving the animal a slightly foolish appearance. The sweat by now was running profusely. Zaleski pictured himself trapped in the bedroom until someone walked through the door downstairs. Whoever it was, there would be no excuse that he might make. He'd committed himself too deeply. There could only be one reason for his presence in Gerber's house and sooner or later it would be determined. He tried to close his mind against the probable sequence.

He was standing at the foot of the bed, facing the dog in the doorway. The window to the right was shut, the frames secured by burglarproof screws. The chow would be on top of him long before he could manage to undo the screws. The dog raised its head fractionally as Zaleski lowered himself onto the bed. For the moment, at least, the animal seemed content to guard the doorway, policing his movements at a distance. A clock downstairs sounded three o'clock. Zaleski wet his mouth furtively, flexing his gloved hands, thinking of an army storage depot outside Giza. Time and again the Arabs had raided it, tunneling under barbed wire like desert rats, literally propelling one another over the top. The commandant, a friend of Zaleski, had lost one eye in an Alexandrian brothel and viewed life sourly through the other. He'd imported six German police dogs trained to savage strangers at sight. Zaleski had sat on a balcony in the moonlight with the commandant, thirty years before, watching the despairing antics of an Arab youth trapped by the dogs between barbed wire and a hillock of canned sausage meat.

He closed his eyes, now, offering himself to the protection of a minor saint who came to mind and went down carefully on his hands and knees. When he opened his eyes again, the chow was up on its feet looking at him curiously. It backed off, still growling, as Zaleski crawled toward the doorway and out onto the landing. The Pole's breathing was coming in short, agonizing bursts. He was past the chow now and at the top of the stairs. There were twelve treads to be taken, head first and on all fours. The chow's nose reached out, sniffing Zaleski's body as he started to go down. It stayed at the head of the stairs, head cocked, rumbling softly, watching Zaleski's progress. The Pole pitched forward, skidding the last few feet on his face. The dog was on him in two bounds. Zaleski lay quite still, with the animal's legs straddling him, its muzzle almost touching his proffered jugular. Suddenly the chow turned away. Zaleski heard it lapping water in the kitchen. He was on his feet and out into the mews in a flash. He slammed the door shut as the animal's body thudded against the other side. His sweater and underpants were drenched, his hands shaking violently. The stretch of cobblestones was empty except for the furniture truck which was still parked at the far end. It was ten minutes after three. There was little that he could do now until Fraser had talked with Gerber.

Chapter Eight

FRASER WALKED WEST on Fulham Road, resisting somehow the urge to turn around or look back over his shoulder. In spite of his inclination to melodrama, Zaleski's warning about being tailed was probably valid. If it was true that the Pole had been turned loose deliberately to lead Raven to the stolen monstrance, everyone connected would be suspect. And the chances were that the name Kirk Fraser would be at the top of the list. He'd gone to the police station. He'd offered himself as a surety for Zaleski's bail. Most damaging of all, maybe, was the fact that Raven had seen Benny in the doorway of the bookstore, rapping away like an old buddy. In spite of what the hood said, Fraser was sure that the inspector had recognized him.

The grip of January had tightened since early that morning. A bitter north wind searched out the ill-clad and feeble, drying the fronts of the buildings and sidewalks. A man wearing a black velour hat banged on the window of the wine bar as Fraser went by. He beckoned Fraser inside but the Canadian kept going. He wanted no part in telling Zaleski's story. He opened up the bookstore. The place was freezing. He sat down in the tiny office, out of sight from the street. His head was still full of Zaleski, a fifty-odd-year-old failure with a track

record of broken promises allied to useless hopes. Only two
things seemed to save the guy from being a barroom bum — a
romantic conceit of himself and the charity of his friends.
Rules meant nothing to him. He'd pulled off the first part of a
spectacular robbery against all odds, blown the rest through his
own stupidity and talked about it all as if he deserved a medal.
The best thing would have been for him to succeed completely, to have taken Hanya to their Lombardy farmhouse and
let her grow her flowers. Jail was not for the likes of Casimir.
One fact niggled — Zaleski's total acceptance of defeat.
There'd been no last-ditch stand of defiance, no rattling of
swords. When you thought about it, Gerber had exploded
Zaleski's last dream, attacked his wife in her own home, put
her in fear of her life. And Zaleski simply shrugged it off. It
was out of character. Fraser checked the time with his watch.
He'd been in the store for ten minutes, long enough for them
to get their men into position. He'd seen enough chase movies
to know that in order to evade your pursuer, you first have to
identify him.

He walked in back to the storeroom and took a look at the
street. A G.P.O. repair truck was parked in front of the
bakery on the corner of Hollywood Road. An inspection plate
in the sidewalk was up. Sitting with his legs dangling into the
hole was a man in blue overalls. He was wearing a pair of
earphones and was holding a clutch of colored cables. From
where he was sitting, he could see both the front and rear
entrance to the bookstore. He did it casually, using his eyes
without shifting his head. Fraser stepped back from the
window and lit a cigarette. *He* was under surveillance while
thugs like Gerber moved around as they liked. Incredible.
Zaleski's instructions had been explicit. The action had to be
set for tonight. Tomorrow would be too late. And whatever

was done had to be done free of police interference. A man like Gerber would react violently to anything that smelled of a frame. A second man had joined the first on the sidewalk, hopping from one leg to the other as if cold and slapping himself. The back of the van was open just enough for Fraser to see the Japanese monkey bike inside. He was suddenly sure that both men were cops. The motorcycle and the truck were going to be used to leapfrog him. The bike would be taken out and ridden past then reloaded into the truck which would repass in turn. That, too, he had seen in the movies.

He buttoned his anorak and left the store by the front door, taking his time about locking up. By the time he had the stationwagon turning out of Fulham Road the repair truck was coming after him. It went by and forked right. Fraser could only see one man in the cab. He turned in the opposite direction. By now the motorcycle should be out of the truck. He picked it up in the driving mirror, a dozen yards behind, tucked in behind a bus. He drove in a sort of square that brought him out in the Worlds' End section of New Kings Road. The blue Honda bike was still there as he turned into the Spik'n'Span Car Wash. Outside were a couple of gas pumps, plate-glass windows displaying tires and accessories and a runway leading to a turntable and washing bay. He wound his window down, reached out and bought a voucher from the vending machine. Two cars were in front of him. He used the interlude to check his recollection of the fireproof door let into the wall. It was there all right, painted yellow and immediately behind the turntable. He glanced up at the driving mirror. The blue bike was propped against the curb, its rider inspecting the tires in the window. A light blinked overhead.

Fraser moved the stationwagon onto the turntable. A

handler swung the car around so that it faced the wash bay. Fraser fastened his windows. Once inside the bay, jets of soapy water rocked the car with high velocity. Washed, it was sprayed free of detergent and polished finally by a couple of blacks waiting beyond the canvas and plastic curtains. It moved forward slowly on the automatic track. As it neared the bay, Fraser slipped out of the driver's seat and ran back, ducking low behind the car on the revolving turntable. The firedoor led to a staircase. He climbed two floors and looked down at the street. The blue bike was still there. The post office repair truck had moved into position, tight up against the curb a hundred yards behind. He walked along a corridor, clattering with the noise of typewriters, rode the elevator down and left the building a hundred yards from where his car was. The keys were in the dash and in any case the hell with it. He'd collect the thing tomorrow. He used two cabs to take him to the Tate Gallery. A cold wind was slicing under Lambeth Bridge, spraying gray water over the retaining wall. He was five minutes early for his rendezvous with Gerber. He used them to obey Zaleski's orders to the letter. He untied his shoelace and did it up again a couple of times, looking east and west along the Embankment. Then he walked around the block and climbed the steps, sure now that nobody was following him.

There was a hush inside the gallery. People seemed to be obeying some invisible injunction to silence. A notice required the checking of cameras and umbrellas. There was a faint smell of lavender and all the furniture carried a rich dark polish. Beyond an archway he could distinguish a massive oil painting, glowing under its light like some fabulous great jewel. He tagged on to a group of New Zealand schoolteachers and had gone a dozen yards when a half-hiss, half-whistle caught his attention. No ordinary cop would have wasted a second look at the well-dressed figure with navy blue homburg and a bloom of purple silk in his breast pocket. Gerber's hand patted the bench. Fraser sat down beside him. The catalogue on Gerber's knees was covered with doodles of broken-nosed cherubs. Gerber lowered his voice, speaking without moving his lips, like a ventriloquist.

"Sure there's nobody on your tail, are you?"

Fraser cleared his throat, trying for the same whispered clarity. "There was but I lost them."

Gerber made a note on the catalogue. "The Pole wants to do business, right?"

An attendant went by, splaying his rubber-soled feet in the gait of the man who walks and watches.

"He'll do business," whispered Fraser. "But it has to be done his way."

"Bollix," Gerber said distinctly. "You people aren't in no position to whack about. What's he want, anyway?"

"Insurance," said Fraser. "He wants to be sure of the women. You're taking everything else away from him."

Gerber put his head back and laughed silently. "Never mind about me, mate. Let's worry about you. Where's the loot?"

"I'll have it in a couple of hours' time," said Fraser. "I'll take it wherever you say. All we're asking for is a little insurance."

"Again with the insurance!" said Gerber. "You people had your chance to earn with me. You don't get a single penny now, but you do get the women back, untouched. That's the offer, and it's all you're going to get."

There was a terrifying finality in the low, flat voice. It was impossible to think of Gerber responding to a plea for charity or compassion.

"We understand that," Fraser answered. "All Zaleski asks is that the exchange goes like this. You release my girl, I give you the monstrance, then you free Zaleski's wife."

Gerber brooded over the spread fingers of his right hand as if the open palm held a message for him.

"You're on," he said finally. "But we'll do it the other way round. Just in case you're up to something. I don't trust any of you. Auntie goes first and then your bird. Can you make it by ten o'clock? If that's too early, say so. Whatever time we agree, you're going to have to be there."

"Sure, I can make it by ten," answered Fraser.

"Good." Gerber released his instructions from the side of his mouth. "You know the bridge over the Serpentine — there's only one. There's a parking place down by the water, dead opposite the Armory. Be there alone with the gear. That's all you have to do — just be there. We'll take care of the rest. Alone and remember — we'll be watching."

If he said they'd be watching, they would. Gerber wasn't the kind to waste time bluffing.

"That's all?" Fraser asked. He was up too tight to do anything about the shake in his voice. "There's nothing else?"

"Just relax," said Gerber. He put his hands on Fraser's knee. "And be lucky. Because if you ain't lucky in this world, mate, you certainly ain't going to be lucky in the next."

The Antelope is one of the few genuine pubs left in the area. Beer is drawn through copper pipes instead of plastic. Credit is given and recorded on a slate. The busty barmaid is flirtatious, and strangers are either welcomed or ignored, according to their preference. A smell of tannic acid rose from the oak sawdust on the floor as Fraser pushed the door of the public bar. Zaleski was sitting in a corner, arms folded, his beret worn at an angle. The pose suggested a Russian general on the eve of Napoleon's retreat from Moscow. Fraser pulled a chair and sat down. There was nobody else in the bar except a couple of regular customers throwing darts. Fraser gave his news.

"It's all set. Ten o'clock tonight. Hyde Park, opposite the Armory. I'm supposed to go there alone."

Zaleski spread a pocket map on the table. His finger traced the course of the Serpentine. He seemed to have been wearing the black kid gloves ever since he left Brixton Prison. His slate-colored eyes were thoughtful.

"Is good place. You see — behind is water."

Fraser bought himself a glass of beer and came back to the table. "You mean a good place for him or us?"

A dart rebounded from the board and landed in the sawdust, quivering a few inches away from Zaleski's shoe. He removed his foot in lordly fashion.

"Where is car?"

Fraser explained, Zaleski listening, stroking the side of his beaked nose.

"Is well done, Kirk. Intelligent."

Fraser pushed his glass aside. The beer tasted flat. "Thank you. I'm glad you approve. Have you any idea what the park's like at that time of night?"

Zaleski's head moved in understanding. "Is why Gerber chose this place. People scared are not curious. I tell you, Gerber is smart."

"What am I supposed to do?" Fraser demanded. He loosened the unfamiliar tie that was choking him. "You want me to go into the park, walking — carrying that goddam cross?"

Zaleski leaned forward heavily. "No walking. Everything is arranged. There will be car. You have detective's telephone number."

"You mean Raven? As a matter of fact I have, why?" He found the card at the back of his wallet.

Zaleski took it from Fraser's fingers. "You see, is not same number he is giving me!"

Fraser shrugged. "All I know is that he said this one would reach him night and day. What is this all about anyway?"

Zaleski tucked the card in the pocket of his duffelcoat. "Inspector-Detective Raven is friend, Kirk. Remember that."

"Detective-Inspector," Fraser corrected automatically. He looked hard but there was no hint of sarcasm — just the old Polish sea dog, beret pulled well forward, collar of his duffelcoat up. "You mean that, do you?" he asked. "Raven's our friend."

"Only friend," amplified Zaleski.

"OK," said Fraser. "God knows I'm trying. For every reason under the sun I'm trying, but this is ridiculous. I firmly believe that you are crazy."

Zaleski tapped the side of his nose, his gold sideteeth glinting. "Polish crazy. Is different. So. I meet you here nine-thirty with everything.

"Nine-thirty," said Fraser and came to his feet. This Pole could follow you through a set of revolving doors and still come out ahead of you.

"OK," said Zaleski and winked.

"That's right," said Fraser. "OK. You're both crazy, you and Gerber. You want to hear the last thing he said to me in the Tate. Be lucky, he said."

Zaleski's grin weakened. "How, be lucky? I do not understand."

Fraser waved farewell. "I didn't either. But I'm beginning to get the drift."

Chapter Nine

THE SMALL PANEL TRUCK had been in the area since early that morning. Gerber had noticed it shortly after the morning papers had arrived, around eight-fifteen. They'd been shifting it every few hours but never more than a few hundred yards away from the mews. The monkeys. The legend on the side of the truck advertized a firm of Hammersmith furniture movers. But according to Gerber's little book, the license tag was one of a batch registered under the name of Caspar Clarke. Caspar Clarke happened to be an assistant commissioner of Metropolitan Police. Not only that, the two men in the truck were typical Old Bills in disguise. Blowing their bleeding noses and looking hard at everything that passed, including the milkman.

The lights were on in the mews, the converted gaslamps that always made Gerber think of the horror films of his youth. They'd made them good then — women running out of the fog with their throats cut. He heard Chang's snuffling long before he pulled his door key out. He let himself in, grabbing a handful of yellowish fur in greeting. The chow's defense of the house was total, a hell of a lot better than some cocky minder who'd remember things that he shouldn't. He turned on the alabaster lamps in the sitting room and drew the curtains, showing himself deliberately at the window. Those slags outside must be working short-handed, jumping in and out of their van like trained seals. They'd probably be on the blower by now, telling Raven that he was back. It was nearly five years since this place had been turned over. In those days it was a habit for all those hard-nosed bastards in the Flying Squad to charge in flashing a search warrant. They'd be wiping their dirty feet on the Persian rugs, drinking his Scotch, looking up the air shafts and in cisterns. They'd make him open up the safe and take away whatever he had inside. The next thing was that he'd have to go to the Yard to reclaim it. The tenth time they'd laid this on him, he'd gone to the Council for Civil Liberties — right mugs, but people who understood what was happening. A couple of days later some chief superintendent had dropped by with a lot of yap about what the police could do if they really started trying. But the raids stopped. His informant at the Yard claimed that his file was still on the ACTIVE list. They pulled it from time to time, as if he was some boy-burglar. For a cop, his man at the Yard didn't seem to know too much about this Inspector Raven. What he looked like was some fag out of one of those Earl's Court pubs with all that yellow hair and the velvet suit. A college boy who fancied himself as a bloodhound, that's what they said. But it had been Raven who pulled Lame Willie Wolff off the plane with fifty-grand's worth of bent gear tucked away in his surgical boot. In other words, the geezer would bear watching.

He went upstairs, the dog padding after him. The fact that he lived in a house worth £70,000 no longer came as a surprise to him. He knew where he'd come from and how — a snottynose who should have been stitching mailbags in some nick, eating porridge with the rest of them. But he'd been too smart, too tough. He'd learned that to give is the same as to lose, that taking is winning. That's what life was all about, no matter what anyone else said. The safe was in his clothes closet, a white-fronted Chubb set deep into the wall. He dialed the right combination and lifted the envelope from the bottom shelf. He carried it to the narrow bed and sat down, the chow lying beside him. The passport and driving license were made out in the name of Philip Bloch. The passport was one of ten stolen in transit to a travel office. Murphy had bought the blank driving license from some broken-down major working for the G.L.C. They all had their price, the bastards, if only you could get to them — even this bleeding judge who lived up the mews.

He slipped the passport and driving license inside his jacket pocket. There was a monkey's worth in the crisp sheaf of Belgian francs — £500. That was something else he had learned, never to be caught short of readies. A quick fifty stuck in someone's fork solved a lot of problems. Not that he expected any problems, once Murphy and Benny had been attended to. Funny to think about it, really — a few more hours and he'd be on his way to Antwerp with what that ignorant slag Benny called "the monster." Emeralds, rubies and diamonds, the like of which those mugs over there had never seen before on offer at one time.

The chow sank its head on his knee. He tugged the under fur behind its ears.

"You got food, mate, and water. Take care of the gaff."

The dog rumbled in its throat. He pushed it away and turned off the bedside lamp. He could see the van from the window, still parked at the far end of the mews, a short distance from where he'd left his car. Patches of light from the neighboring houses lay across the cobblestones. He could just make out the figure of a man standing close against the wall, forty yards away. They must take him for a right charley, he thought, angered by the lack of respect. He pulled on a pair of sneakers and hung his shoes around his neck. There was a hatch in the ceiling above the landing outside his bedroom. He used a kind of boat hook to pull down a flight of collapsible steps, kicked the dog aside and climbed up into the loft pulling the aluminum steps after him. A faint glow came from the skylight let into the roof. He perched on the water tank, lifted the window and crawled out onto a duckboard fastened to the tiles. The angle of the roof hid him from anyone in the mews and he was too high to be seen from the back. He rolled sideways, body flattened, past a cluster of bricked-up chimneys and onto the next roof. There was no duckboard here to help his progress. He went more slowly, his rubber soles braced against the guttering. He negotiated five roofs in all, varied in slant and in width. An iron frieze marked the last house in the row. He held on to it tightly, swinging himself out and past and then down onto the wall, still out of sight of the mews. His feet thudded into soft earth. He picked himself up, changed his shoes, leaving the sneakers under a large flower-pot. Then he walked out through the side entrance to a house on Redclyffe Gardens.

He crossed Old Brompton Road, strolled down a garage ramp and rang a bell. An attendant came out of the office.

"The name's Bloch," said Gerber. "I called you about a car this morning." He tendered the phony license.

The man took it and consulted a book in the office. "That's right — an Anglia, wasn't it. If you want to come this way . . ."

He led Gerber to a small black Ford that was almost new.

He copied the particulars from the license as Gerber checked the fuel and lights.

"Right you are, sir. All I need now is thirty pounds deposit."

Gerber peeled off three bills. By the time he reached King's Road, he was certain that nobody was following him. He forked left and minutes later was crossing Battersea Bridge, the sweep of the Thames to the west. The *M. V. Sauerland* was lying in moorings, fifteen miles downstream. By now she'd have cleared customs, awaiting the turn of the tide and her pilot. The wind had freshened considerably, and his stomach bucked at the thought of the trip from shore to ship. The last time he'd made it, he'd sat hunched in the dinghy, vomiting over the side, water soaking into his clothes. But the route was a safe one and guaranteed, three thousand D-marks for a landing with no questions asked. He turned right, skirting the south edge of Battersea Park. Police photographs had been circulating in London since the previous morning, blown-up colored prints of the stolen monstrance. The dealers in the café near the Diamond Bourse had been passing one around, speculating on the fate of the stolen jewels. He'd held the picture in his hands, gloating over the glory of hundreds of jewels pushed into pure shimmering gold. The crappy way the stones were set, some of them literally hammered in would make the monstrance difficult to break up. But old man Davidoff had the right tools and had spent his life at the game. He was there waiting and prepared to work through the night. Gerber had no intention of leaving him either, not till the last gem had been pried loose, sorted and weighed.

He parked the Anglia and walked back toward the mansions, reading every sound and shadow as far as the entrance. He stayed for a while in the darkened hallway then ran up the stairs and tapped softly on the door. It opened to the coded signal and he slipped inside, taking off his hat and coat. There was a tray on the floor by the closed bedroom door. The cups had been used but the plates of sandwiches were untouched. Benny gestured with the gun he was holding.

"They've gone on hunger strike, the pair of them, since this morning."

Gerber stepped sideways smartly. "How many more times I got to tell you never to point that fucking thing at me. Give it to me!" He dropped the gun in his jacket pocket. "Where's Murphy?"

Benny opened his arms wide. "I done what you said."

Gerber frowned, glancing across at the bedroom door. "On your own or did you bring someone else in? I don't want no lies!"

Benny's eyes were evasive. "Don't you trust me, Sam? I done it on my own. If they find him, they won't bleeding well recognize him. Just like you said."

Gerber's arm snaked out, his hand catching the smaller man's knitted jacket and driving him up against the wall.

"Like *I* said, you rat-bastard! I don't know what you're talking about." He turned his wrist, increasing the pressure on Benny's throat. Then he opened his fingers. "Say it, Benny," he insisted.

Benny's hand flew to his throat. He choked out the denial desperately. "You don't know nothing, Sam. For crissakes, I'm your friend."

Gerber shoved him away contemptuously. "Wrong, Benny. When you've done one, you're nobody's friend. How'd you get him out of here?"

Benny's fingers were massaging his throat frantically. "About five this morning. He thought we were meeting you outside. I gave him a little whack in the car. He was still out when I done the rest. I put him in that crusher we saw."

"*You* saw," corrected Gerber. The crusher was a half mile away on a wharf building site. It started up at eight every morning, feeding granite into the cement at the bottom of a new pier support. "You've been drinking, haven't you?" he accused. He hadn't made up his mind yet what to do with Benny. He needed him for a few more hours at least.

Benny grinned, measuring off an inch or so with thumb and forefinger. "I was nervous, Sam. It was one of those things. I dunno. I was just bleeding nervous," he repeated.

Gerber looked at the wafer-thin watch on his wrist. "The deal's on. We're going to dump this pair in the park then you take me to Tilbury. You'll have to drive the car back. Got it?"

"Got it," said Benny. His face had taken on the look of a trapped animal that has seen the chance of escape.

"Open the door," ordered Gerber.

Benny crossed the room and unlocked it. The two women were huddled together, sitting on one of the beds, blankets wrapped around their legs. Murphy had done a good job boarding up the windows. The screws holding the planks were driven deep into the framework. Gerber lowered himself down on the free bed.

"I've got some good news for you. You're going home."

The girl moved quickly, taking Mrs. Zaleska's hand in hers. She sat there, kneading the older woman's flesh with her fingers.

"Well come on!" urged Gerber. "Aren't you going to say something?"

Mrs. Zaleska looked as if she hadn't heard. The girl stared back at him, hollow-eyed. He spread his legs comfortably.

"Suit yourselves. So if you don't want to talk, listen! It's not me the police are looking for remember — it's your husbands. If there's any trouble at all, that pair of slags won't see daylight for the next fifteen years. Behave yourselves and everyone's happy. It's up to you."

Mrs. Zaleska continued to look at him blankly. It was the girl who finally answered.

"We'll do whatever you say, of course. We never had a chance to do anything else, did we?"

Gerber shoved himself up from the bed, smiling. "That's more like it, sweetheart. Now then, we've still got plenty of time, you might as well make yourselves pretty."

He could hear them from the front room, talking to one another, their voices low. Benny was sitting near the half-closed door, fiddling around with his nails. He'd have to think hard about Benny — real, real hard.

Chapter Ten

RAVEN bumped the MG over two sidewalks, unlocked a padlocked gate with one of his false keys and parked in the musical director's slot. The Albert Hall wasn't in use that night. The railed-off enclosure was unlit and deserted and he needed somewhere to sit — to lick his wounds and compose his letter of resignation.

Detective-Inspector Raven presents his compliments to the Commissioner of Metropolitan Police and informs him that he can stuff his job . . .

Dear Commissioner: There has been a growing feeling in my mind . . .

I resign. *Raven* (*Detective-Inspector*).

Something on the order of the last would be the most satisfactory. Something that would be remembered as the shortest resignation in the history of the force. However it was worded, he ought to have it in the mail before midnight. He'd no intention of turning up at the commissioner's meeting. He could see Drake's face when he heard the news. The Dante Gallery case would be officially closed, the failure of the investigation blamed on an incompetent and undisciplined cop who'd resigned rather than face just criticism. It was strange to think that the few hours of active duty remaining could well be the most disastrous in the whole of his career. Instead of going out with two fingers up and a hero's farewell he'd be recalled as the man who'd tried playing Inspector Javert once too often and been finally suckered. The truth was that since Zaleski's release on bail nothing had gone right. He'd started the day with five suspects. Five suspects under observation by a squad of trained men. Now each and every one of them had vanished like stage demons. Four of them, anyway. No one knew for certain where Gerber was, in his house or out of it.

He lit one of his yellow-papered cigarettes, staring out beyond the lights of the passing cars. The wedding-cake edifice reared against the night sky, a queen's vulgar tribute to her pious bore of a consort. Behind it lay the park. He'd patrolled it both in sunlight and in moonlight as a rookie cop all those years ago. He still remembered the evil engendered once night had fallen. The lonely, the predators, the troubled in spirit who sought self-destruction. He'd once helped an Irish sergeant cut down a boy hanging dead by the neck from an ornamental cherry tree in full blossom, at six o'clock of a sunny June morning. He recalled every detail, the boy's odd socks — one blue, one brown — the note in his pocket, started but never finished, the collection of pawn tickets. Even then he'd thought that the chase of the ignoble was unworthy and somehow poisonous. He'd used the phrase and thought in a thesis written at police college and found himself saddled with an extra period of fatigues.

He flicked the cigarette butt, watching the glow spiral through the open window. The phone bleeped under the dash. He'd had it switched off for the last half-hour. The girl at the telecommunication center was crisply correct. Obviously she'd just come on duty.

"Inspector Raven? I have Sergeant Hobbs on the line for you."

Hobbs came on. "They said you were off the air, sir. I've been trying to contact you. A man called at eighteen hours forty-two and asked for you personally. He wants you to meet him at twenty hours thirty tonight in the foyer of the Royal Court Theater. That's Sloane Square, sir."

"I know where the Royal Court is." Raven jammed his long legs against the floorboards, but his seat was as far back as it would go. "Did he leave a name, this man?"

"Yes, sir, he did. As a matter of fact, he spelled it. Z-A-L-E-S-K-I."

Raven's batteries suddenly took on a new charge. "Listen, Bill. How many people know about this besides you and me?"

"Just the girl on the switchboard, if she's listening. Otherwise nobody, sir. He came straight through on the extension. Is there anything you want me to do?"

"Yes," said Raven. "Vanish. Get the hell out of that building before anyone starts asking you questions and keep this under your hat, Bill."

"Understood," said Hobbs. "I'm on my way."

Raven drew a deep breath and thumbed another cigarette out of the pack. He sat for a moment, listening to the torn bill flapping on the nearby board. Then he picked up the phone again. He located Gifford three miles away at the west end of Fulham Road.

"What have you got?" he demanded.

The sergeant's voice sounded dispirited. "Not much, sir, I'm afraid. The lights are still on in Gerber's place, but there's no way of telling if he's in there. We've definitely lost the others."

Raven flicked away the curling ash. "And that's it — there's nothing else?"

Gifford hesitated. "You're not going to like this, sir. But Carter and Goss, they're the men I've got on Gerber, reported that Zaleski went to Gerber's place this afternoon. Gerber was definitely out. Zaleski went in with a key and came out again a quarter-hour later. He wasn't carrying anything either time."

Raven grimaced. "You mean they both sat on their asses, watching our number-one suspect walk away. No one had the fucking sense to get on his tail again? Is that what you're telling me, Sergeant?"

Gifford cleared his throat. "My instructions to them were to stay with Gerber, sir. I'm ready to take full responsibility. By the time they got me on the phone he'd gone."

"Well, I'm meeting him at half-past eight," Raven said without further explanation. "I want you to pull in all your men and vehicles and assemble them in the Sloane Square area. Tell them to split up and try to act as if they really belonged on the Serious Crimes Squad. I'll be in constant touch."

He called the telecom center and asked for the frequency he was using to have priority clearance. Thought of the coming meeting made him nervous. He felt like a man about to play poker for high stakes with everyone at the table prepared to cheat. The fact that Zaleski wanted to see him sounded like a deal. Yet how *could* there be a deal with Gerber in on the caper. And whatever the proposition, the monstrance would have to come back. That much was crystal clear. It was eight twenty-five when he walked around the corner on to Sloane

Square. He left the MG behind the Church of Christ Scientist. They could burn the car, bomb it, tow it away — anything they liked as long as they left him somewhere near a phone booth. He was nearing the end of the road and suddenly it no longer mattered about the law and Zaleski. His real battle was and always had been with Drake and people like him. To fight and come out the winner meant more than the abstract virtues people paid lip service to.

The lobby of the Royal Court Theater was empty. It was an early show and the ticket office was already closed. Raven waited at the top of the steps. Five minutes passed then ten. A doorman carrying in a QUEUE HERE sign glanced at him curiously. The clock in the vestibule had the same time as Raven's watch, twenty minutes before nine. He buttoned the blue gaberdine, looking across at the lights around the square. They burned with the special brilliance of a winter night, pinpointing the passage of a piece of paper blown by the cold wind roaring down Sloane Street. There was no sign of Zaleski. Raven's thin face betrayed none of his frustration and uncertainty. Another ten minutes, he told himself. The feeling was growing that he'd been hoaxed. By whom it didn't matter — the Poles, Gerber or even Drake himself. Whoever was responsible was out there in the darkness under the trees, laughing at him.

And then he saw Zaleski over by the taxi stand. The Pole moved into the light of a streetlamp, deliberately facing the entrance to the theater. Raven hurried down the steps. By the time he had threaded his way through the traffic, Zaleski was back in the shadow. The two men moved to one of the benches.

"You wanted to see me," said Raven. "I'm here."

Zaleski was wearing a duffelcoat and beret. A trick of light, the way he carried his head and shoulders, gave him the appearance of a man twenty years younger. He was smoking a cigarette through a six-inch holder, his manner supremely confident.

"So are meeting and talking as man to man. Is pity we have not done before. You still think I robbed gallery, Inspector?"

Raven shifted his bony shoulders. "Let's not spoil things by insulting one another's intelligence. What *kind* of a rogue you are I'm not quite sure, but you're certainly a rogue."

Zaleski lifted his nose like a boyar scenting a serf. Something about the Pole's indomitable stand reminded Raven of a headstone in the village where he was born. The inscription had been over an anonymous grave.

A FINE NATURAL BLACKGUARD
WHO GAVE GREATER JUSTICE THAN EVER HE GOT

The critical part of his brain revived the words and wondered how far they were applicable to the man sitting beside him.

Zaleski waved a black-gloved hand. "For British people, all Poles are rogues."

"That's balls," said Raven. "My sister happens to be married to a Pole. He grew up in an English orphanage. He lectures in economics, writes poetry and loves his family. I never heard him say a single word about the treatment you people have had in this country."

Zaleski answered with the determined courtesy of someone giving a stranger the benefit of the doubt.

"Is another generation. No traditions. No memories. Different beliefs."

The double-decker buses swayed past top-heavily, the passengers like cutouts pasted against the windows. The constant rush of vehicles made an island of the center of the square. Pedestrians used it briefly and without even a glance for the two men huddled on the bench.

"Beliefs," repeated Raven. "And what the hell do *you* believe in, Zaleski?"

It wasn't the sort of question that went with a police investigation of a robbery. But then Zaleski wasn't an ordinary thief. The Pole's reply came too quickly to be anything but genuine.

"Honor, Inspector-Detective. Honor and friendship. These things I believe in."

Raven nodded, feeling that an old rogue-lion had stepped slap-bang into his sights, toothless and defiant, with a lifetime of subterfuge behind him. Raven took his finger off the trigger deliberately, suddenly understanding. He spoke impulsively.

"I've got a feeling that you're going to try the biggest con of your life on me. Before you do, there's something I'd like you to know. I won't *be* a cop this time tomorrow. I'm retiring."

Zaleski's head turned slowly, the glow from his cigarette showing his twitching cheek.

"And now — tonight? Another detective is in charge of case?"

It was cold and Raven shivered. "No. I'm still on your trail. Tomorrow it'll be someone else. There's a good chance that one way or another they'll nail you."

"Not nail," said Zaleski, shaking his head decisively. "Is impossible. Is no evidence. Poles are not stealing monstrance, Inspector. Like newspapers are saying, *professional* criminals are doing job."

Raven's fingers dug deep into the pocket of his coat. He'd carried the badge with the bison's head for three days now like a talisman. He had a sudden urge to shove it into Zaleski's palm and walk away.

"Look," he said patiently. "I know what happened up in that monastery all those years ago. I can even understand how you and your friends feel about the way you've been treated. But I'm a cop until midnight, Zaleski. I want to stop you people making fools of yourselves."

Zaleski looked unimpressed. "You came to my house and arrested me for something I did not do. You know this?"

"I know it," Raven admitted, putting his collar up.

Zaleski spread his hands. "So is frame-up."

"It's freezing cold," said Raven. "Let's get the hell out of it. My car's across the street. We can talk better there."

The clock hanging outside the Royal Court Hotel said ten minutes of nine. The MG was still behind the church and unvandalized. Raven took this as an omen. The Pole climbed into the spare seat, his pebble eyes fastening on the radio-phone under the dash. Raven lifted it off its rest.

"You wanted to talk. Well, here we are, the two of us. No one's ever going to know what was said."

Zaleski glanced at Raven shrewdly. "You want justice. OK, or not?"

Raven shrugged. "I do one job. The judge does another. Call it what you want."

The answer seemed to satisfy Zaleski. "I want to make proposition. A good one for you. You give me help. I give you back monstrance."

"I thought you didn't know anything about it," said Raven. "But we'll let that go. The important thing is does your friend know you're here?"

"Which friend?" parried Zaleski.

"Gerber. Any deal that involves him is out."

"You are wrong, Inspector-Detective." Zaleski blew his nose into a large square of silk then wiped the corners of his mouth carefully.

"I'm *not* wrong," Raven retorted. "I don't know how you came to be mixed up with a bastard like that, but let me tell you a story about him. A true story. Did you ever hear of the City Bank robbery? It happened last year. A hundred-thousand-pounds' worth of jewelry was stolen and a security guard had both eyes shot out."

Zaleski's fingers found the bridge of his nose. "I remember."

Raven's lighter flared. He passed it to Zaleski along with the pack of Gitanes.

"Gerber set the job up. He knew the place from the inside. Friends of his used the safe-deposit boxes — Hatton Garden jewel dealers. He was supposed to fence the proceeds. Ten minutes after that guard died — the loot was already in Gerber's hands — the Yard had an anonymous tip about three men, giving the number of the car they were driving. Forensics did the rest. It was all there, flash burns from the gun they used, dust from the bank, threads from their clothing were found under the guards' fingernails. They all got life. The point is, it was your friend Gerber who turned them in."

Zaleski spoke with his head down, blowing a thin stream of smoke at the floor.

"This man is no friend, Mr. Raven. Is enemy. If you agree I give you Gerber *and* the monstrance."

Raven's long, thin jaw set. His face revealed none of his inner excitement.

"You mean you can arrange things so that I can grab Gerber with the monstrance in his possession?"

Zaleski wiped his mouth again as if tasting something bitter. "I can do more. You want to know why — I tell you. This man took my wife prisoner. Fraser's girl, too."

Facts slotted into Raven's brain like program cards into a computer. "Then Fraser *was* part of it!"

Zaleski's head moved from side to side. "Is difficult to explain."

Raven pushed the phone back on the rest. The Pole only grinned. "Why didn't you come to me sooner," demanded Raven. "These women are in very real danger. Gerber doesn't bluff."

"Is no danger," Zaleski said calmly. "Not any more. You see, Gerber and I do business together. He gives me my wife and Ingrid. I give him monstrance. Is simple."

Raven leaned forward, coughing the salt burn of tobacco from his lungs. *"Christ!"* he complained, wiping the wet from his eyes. "There's something I have to know, Zaleski. Why were you in Gerber's house this afternoon?"

A door opened in a nearby house, shafting light into the car. A look of savagery had replaced the Pole's irony. The door shut and the car was in darkness again.

"The keys to Dante Gallery are in mink coat hanging in bedroom. Gerber doesn't know."

Raven whistled softly. He put them both to the test, himself as much as Zaleski.

"What you're doing, of course, is asking me to compound a felony."

"Why not?" Zaleski said coolly. "You arrested me falsely — for something I am not doing."

Raven drew his knees up, hugging them with his arms and chin. "And you still trust me?"

Zaleski's stocky shoulders rose and fell. "In Polish we say 'good enemies better than bad friends.'"

Raven's gaunt face creaked into a smile. "I think I'm going to remember you for the rest of my life. How much time have we got?"

Zaleski glanced at the clock on the dash. "Fifty-five minutes. You gamble with me or not, Inspector?"

There was something courtly in the way he put it, as if the issue was at least between gentlemen.

"I'll gamble with you," Raven said deliberately.

Zaleski removed the glove from his right hand. His grip was warm, brief and firm.

"Gerber is big catch, Mr. Raven. I know this. Perhaps you will change your mind about not being policeman any longer."

The question bobbed like a balloon in Raven's brain. He punctured it, ending all further doubt.

"No chance. No matter what happens, there's no chance."

"I am glad," said Zaleski. "Then you will come to Wielkapolska later tonight. Any time. You will meet my wife, my friends. And perhaps you will understand more. Now, Gerber — I tell you what you must do."

Raven listened with growing respect. You took an abstract — a moral virtue called justice — and administered it through people like Drake and himself. You put a judge up on a bench, a man whose interior torture impelled him to the role of defender of morals and who hanged himself in a noose made of women's underwear. Zaleski's values were more primitive, but at least he salvaged his honor.

"We'll do it the way you say," Raven agreed finally. "No

move will be made till we're sure that the women are safe. You'd better go now."

Zaleski pulled back the catch on his door. "Remember, good enemies always better than bad friends." He smiled, turned and strutted away without looking back.

Raven picked up the phone. Gifford's team was riding in three vehicles, circling the area. He gave his instructions quickly, alive to the excitement in Gifford's voice.

"After all these years," the sergeant crooned. "To think that bastard's finally come unstuck! There'll be some cheering over this one, sir."

"Not if you don't keep your mouth shut," Raven warned. "We've been had. It's as simple as that. Those Poles were no more than errand boys, and we're going to forget about them. Services rendered. There's no evidence against them anyway. Oh, and Sergeant . . ."

"Yes, sir?"

"Your men made a mistake this afternoon. That couldn't have been Zaleski they saw. It must have been someone else. Incidentally, the keys to the Dante Gallery are in Gerber's house, and you and I are going to find them."

The pause lasted for thirty seconds then Gifford's voice was noncommittal. "I thought they were wrong at the time, sir. As you say, it must have been somebody else."

Raven clicked the phone down. There was no need for Gifford to have said any more. Expediency had a way of replacing justice, and the sergeant was well aware of it.

Chapter Eleven

THE LIMOUSINE THAT Czarniecki had borrowed was a Rolls usually engaged on the airport run. It had walnut paneling, dark-red leather upholstery, a drink cupboard with cut glass and a bearskin lap robe. The giant Pole was wearing a chauffeur's cap on his bald head. Sobinski lolled by his side, silver-haired and watchful, a man of distinction in spite of his missing arm and cheap, ill-fitting clothes. Fraser and Zaleski were on the back seat. The Canadian hadn't opened his mouth since they had climbed into the Rolls — Zaleski couldn't make up his mind why. The Pole was still thinking about Raven, whistling softly as he did so and tapping out the rhythm with his fingers. Policemen were made of the same stuff as noncommissioned officers — obedient, zealous in authority and possessed of the imaginations of slaughterhouse attendants. Raven was apart in everything. The way he dressed, the raincoat with dashing brass accouterments, his velvet suit and elegant shoes, his long yellow hair. Zaleski recalled similar faces, thin, mobile and sensitive. There had been one at school, a Jesuit priest. There'd been a French colonel he had met in the desert — others he could no longer identify. But he remembered the same quality in each — an integrity that gave their word the right to be believed.

He leaned forward and touched Czarniecki's shoulder. The Rolls floated to the curb. They were in back of a school. Lights across the deserted playground showed that night classes were being held. Zaleski walked around and into the cul-de-sac. Englishmen claimed that their homes were their castles. The image was just. The short street was full of tiny castles each with its drawbridge up. Beyond the moats, children played safely and happily while women dreamed as Hanya once must have dreamed. He passed in front of the undrawn curtains, excluded from the scene within as his countrymen were excluded, pariahs. He was suddenly proud to be Polish. He had promised Bogdan and Stanislas a miracle, and he had failed. Yet his failure was accepted without bitterness. The churchyard gate was shut. He lifted the latch and slipped inside, pursued by the plummy voice of a television announcer coming from the house across the street. The overhead window lifted easily under the pressure of his gloved fingers. The unfastened catch had gone unnoticed by verger or cleaner. He dropped into the musty odor of stale incense. The red lamp was burning steadily in front of the altar, lighting the plaster figures with hands raised in benediction. He threw a leg over the iron frieze surrounding the tomb and yanked open the sanctuary door. The weight of the monstrance sent him toppling sideways as he landed in the churchyard outside. There was nobody to notice him hurrying back to the Rolls. Fraser's silence seemed to have infected the other two. No one spoke as Zaleski hefted the canvas bag onto the floor. The two Poles stared down over the front seat as the flame of Zaleski's lighter caught the scintillations of a thousand jewels. He snapped his lighter shut, extinguishing the dream. The gray days would continue and they would somehow survive. A single tear rolled down the side of his nose, unchecked. He removed his glove and wiped his nose with the back of his hand. Czarniecki's breath reeked of garlic sausage.

"The angels were against us," he said in Polish.

Sobinski's seldom-used smile mocked both success and failure. "Bogdan is right. It is the immorality of the lives we lead that surely offends them."

Zaleski zipped up the bag. There was nothing left to be said among the three of them. As the years passed, they would no doubt remember the incident in a different way. He twisted sideways toward Fraser, in a hurry to explain.

"You see — for Poles is *never* defeat!" Faith gave his statement the ring of sincerity.

Fraser looked at each man in turn then nodded as if he had just extracted a long-withheld secret.

"You guys were born a couple of hundred years too late."

"God is taking long holiday," smiled Sobinski. It was the second or third time Zaleski had ever heard him speak in English and the words sounded strange in his mouth.

Zaleski moved uncomfortably. Mention of God reminded him of the desecrated church, and he tried to recall his virtues. The self-analysis did nothing for his peace of mind. Ah well, he thought, Hanya would have to intercede for him.

It was now twenty minutes of ten. The Rolls glided to a halt on the carriage way leading to the Serpentine. The one bridge across the mile-long lake was a couple of hundred yards away. It was a simple structure that carried the main stream of traffic from Knightsbridge to Bayswater. The restaurant overlooking the water was a haven of light and warmth in the cold night. The headlamps of the cars in front crisscrossed, occasionally displaying the functional ugliness of the Armory across the bridge. Opposite the Armory was a space the size of a tennis court, bounded by the carriage way, trees and water. There was only one way on or off for a car, though a man on foot could reach it from the trees or along the path leading from the boathouse. Traffic going north or south approached the small car park at a right angle. There was no possible reason to stop there at ten o'clock on a January night. The odd bluster of wind had blown water across the tarmac, and it lay desolate in the lights of the passing cars.

Beyond the lake, dark acres of grass and woodland stretched in three directions. Zaleski leaned forward, pointing over Czarniecki's shoulder and speaking to Fraser.

"You see, is nobody. Nobody at all. So you go there now and wait for Gerber. OK?"

The two Poles climbed into the back. Fraser took the wheel, trying the controls nervously. Zaleski lifted the heavy canvas bag and threw it onto the seat beside the Canadian.

"OK?" he repeated.

Fraser wiped his forehead. The back of his hand showed sweat. "For chrissakes stop saying OK? How many more times do you want to hear it! I concentrate on Hanya and Ingrid. No matter what else is going on, the moment they're in the car I *move*."

Zaleski nodded unruffled. "And driving to Wielkapolska and waiting there, Kirk. So long and good luck."

He shut the door of the Rolls, holding the battered leather case that Sobinski had provided. The German navy binoculars it held were designed for submarine work. Specially ground lens made night vision almost as clear as day. The three Poles stood in the shadow of a tree, watching the taillights of the

Rolls across the bridge. Czarniecki shoved his chauffeur's cap and scratched his bald scalp. He grunted and spoke in Polish.

"A man without honor would continue to drive. He would drive on out of the park and into a world where the values would be false, the champagne properly iced and the women beautiful."

Zaleski saw the taillights leave the stream of traffic, glow for a moment by the edge of the water and then go out. Wind shivered the branches over their heads. He looked at his friends with sudden compassion. What right had he to wear cashmere when they went so shabbily. Somehow he must find the means to put silk shirts on their backs — to provide a weekend for the three of them in Paris. Thoughts came to him, ways of publicizing the restaurant. He saw a long room with mirrors reflecting the glittering chandeliers, violins, perhaps — the spirit of Old Poland. He wiped away the second tear of the evening, this time surreptitiously.

"Now," he said, clapping his gloved hands together. "Let us take up our positions."

Chapter Twelve

THE SECOND STORY of the old-fashioned apartment building had been without a lamp ever since Gerber had appeared on the scene. As soon as the janitor creaked up from below with a replacement, Gerber had it removed. Tenants living on the floor had learned to negotiate the shadows, relying on the light from the staircase. Occasionally they wrote letters to the building manager that remained unanswered. None of them was aware that the door of 2B had just been opened and closed on a party of three people. The two women went first; Ingrid with her trailing skirt and long hair like a moth against the pale wall, Mrs. Zaleska more slowly, one hand gripping the banister tightly. Benny came close behind, hustling them through the hallway, down the steps and into the waiting car. The headlamps flared briefly, picking out the sweep of railings circling Battersea Park.

Gerber was standing in the entrance to a neighboring block. He scanned the street both ways, looking for the slightest sign of danger. Then he walked down the steps, lifting his homburg to an imaginary host and hurrying fifty yards to the parked Rover. He'd left the rented Ford a quarter mile away. He unfastened the door on the driver's side, glancing across at the woman sitting next to Benny. Mrs. Zaleska turned her head slowly. The lipstick and powder she had used hid the suffering on her soft-fleshed face. The look of contempt in her dark eyes was something she could do nothing about. Gerber felt the hot flush rising above his collar.

"Up yours, too, Auntie," he said deliberately. Mrs. Zaleska just looked.

Benny turned his wrist. He tapped the face of his watch with a brown-stained forefinger. His voice cracked nervously.

"Nine-twenty. I'd better get going. There's no change, is there, Sam? Nothing else you want to tell me?"

Gerber shook his head, dragging his eyes away from Mrs. Zaleska. An old bag like that, he wouldn't have wash his balls. Pity he didn't have time to teach her a lesson.

"You know what to do," he said. "Keep driving around in the park. Don't show before ten. The moment you're shot of this pair, shoot out through Lancaster Gate and dwell by the underground station. I'll be right on your tail." He closed the door quietly and stood by the railings, following the Rover till it turned the corner.

He walked back to the rented Ford and pulled the letter from the glove compartment. He'd assembled it from a couple of newspapers, using a pair of scissors. The letters were pasted onto a piece of hotel stationery, the envelope addressed to the Commissioner of Police, Scotland Yard.

JuNior MuRPhy iS iN cEMent undER nEw peeR AT tireLS WArf BumenSEY BeNNY the BOokeppER doNE him oVer the Dante GaLLURy Job.

He sealed the envelope thoughtfully. The misspelled words gave the message the right touch of kosher. It was the sort of brief that the law loved. The anonymous tip wasn't as final as a shot in the head, but it would keep that slag Benny busy for a few years. He'd wait for a bit outside the underground station, watching the cars coming out of the park. Then he'd go home and start scheming. He wouldn't panic till Old Bill arrived and then he'd cough his guts. But by that time Lucky Sam would be in Antwerp, two days later in Mexico. He wouldn't sell a fucking stick of what he had in England — why should he? Nagel could take care of old Chang. Gerber grinned, thinking of the dapper lawyer lumbered with a dog who'd chew his arm off for a look. He'd miss old Chang. But he'd be back, if not this year then next. As soon as the word came that he was sweet. If the law brought a case about the monstrance, good luck to them. There wasn't one piece of real bleeding evidence against him. Abduction he knew nothing about. Nothing at all. He'd arrange for the frighteners to be put on those two women, and it would be no more than his word against Benny's. Lucky Sam, he thought. Falls in the shit and comes up smelling like a rose.

He stopped the Ford on the corner and dropped the letter in the mailbox. Ten minutes later he was in the car park adjoining the lakeside restaurant. He cut his motor, leaving the car keys in the dash. The attendant was twenty yards away with his back turned. Gerber unfastened the door on the far side and ran down the slope, away from the lights and toward the lake. The bridge arched gently away from the sodden turf. He slithered down to the edge of the water and groped along the stonework. The dinghy he had rented earlier was in the darkness under the bridge, secured by a rope attached to an iron hoop he'd sunk in the grass. People rented boats, ran them aground, capsized them and walked away without bothering to report to the boathouse. The men there made their rounds in the morning, collecting any craft that were missing.

He retraced his steps, bending low in front of the lighted facade of the restaurant then around to the back of the premises. Figures floated behind the steamed windows of the kitchen like fish in a bowl. Pale filtered light illuminated the clinkered yard outside. Opposite a row of garbage cans were some motorcycles. He trod carefully, keeping close to the wall as he made his way toward the machines. The Yamaha at the end had a large wooden box strapped to its carrier. Gerber stopped dead as the door opened. The sound of a kitchen going at full blast blared out across the yard. A man wearing a tall chef's cap and a napkin around his neck peered up at the sky, shrugged and shut the door again. Gerber unfroze, sure of himself in every gesture. He unlocked the padlock fastening the wooden box. Inside was a leather helmet, a pair of goggles and a dirty raincoat. He carried them out of the light and transferred the contents of his pockets to the raincoat. False passport, money, the key to the Yamaha. He tore the lining out of his homburg. There was no tailor's label in his overcoat. He stuffed hat, lining and coat deep down in three different garbage cans. The small revolver he kept. With this kind of money at stake, a man had to take chances. He locked up the box again. He knew the measurements by heart. There was plenty of room for what he was going to put there.

He used wet soil to scuff his shoes and dirty the bottoms of his trousers. A mug wouldn't have remembered details like that, he thought, sliding back down the slope. No more than the cloths tied on the oars to stop the splashing. A Kensington clock banged out a quarter-to-ten as he pulled the dinghy across the lake, hugging the stonework of the bridge and heading for the empty car park opposite.

Chapter Thirteen

ZALESKI'S CHOICE OF position was instinctive, the choice of a cavalryman as opposed to a footslogger. He was standing on the top of a wooded knoll that dominated the lake. The slope was dotted with oak trees planted by the Stuarts, old bare trees smelling of damp and vinegar and trailing last year's nests from their branches. The darkness behind Zaleski stretched unbroken as far as the northern perimeter of the park. The wind had blown water across the hardtop below. The headlamps of the passing cars shone briefly on the glistening surface as the drivers made their right-angled turn from the bridge.

A branch groaned above Zaleski's head. He shifted the cumbersome flare pistol from his left hand to his right. The short, stubby weapons were used at sea to send up distress signals. The miniature rockets were capable of a high trajectory and the idea was Zaleski's. The Poles had employed flare pistols in the desert war of nerves. Now, once he pulled the trigger, Raven would send his men into action. Sobinski was behind a tree somewhere off to the left, Czarniecki to the right. Zaleski could sense the presence of the police without actually seeing them. The night glasses had caught a flash of movement a few minutes before, the powerful lens dragging the image closer till he could distinguish a car without lights parked close to the Armory.

From where he stood, the restaurant could have been the saloon deck of some ship at sea, the passengers sealed behind plate glass, the broken image below reflected on the surface of the windswept lake. He shifted the binoculars again, detecting a slight change of pattern. Something was moving immediately beneath the cars crossing the bridge. He probed the darkness between the spans. The movement was that of a dinghy close to the stonework. He could see the faint splash as the oars broke the surface of the water. The rower was pulling the boat sideways across the current, staying well under the bridge. Zaleski followed the dinghy's progress till it finally disappeared at the end of the bridge. A couple of minutes later, a man slipped out, standing close to the stonework of the pier as he scanned the wet, deserted stretch of hardtop. It was Gerber, all right, wearing some kind of leather helmet and motoring goggles. He put his head down and ran for the trees at the bottom of the slope facing him. Zaleski strained his eyes, but there was no trace of movement below, nothing to indicate Gerber's position. Zaleski shivered with excitement. He'd been sure of some kind of treachery and his hunch was vindicated. He laid the binoculars at the foot of the tree, leaving his hands free. A faint cough came from his left and he shut his eyes. *Sobinski.* If the others hadn't seen Gerber's arrival there was no way now of warning them. The soft, bleating cough sounded again. He could only hope that Gerber would mistake it for a sheep. *What happened to the accursed sheep at night!*

Zaleski inflated his chest, the east wind stiffening the hairs in his nostrils. There was little chance of some stranger wandering into the action. The nighttime park hustlers and prowlers confined themselves to the Marble Arch and Park Lane areas.

At this end, there was nothing but the steady swish of the north-south traffic with occasional stops at the restaurant. He picked up the binoculars as a car halted at the near end of the bridge, indicating a right turn. Passing headlamps spotlit the driver's face for a second, and Zaleski breathed easier. The Rolls coasted down the slope to the parking place then the lights went out. Zaleski checked his watch. Seven minutes to go.

He shivered again, this time it was the wind, slicing through the oak trees from the east. The humiliation of his arrest and imprisonment were forgotten. He saw himself now as commander of a rescue force without whose help the police were lost. His ears caught the chime of a clock. He counted the strokes, his eyes fixed on the entrance to the parking space. A car pulled off the carriage way, came down the slope and stopped twenty yards from the Rolls. The driver cut his lights. It was difficult to see without the field glasses, but Zaleski's ears helped his eyes. He heard the sound of a car door, footsteps crossing the tarmac. He recognized his wife's back as Fraser helped her into the Rolls. The figure at her side turned, the man moving awkwardly under the weight he was carrying. The car door banged a second time. Fraser's girl scuttled into the light, protecting her head with an arm as if in fear of a blow.

The Rolls drove off immediately, pulling back onto the carriage way. The other car was still stationary. Zaleski lowered the flare pistol. He could just make out the shape of the bag on the seat next to the driver, but there was no sign of Gerber. The parking lights came on and Gerber stepped from the shadow, approaching the car from the off side. He opened the door, leaned in and came out holding the bag. Tires hissed as the driver trod hard on the gas pedal. The car skidded up the slope, leaving Gerber standing with the canvas bag at his feet. Zaleski lifted the flare pistol, his mouth dry, watching the helmeted figure carry the bag toward the darkness at the end of the bridge. Zaleski's arm was straight, the barrel of the gun pointing up and away from the trees. He pulled the trigger firmly. Nothing happened. He tried again, using both hands, but the mechanism seemed to be locked. Gerber was already hidden behind the stonework.

Zaleski charged down through the trees, arms flailing in an attempt to hold his balance. He thudded across the parking space, up the incline and onto the sidewalk that crossed the bridge. Cars hurtled by, the occupants oblivious to the stocky man running beside them. Zaleski's breathing had become a rattling wheeze. Flagging leg muscles pumped him forward painfully. He turned left at the end of the bridge in time to see the empty dinghy drifting away on the current. There was no sign of Sobinski or Czarniecki. No sign of anyone. He slowed to a trot, conscious that he'd lost his beret somewhere. A ring of cars was parked outside the restaurant. Gerber had to be out there, making his way between the lake and the buildings. An attendant loomed up, barring Zaleski's way with outstretched arms. His eyes fastened on the pistol.

"What's coming off here? What are you supposed . . ."

"Police," gasped Zaleski.

The attendant aimed a shrewd kick at the Pole's testicles. Zaleski stepped sideways chopping down hard with the pistol at the man's lifted leg. He dropped like a shot bird, groaning. Zaleski rushed through a group of diners leaving their car. A woman shrieked. He vaulted a low brick parapet onto wet, slippery grass. The restaurant windows were overhead, animated faces inside conversed without sound. Zaleski followed the line of the parapet to the end of the building and turned back into comparative darkness. The weight of the monstrance must be slowing Gerber. Zaleski's nose told him that his quarry was not far away. Gerber would have some form of transport. He remembered the helmet and goggles. *A motorcycle, of course.* Zaleski was in back of the kitchens now, creeping along an asphalt path toward a nimbus of light. Feet crunched across crushed cinders. He flattened himself against the wall, feeling his way to the corner. His view widened as he moved forward. Garbage cans were lined up on the left side of the kitchen yard. On the far side of the steamed windows were some propped motorcycles. Gerber was straddling a Yamaha. The bag was missing, but there was a large box attached to the carrier. Gerber's weight bore down on the kick start. Zaleski slipped out from cover, still holding the useless flare pistol. The staccato roar of the motor echoed in the yard. Cinders hailed against the kitchen windows as Gerber put the machine in gear and drove it straight at Zaleski. The Pole shut his eyes and pulled the trigger, the action purely reflexive. The jarring impact of the blow he had dealt had freed the mechanism. The small rocket soared over the kitchen roof, trailing brilliance across the surface of the lake. Zaleski threw himself sideways as the Yamaha bucked, lifting its rider as a Brahmin bull does a rodeo star. Gerber fell awkwardly but away from the still-spinning wheels. Zaleski was on him gladly, whispering obscenities as his thumbs choked his quarry into submission. Arms dragged him away. He shook himself free, standing in the glare of headlamps. For a second or so he was blinded, then he walked toward a familiar face.

Chapter Fourteen

IT WAS MIDNIGHT when Raven passed the Houses of Parliament on his way back to the Yard. He'd left Gerber lodged in the cells at West London Central. They'd put everything out on the charge room table for him to see. The monstrance, the pistol he'd been carrying, forged passport, the keys that had been found in the upstairs clothes closet. He'd listened to the charges, sneering as he leaned against the desk. They'd hit him with Breaking and Entering, Stealing and Receiving, Being in Possession of a Forged Document, Possessing a Loaded Firearm without a License. He admitted nothing, saying no more than that he wanted his lawyer to be informed of his arrest. Then Raven had broken the news that the chow was dead. The animal had savaged Gifford badly. An R.S.P.C.A. inspector had fired a drugged dart at the dog. Fifteen minutes later it died in convulsion. The news turned Gerber into a beast himself, snarling threats till the sight of a strait-jacket finally quieted him.

Raven unlocked his room, heated water and made himself a cup of coffee. He put his jacket on a shaped hanger behind the door and sat down behind the loose-jointed office typewriter. He flexed his fingers, a yellow cigarette hanging from his mouth, and started to type his report. From time to time he stopped to pry out a stuck lever. He read from his notes, transcribing them into an eight-page account of the Dante Gallery robbery. Eight double-spaced pages, say two thousand words in all. He initialed each page and scrawled his signature at the bottom of the last. He added no rank or qualification. It was past midnight, and as far as he was concerned he no longer *was* a cop. Apparently Drake was on his way over to West London Central. Someone in the Commissioner's Office had pulled the coordinator out of his bed. He'd snuffled around, accepting congratulations cagily like a suspicious wart hog. The Italian ambassador had already been informed that the monstrance had been recovered. The ministries concerned were trying to arrange things so that the jeweled cross could be freed from production in court. Raven had no intention of waiting to see Drake. That particular contest was over. Cop or no cop, regulations required him to give evidence at Gerber's trial. The coordinator was bound to be present, running the case in Raven's place. That meeting was something to look forward to.

He put the cover on the typewriter and cleared the drawer of his cassette player and cartridges. There was little enough for him to take at the end of it all. His sister's picture, the Portuguese bedspread from the wall. The plaster looked drab without its vivid colors. The rugs and the curtains they could have. He put his coat on and shut the door for the last time, leaving the key in the lock. The corridor downstairs was crowded with people coming from the pressroom. He brushed past hands grabbing at his sleeve, ignoring the barrage of questions. He had no time for reporters in general, disliked their purpose and methods. They were dogs that attacked from behind, baying with enthusiasm as they brought their prey down. He was past them and almost at the door leading out to the car park when he heard his name called.

He turned, recognizing the voice. Noel Armstrong worked for a television news program, a middle-aged man with a wry smile and dusty shoes. Raven often talked with him, ever since the day they'd met at a Scarlatti concert. Armstrong planted himself squarely in front of the man who was following him.

"Piss off!" he said over his shoulder. The man went. "Got a minute for me?" Armstrong added.

Raven gestured at the door. "Let's go outside. "It'll smell better. We can talk in my car."

Armstrong was on the large side and hard pushed to find room in the small bucket seat.

"Is this stuff true that I'm hearing?" he demanded from the middle of a cloud of tobacco smoke.

"About Gerber?" parried Raven. "It's true enough, yes. The bastard slipped up at last. There's no way out of this one. We've got him bang to rights. Keys to the gallery, false passport *and* the monstrance. Another couple of hours and he'd have been out of the country."

"I don't mean that," said Armstrong, rapping his pipe on the dashboard. "I'm talking about your retirement. Someone said you'd turned it in as of today."

"That's right, too," admitted Raven. "No more of those cosy cocoa hours, Noel. I'm going to retire to my houseboat and take tango lessons."

"Good for you," said Armstrong, cocking his head. "I'd like to be able to join you. Don't believe this junk you hear about Sam Fury, the Fleet Street scourge of the wicked. All I want to do is put my bloody feet up."

"Yes," said Raven. At the end of a minute's silence he made

up his mind. "How would you like a good story, Noel — a real steal from all those bastards in there?"

"Try me," said Armstrong. He switched on the dash light, a felt-tipped pen hovering over the scribble pad on his knee."

"Right," said Raven. "There's this Pole running a restaurant on Fulham Road, opposite Saint Stephen's Hospital. It's called Wielkapolska." He spelled it twice, Armstrong's stubby fingers flying in his own brand of shorthand.

"This Pole's an ex-commando," Raven continued. "In fact he's one of three survivors from the original team that rescued the monstrance from the Germans. Incidentally, it was the *Poles,* not the British. OK?"

"OK," said Armstrong, turning the page.

Raven juggled with a hand. "You know the way these Poles are."

"No, I don't. Tell me," Armstrong said pointedly.

"Well, they're East Europeans," said Raven. "Slavs. You know, romantics. This one's straight out of Alexander Dumas. He read about the theft of the monstrance and vowed to track the thieves down."

"Did he now?" said Armstrong. "And just how was he going to do that?"

"Faith," Raven said gravely. "It works miracles, remember. He also suspected Gerber."

Armstrong's face was frankly dubious. "This thing isn't hanging together. *Gerber* puts himself in the hands of a Polish eating-house keeper? Look — I know the man's form as well as you do. It doesn't make sense."

"It'll do," said Raven. "There are special circumstances that we won't go into. Anyway the Pole followed Gerber to the park tonight, having got in touch with me. He'll be a crown witness at Gerber's trial."

Armstrong shifted his pipe and opened his window, coughing. "You know, I've got a hunch that this could be a send up."

"With *you*, Noel, never!" Raven placed his hand on his heart. "Gospel, every word. I want you to call your outfit on this phone now and get the lights and cameras over to Fulham right away. They'll be in the restaurant celebrating. You'll find Zaleski in the right mood for some good quotes. Do your best for him. Wartime hero — romantic background — I don't have to tell you. The name is Zaleski. Casimir Zaleski. Here."

He pushed the phone into the reporter's hand.

Armstrong talked for a few minutes, brushing aside demur and argument till he had what he wanted. He put the phone down.

"They're on their way. I'd better get over there myself. And thanks."

Raven turned the starter key. "I'll drive you. It just so happens that I'm on my way there. Fasten your seat belt."

"There's just one thing," Armstrong said, finding the buckled ends.

Raven lifted a hand at the cop at the exit. That, too, was for the last time. "Yes?"

"What's Gerber doing in the park in the first place? Ten o'clock at night, carrying half-a-million quid's worth of stolen gear!"

"He didn't say," Raven answered equably. He turned his head and winked. "But my guess is that he was probably there to meet someone."

The sound truck was already outside the restaurant by the time they reached Fulham Road. Electricians huddled in the doorway. The power cables they were waiting to connect squirmed across the sidewalk. A man in a fur jacket and earmuffs was talking to a couple of uniformed policemen in front of the truck.

"Looks like trouble," Armstrong said quietly. Raven slammed the off-side wheels up against the curb. The man in the earmuffs hurried across to meet Armstrong, his breath ballooning in the freezing air.

"I *love* working with you!" he said bitterly. "A quarter-to-one in the morning, our balls dropping off from the cold, and this character won't even talk to us."

"He probably hasn't heard you," said Raven. The din was incessant inside the restaurant. Someone was banging on a table, accompanying a man singing. The faded velvet curtains were drawn across the front window, blocking the view from the street. Raven shoved his way through the group of technicians huddled in the entrance and beat on the door with both fists. The noise inside seemed to hang suspended. He used the break to bend down and shout through the mailbox.

"Zaleski? It's me, Raven!"

Seconds stretched in silence, then Zaleski's voice was close. "Inspector-Dective?"

"Open up!" said Raven. "I want to talk to you." He motioned the men behind to clear the entrance.

The door opened wide enough to let Raven in. Tables had been pulled together in the center of the room and spread with a large cloth that was littered with the remains of spareribs. The faces round the table were familiar. Zaleski's empty chair was at the head, the Canadian's girl on his right. A bald-headed giant like a carnival freak sat between the girl and Mrs. Zaleska, then came Fraser. The last guest was a man

with smooth white hair and a missing arm. Raven recognized
the two Poles and Mrs. Zaleska from the pictures supplied
by the Aliens Office. The big Pole and the girl had turned
their heads so that all five were looking at Raven. The white-
haired man tilted a champagne bottle and drank, his toast
ironical.

"Attention!" called Zaleski from behind Raven's shoulder.
His right cheek was twitching and he looked both drunk and
triumphant. He was wearing a chaplet of grease beads on the
front of his sweater. He was the only one making any noise,
but he fixed his eyeglass and bawled louder. "Why not paying
bloody attention! Champagne for my friend, Inspector-Detective."

It was vintage Krug and perfectly chilled. Raven put his
empty glass down. "I wanted to have a word with you,
Casimir."

Zaleski flung his arms wide. "Speak! In this room are no
hearts with secrets."

Raven glanced across at the table. The big Pole's eyes were
glazed. Mrs. Zaleska nodded, still wearing her hat like a
modish Warsaw matron at a tea party. Fraser's head was
hanging, his eyes tracing the doodles he was making with his
fork.

"There's a television crew outside," said Raven. " 'Window on the World.' They want to interview you."

Someone at the table said something in Polish. Zaleski
steadied himself against the wall, his small slate-colored eyes
almost disappearing as he concentrated. Raven took his elbow.
"It's a chance to tell people what really happened up in that
monastery," he urged. "Fifteen million of them."

The voice said something in Polish again. It was Sobinski.
Raven dropped Zaleski's arm and craned down over the
table.

"You speak English, don't you?" he demanded.

Sobinski nodded, rolling his cigarette between thumb and
forefinger.

"Then don't try to screw his chances," said Raven.
"Fraser!"

The Canadian raised his head. "What's on your mind?"

Raven jerked his head toward the street. "This could be just
the thing for him — publicity. I know the man who'll do the
talking. He's absolutely straight."

Fraser shrugged but Zaleski came off the wall, bracing his
belly with great dignity. "I talk to these people. Bring them
into my house and I talk."

He unlocked the street door, standing aside courteously as
the crew stumbled in ashen-faced from cold. Zaleski busied
himself with coffee and brandy, bustling around and smiling
broadly as he helped arrange the lights and camera. He was
everywhere at once, his stained sweater hidden under a blazer,
chatting with Armstrong as if the two men had known one
another for years. It was some time before Raven managed to
attract his attention, calling the Pole over to the entrance. The
others were at the far end of the room.

"I'm off," said Raven. "There's something I wanted to
leave with you — a souvenir."

Zaleski opened his palm on the bison badge. He looked at it
for a while and then stuck it in his lapel.

"So," he said, pushing his hand out. "So long, Inspector-
Detective. Come again."

Raven drove home. He sat for a while in the car, looking out at the swamped pavement. The wind had blown a hole in the night, a gray rent like a torn sleeve showing a lining. The moon was somewhere on the other side. He climbed the yawing gangway, tired — exhausted even in the way that a steam bath left him, but strangely at peace.